Ivor Johnson's Neighbours

A Love Story

Bruce Graham

Pottersfield Press, Lawrencetown Beach, Nova Scotia, Canada

© Copyright 2004 Bruce Graham

All rights reserved. No part of this book may be reproduced, stored in a retrieval system or transmitted in any form or by any means without permission in writing from the publisher. In the case of photocopying, permission must be obtained from the publisher or from Access Copyright, 1 Yonge Street, Suite 1900, Toronto, Ontario M5E 1E5.

Cover design: Dalhousie Graphics

Front cover image: "Parrsboro, NS, From Shore Road" History Collection, Nova Scotia Museum

Editor: Julia Swan

Printed in Canada

Pottersfield Press acknowledges the support of The Canada Council for the Arts and the financial support of the Government of Canada through the Book Publishing Industry Development Program for our publishing activities. We also acknowledge support from Cultural Affairs, Nova Scotia Department of Tourism and Culture.

Pottersfield Press
83 Leslie Road
East Lawrencetown
Nova Scotia, Canada, B2Z 1P8
Website: www.pottersfieldpress.com
To order, phone toll-free 1-800-NIMBUS9 (1-800-646-2879)

National Library of Canada Cataloguing in Publication

Graham, Bruce
    Ivor Johnson's neighbours : a novel / Bruce Graham.
ISBN 1-895900-60-3
    I. Title.
PS8563.R3143I86 2004   C813'.6   C2003-907226-6

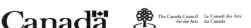

Author's Note

If you lived in the middle of New York City and were a member of a large family, you might become acquainted with a few hundred people well enough to know what they did for a living, learn the inside scoop on their families and their traits and idiosyncrasies. If you lived in a small town in the 1950s you'd be acquainted with five or six times that number. Small towns permit you the luxury of elbow-to-elbow living if you want it and that disadvantage if you don't. No one is lost in the swell of humanity in a small community. In other words, everyone counts and everyone stands out.

I was lucky enough to live in a small town during the 1950s. It wasn't all good times and it wasn't all laughs. For many folks there was not enough work and too much poverty. There was the chill of the Cold War and Communism. Many things seemed important in those days before television – church, an absolute sense of right and wrong and of course story telling, where a sense of humour was an asset more admired then than now.

Ivor Johnson's Neighbours is fictional. However, astute readers know that through all fiction flows a stream of truth. The stream is wider and deeper in some chapters than in others, but it is always there.

There are people I wish to thank for either widening the stream or providing additional information about the 1950s. First my father, George Graham, a gifted storyteller in his own right. My long-time friends Doug and Linda Hatfield recall much from those times. Marion Wasson provided funny stories from her early married life. Her husband, Ralph, contributed comical tales of Whitehall.

As always, I want to thank my publisher Lesley Choyce of Pottersfield Press and editor Julia Swan for their consideration and care.

Bruce Graham
March 1, 2004

To Helen
a Whitehall girl
herself

1

More than one child had been conceived under the Whitehall Bridge. Unkind as it was, scurrilous boys jokingly nicknamed one such offspring Bridget. Until she grew up to be beautiful, smart and a lawyer.

Under the bridge was a gathering place for youngsters. A retreat where you could skip rocks, play hide and seek, smoke your first cigarette, and steal your first kiss. On lazy summer afternoons boys gathered to brag and catch minnows. If you could find a girl adventurous enough, the two of you could crawl up the steep bank to the centre pylon, which wasn't at all cold and clammy. Under the bridge wasn't exactly private but it was more private than most places. It was a good spot to daydream and sort out your thoughts. You could listen to the cars rumble overhead and watch the incoming tide fill up the space between the banks.

The bridge spanned a tidal brook that ran from the inner harbour – a mile long finger of salt water. At low tide when the water was gone, the inner harbour was marsh and mud, but when the tide was high it was a short, inland waterway leading from the lighthouse to the very edge of town.

The lighthouse had a foghorn that warned Minas Basin fishermen they were in treacherous tides, the highest in the world. The foghorn should have sounded too when there wasn't any fog, as a way of warning clam diggers that the tide was turning. Every season, greenhorns intent on extricating the tasty, soft-shelled morsels from the mud suddenly found themselves surrounded by water. Most waded safely back to shore. Those closer to the islands were forced to abandon hope of reaching shore and retreat to the only dry land available. Spending a dozen hours on an island isn't always a holistic experience. Of course, concerned parents were quick to tell their children that some of those stranded didn't reach either shore or island. In young minds such warnings conjured up images of a slow and horrible death by cold, creeping seawater.

Because it spanned a tidal stream, conditions under the Whitehall Bridge were constantly changing. One moment you could wade in ankle-deep water to the other bank, a few hours later it was over your head.

A mile from the bridge, at the big clearing known as McCurdy's Meadow, two streams joined together. Now called Dyas's Brook, it meandered past grassy banks shaded by thickets of stubby spruce and alders until it finally met the tidal stream flowing under the bridge.

Under the bridge was a place Edger liked to go so he could sit and figure things out, particularly at night when he was apt to be alone. Life had become considerably more complex for him, and he needed a hideaway to contemplate the various inconsistencies of his existence.

An occasional car rolled overhead. The low muffled rumble, rumble, rumble of a passing vehicle always gave Edger a sense of security. A feeling that his spot was special. He lit a cigarette and looked down at his new PF Flyers. He had bought them uptown yesterday and they still had the good smell. The black canvas sides were stiff. The white soles and the wide white rubber bands connecting the soles to the canvas sides were not yet scuffed. He loved the smell of new things. If only somebody could find a way to keep things smelling new. What an invention! He thought of writing the B.F. Goodrich company to see if anyone was working on such a project. Even if you didn't kick cans, walk in the ditch or wear them digging worms, sneakers got old fast. Somebody must be working on it.

Funny about clothes, Edger thought. He hated new blue jeans with their stiff legs and the scraping noise they made when you walked. He and Ledger would pester Tess to wash new jeans several times to soften them. Sneakers were the opposite. You wanted them to stay new. Sitting under the Whitehall Bridge, Edger wondered why this was. Why were there some things you wanted to be new and look old, and some things you wanted to stay new always?

He loved new. When next year's models arrived at MacIntosh Motors, Edger was one of the first to open the doors and smell the dash and upholstery. The trunks always had a special aroma. Edger wondered if you never opened the trunk of a new car, ten years later would it still smell like that? As with so many of his questions, nobody had an answer.

Edger wasn't alone when it came to liking new cars. Lots of people would be there the day new models arrived. Old men would run wrinkled hands over the dash and whisper, "Oh, yeahhh," and nod with approval. Edger even liked the smell of the tires, and he was not above getting down on his knees for a good sniff. After all, new cars only arrived once a year. Nothing smelled as good as newness.

He noticed that the people hanging around the dealership passing judgement on new models never actually bought a car. They were what Ivor Johnson called gawkers. Cumberland County was, Ivor said, famous for gawkers.

"Am I a gawker?" Edger asked Ivor.

"You've got the makings," Ivor replied.

A one-ton truck rolled over the bridge, disturbing Edger's dreaming. He knew the weight of the vehicle by what happened under the bridge. A vehicle under a ton caused small deposits of dust to drop between the planks. Above a ton and the bridge slightly reverberated, loosening not only dust but globs of goop and mud as well. Having a lot of experience under the bridge, Edger knew exactly what was rolling overhead. He also knew where to sit so he wouldn't get dirty. He had his special space, way at the back where you could rest against the middle pylon, smack dab in the centre of the bridge.

Another car rumbled over him as Edger watched a seagull float by. The gulls often drifted under the bridge, taking a free ride up to Frog Hollow where someone might be cleaning fish. Corky Langille had shot a seagull under the bridge once and Edger remembered the noise the gun made. Corky took the dead bird home and cooked it. "Couldn't eat it," he said, "too fishy. You want a bird that tastes like a bird, not like a fish."

Edger continued smoking and admiring his new PF Flyers. The aroma of the canvas reminded him of a pup tent he and Ledger had when they were young. They used it as a fort and took prisoners until Tess made them stop.

He smiled, thinking of another time when he and Ledger climbed a tree and refused to come down, even when Tess threatened to call the fire department.

Again something interrupted his daydreaming but it wasn't a car. He heard the low scuffle of footsteps crunching gravel on the other side of the bridge. He put out his cigarette and listened. Someone was coming, sliding a bit on the embankment. Edger could see a human form coming under the bridge, crouching, working its way towards the centre pylon directly across from him. He sat very still and squinted to see better. A number of noises were coming from whoever it was. There was a mixture of muted sounds that didn't fit the silhouette. It was a woman sobbing. Edger knew it was Pearl but the other small sound truly alarmed him. He had untangled the shrill, high-pitched halting cry that mingled with Pearl's sobs. Her baby! The other sound was her baby. They were both crying, Pearl and her baby. Edger froze. While it was alarming to find Pearl under the bridge, bringing her newborn child spelled something else Edger didn't want to identify, but it filled him with a profound sense of panic. A chill raised goose bumps up and down his arms and created a tingling shiver that made the hair on the back of his neck stand up.

He wondered if he should shout something across the water. What, exactly, he didn't know. "Why are you crying?" seemed rather feeble under the circumstances and Edger had some idea of the circumstances. He knew Minnie had flatly refused to have anything to do with the baby and had told Pearl to give it up for adoption. Pearl, hurt and indignant, had moved in with Gabby until things got straightened out. Minnie would accept the child, nurture and love her if only Pearl would 'fess up as to who the father was. But Pearl wouldn't tell and that got Minnie's dander up. Even though Duddy was coming down to Gabby's every day to see his granddaughter and Fudd was going around calling himself Uncle Fudd, it didn't help. Mother and daughter were estranged and that daughter with her baby was sitting on the other bank under the bridge, they were both crying and the tide was coming in. It was creating turmoil in, and tearing the heart out of, poor Edger.

He had always carried a torch for Pearl, maybe more so because she would never give him the time of day. Pearl could be blunt, brutally frank in fact. She never cared for him and it hurt. It hurt worse because Edger suspected he knew the identity of the child's father.

He could hear Pearl's feet on the gravel. She was getting up, standing as straight as she could in the cramped space, looking at the water. Another shiver went through Edger. God, what was she going to do? What if...? No, no she wouldn't. Edger sat very still and his head almost exploded as it usually did when he was faced with too many thoughts at once. He was sure Pearl could hear his heart pounding from a hundred feet away.

Was she going to toss her beautiful little baby into the tide? What would he do? Did he have the guts to jump in and save the child? Edger was no hero. He could stay where he was until the water reached him and he'd eventually drown. Or just wait with his hands pressed tightly over his ears until Pearl had done the awful act. He could wait for her to leave and scamper out and tell nobody of the murder. What if the child cried in the water? It certainly would. What then? This could be his brother's child. He could be the baby's uncle, for Christ's sake. Did that make any difference? He tried out "Uncle Edger" several times, silently rolling it over in his mind to see what it sounded like. Not bad!

Pearl was sitting down again. Her crying had changed to a slow whimpering as if she might be sick. The baby was crying harder. Then it stopped. Pearl was giving it her breast. She couldn't be considering doing something awful to the child just after feeding it, could she? Or maybe she just wanted to keep it quiet. Edger shivered at that thought. It was September. The water was cold and Edger acknowledged again he was no hero, uncle or no uncle.

He was trying to get it straight in his mind what to shout across to Pearl. He didn't want to startle her, cause her to lose her footing and fall down the embankment into the water. What the hell was there to say anyway? "Pearl, don't do it. If my brother doesn't want you, I do."

She'd jump for sure.

Edger looked at his new PF Flyers. Oh no, he was not jumping into that water in his new sneakers, baby or no baby. The wide, white rubber bands gleamed in the darkness. There wasn't anything else as bright under that bridge.

Edger's head ached with all the possibilities confronting him. Having to jump into the water to save the baby on a September night was not something he wanted to do. Then another horrible thought: the possibility of Pearl jumping too! Oh my God, which one to save? Would he freeze and die in the attempt? The three of them found dead. What would people say, a tragic love affair?

Edger didn't mind that bit of speculation. At least he would go out with a little glamour. Then he looked at the water again. The space between the embankments was filling up. The water was well over his head and getting deeper by the minute. Would they all die? Why didn't Pearl love him? He wished it were his baby. Why was his brother not taking care of things?

They were all just empty, pointless questions that wouldn't matter a damn if that stupid Pearl threw herself or her baby into the water.

My new PFs ruined, he thought. His cigarettes would be no good either, and darn his luck! Of course, he had just bought a new pack. Edger sighed and took his cork-tipped Black Cats out of his shirt pocket and set them down next to him. Pearl was sobbing quietly, almost noiselessly. Edger started to get ready just in case he decided to do something. He was saving his sneakers first. He pulled at the laces. Even they felt new, silky and soft. Laces lost that feeling too, just like the rest of the sneaker. He put the PF Flyer for his right foot next to his cigarettes. His sock was damp. The night was cool and Edger felt chilly, yet he was perspiring. His forehead was wet. He shivered. God, that water was coming in from the sea. If only he could think of something to shout that would not scare Pearl. As he tried to untie his left sneaker, the lace turned into a knot. He made the mistake of pulling at it and the knot got tighter. He struggled to undo it, struggled to find something to say, struggled to find the courage to conduct a rescue. His head ached and he shivered and swore he was never coming under the bridge again.

The stream was becoming a river, the water was the length of a broom handle from his feet. Edger would soon have to show himself, shout something, jump in the water or at the very least get his feet wet. He silently swore at his knotted lace while Pearl struggled to get up again. Edger held his breath. She was on her feet, unsteady as if she were dizzy.

Pearl stood staring at the water. Edger felt the muscles in his stomach tighten. Then she slowly made her way out from under the bridge. Bits of gravel slid into the water. When her feet stopped crunching the gravel he knew she had reached the road.

A wave of relief swept over Edger, causing him to tremble. His teeth started chattering. Although Pearl was gone there were still his sneakers to consider. If he got them wet the saltwater would leave a stain. He had one on with a knot in it and one off. He hesitated because any decision made his head ache even worse. He had to leave the knot alone and put the other sneaker on or scramble out with one on and one off. There were only two choices, why did it hurt so much? He put the sneaker on and grabbed his cigarettes. When he reached the road he couldn't see Pearl but he knew she had walked in the direction of the Snake, towards Gabby's house.

2

Snake Road got the name from its shape. It was bent like the letter S as it slithered away from the longer, more populated Whitehall Road that ran to town. Snake Road was just a twisty little street with half a dozen small wooden frame houses.

On the first curve of the S lived Minnie and Duddy, Pearl's parents. You could tell their house because of the piles of two-by-four and four-by-eight boards, laid against the little shed. Duddy had other aspects of his business in the yard. Two ladders leaning against a tree, bits of scaffolding, pieces of plywood, two sawhorses and the rusted frame of an old bench saw. Fudd's toboggan, left there last winter, rested against the scaffolding. Except for the toboggan, the yard was messy but somehow purposeful. On the far side of the house there was a small lawn and four large maple trees. It was from one of the maples Pearl's brother Fudd caught Edger trying to get a peak at Pearl undressing. Fudd told everybody of course, calling Edger "the peeping pervert, who was so hard up he tried to see Pearl's snatch." Which as far as Fudd was concerned was the ultimate in desperation.

After that, if Pearl's nose could get any higher in the air when she passed Edger, he figured she'd get a crick in her neck. Of course like most things on the Snake, it all blew over in a day or two.

Edger knew he was lucky he hadn't been caught earlier. For months he had been climbing the tree that gave him the best viewpoint directly into Pearl's bedroom. Every night when he climbed down he swore he wouldn't go back, but back he went. He had just enough success to continue. On several nights Pearl had not quite closed her curtains. She had been revealed in various stages of undress. Twice he'd seen her in bra and panties and once – just once – her bare, soft white, beautiful bottom. There was no ass in the world quite as beautiful as Pearl's.

Oh God, Edger carried a torch for Pearl all right, a torch that drove him to personal injury. It had happened at the moment of full bliss, when Edger was filling his hungry eyes with the image of Pearl's lily-white bottom and Pearl started to turn, stark naked, to face the window. It was all too much for Edger. He had taken a step off the branch, trying to walk on the air to get a closer view. So breathless and light-headed had he become, that he tried to traverse the space between tree and bedroom and of course he'd landed with a thump on the ground.

Hurt and humiliated, Edger stumbled across the street and sat on Royal's front yard. He plunked himself down on the thorny runner of a yellow hybrid and the sharp barbs bit into his own rump, still smarting from the fall.

Royal's house was across the street from Duddy's and a little farther along the first curve of the S. He was a gardener. His front yard displayed what was, for Royal, more than a hobby. Roses were his passion. As boys, Edger, Ledger and Fudd had carried out several search and destroy missions on the roses. But the plants withstood such adolescent assaults. The boys could swat the yellow, pink, white, and deep red flowers with their baseball bats and make the petals fly, but the bushes survived and proved more stubborn than those carrying out such thoughtless destruction.

Roses surrounded Royal's house. His front, back, and side yards were a festival of colours.

Royal talked more to his roses than he did to people. He and Ivor were both men of quiet demeanour, but beneath Royal's quiet internal stream was a rocky bottom of fixed opinions. When he opened his mouth it was usually a declarative statement rather than a question. Unlike Ivor, people seldom came to Royal for advice because they already knew what he thought. Royal's mind was focused on a fixed track. What he believed he believed firmly and what he didn't believe he dismissed as unimportant. People liked him more for what he did with plants than for his personality. Royal didn't display much on the surface. Most of him was well underground, dragged there by personal agony. God, how life can drag you down. But without complaint, the Rose Man of Snake Road let the barbs scratch his slender six-foot-two frame, because his pain was somewhere else.

Next door to Royal was Ivor Johnson's tidy little house, where there wasn't a flower in sight. The small lawn was cut short. Two whitewashed tires marked the end of the driveway. The tires contained flowers once but not in recent years. Ivor whitewashed the tires every spring but never planted anything in them. Ivor's place was total neatness and order where nothing was enhanced. No blade of grass allowed higher by half an inch, no weed permitted. Painted, pruned, trimmed and cleaned. Almost antiseptic.

Across and up from Ivor Johnson was the mansard-roofed little two-story, where Edger and Ledger lived with their mother. They had never called her "Mother" or "Mom" or anything smacking of a maternal connotation. Why? Nobody could remember. She was just Tess, always had been.

Gabby lived on the last curve of the Snake, next door to Ivor Johnson. Gabby wasn't a bootlegger. She didn't sell anything, but over time her porch had evolved into the street's social centre. It was the back porch, away from the street, making it more difficult for gawkers who drove by to see who was coming and going.

Most nights there were people at Gabby's. Royal, Ivor and Mink were the regulars. Tess sometimes, Minnie hardly ever and Duddy quite often. Now that Edger, Ledger and Fudd were older – although not quite legal drinking age uptown – but on the Snake, well – everything on the Snake was just a little lower key and a little more relaxed.

Just around the last curve of the S was the ramshackle trailer of Mink Martin. The engine block of a Ford truck and parts of a '49 De Soto littered his front yard, except you could hardly call it a yard. It was more a place for his old German shepherd to sleep, away from the numerous cats in the trailer. The dog had made a bed for itself in the middle of an old block and tackle, the ropes rotting and splayed.

Snake Road, locally referred to as the Snake, wasn't a busy or noisy street. Yet there was always something going on.

A minister's wife, who had lived uptown for several years, had unkindly remarked that Snake Road had more oddballs than any street in Cumberland County, which was saying something. But nobody could pinpoint who was so very odd. Individualistic, yes. Some rather peculiar perhaps, but surely no more so than other people in other places.

Ivor Johnson and Royal were drinking beer in Gabby's porch when Edger came in, trying to look nonchalant, which he could never do. Edger was certain Pearl didn't know he had been under the bridge so he decided not to mention it to anyone. He did want to know whether his brother had put the poor girl in this predicament. If so, why wasn't Ledger taking responsibility for it? Edger knew that Ivor Johnson would agree with him. Ivor believed in responsibility. If you do something, take responsibility for it, was his motto.

The box of beer was on the floor by the table. As was the custom at Gabby's, Edger helped himself. The rule was, you could drink as long as you made sure you brought a few bucks every Saturday. Also, you were required to show up with a case of twenty-four once a month. That was your contribution. Even if Gabby wasn't home her porch was open. She always knew who paid and who hadn't. There were men, thousands of miles away working up north, who were gone for months but still sent Gabby beer money.

Ivor Johnson and Royal were in a serious discussion about the Boston Red Sox when Edger walked in. Gabby was on the telephone in the kitchen. There was no sign of Pearl.

Edger realized his forehead was still damp. He was experiencing recurring relief for not having to be a hero. It dazed him, reliving the near experience of pulling Pearl and her baby from the frigid waters of the Minas Basin. "Local man saves mother and child." Edger was visualizing the headlines when Royal said, "New sneakers, Edger. That your blueberry money?"

"Yeah, part of it. I'm looking for a car but can't find nothing."

"You make enough scooping blueberries to buy a car?" Royal asked.

"Plus working in the mill and on the truck. I got a little. Five hundred anyway."

"You aren't going to find much of a car for five hundred," Royal replied.

"I know, but something to get me around."

Gabby got off the telephone and came down the hall to the porch. "Edger, you look pale as a ghost. You not feeling well?"

"Sure, I'm okay." Although he didn't want to, Edger couldn't help himself. He blurted out, "How're you making out with the baby?"

Gabby shrugged. "Pearl's up with her mother. She's been in an awful state most of the day. Duddy's been down a couple of times and he took her up tonight. Says he's going to make Minnie listen."

Surprised, since he'd just seen Pearl under the bridge, Edger's mind was racing like a runaway train. He was trying to apply the brakes but couldn't. "When did he do that?"

"Do what?" Gabby asked.

"Take her up to Minnie's."

Edger was too eager. Royal was concentrating on peeling the label off his beer bottle, but Ivor Johnson had him fixed with a straight gaze. Ivor always knew what Edger was thinking and it always made him nervous.

Once, he and Ledger took all the Snow Whites off Ivor's big apple tree. Ivor never said a thing to them. He simply came out of his house and stood on his front step whenever they passed. He would come out day after day, following them with his gaze until they were out of sight.

Ledger, always the brave one, tried staring back once. He stopped in the middle of the street and tried to stare Ivor down. Passing cars never disturbed his brother and for an hour he and Ivor just stared at each other. Thirty minutes into the test of wills, Ledger started swallowing hard and blinking but Ivor never moved. It sent shivers down Edger's back the way Ivor never flinched. The minutes dragged on with Edger sitting by the side of the road, an onlooker wishing it would end, but afraid to break the competition. Ledger tried to steady himself by shifting his feet. He nervously licked his lips. He was breathing hard like he was running a race. Finally, his legs unsteady, Ledger shouted at the top of his voice at Ivor, "Who cares?" and walked away.

The brothers never stole another apple from Ivor Johnson.

At the moment, Edger felt Ivor was reading his mind like an open letter and Pearl was on every page. The harder Edger tired to conceal his deepest thoughts the more they seeped out of him, like porridge through a screen.

"No, I just wondered," he stammered. "I thought I saw Pearl up the road by the Whitehall Bridge."

"Not unless she's already left her mother's. Did she have the baby with her?" Gabby asked.

"Ah, yeah. I think so," Edger said, trying too hard to look relaxed. He took a swig of beer. It was warm and bitter. Mixed with the latent fear from the bridge and the new nervousness arising in him, the beer was a potent cocktail sending shivers in waves, circumnavigating his back and running around to his rib cage.

Maybe he was coming down with something. When he looked again, Ivor Johnson was grinning at him. He knew! Damn it, he knew.

Suddenly the door swung open and Pearl rushed in looking tearful and upset. She held the baby tightly in front of her. Her father followed, making faces and nodding to everybody. Pearl spoke to no one. She breezed by Edger, so close he could smell the evening mist in her hair. She didn't look at him. He was used to Pearl snubbing him. It was worse than a snub really, it was as though he wasn't there. There was no such person as Edger. He was nonexistent in Pearl's eyes.

It had started with the spider. Pearl never forgave him. Ledger, who had put Edger up to it in the first place, came to Pearl's defence. He helped the hysterical girl unzip the back of her dress and Ledger got to put his hand down her back and get the insect. Then he cuffed Edger for doing such a mean thing.

Ledger the hero. Edger the villain. Pearl the victim. It had always been like that. Her refusal to forgive him drove Edger to pester her more. It bothered him being hated and he failed to see it was part of the attraction. Pearl was unreachable; she had built a wall between them.

Pearl was in the house with Gabby and Duddy for a few minutes when Gabby called out for Ivor to join them. Royal finished peeling the label off his beer bottle and got up to go. He slapped Edger on the shoulder. "True love never runs smooth," he said and was out the door.

Edger sat at the table by himself. He could hear Gabby, Pearl and Duddy talking in the living room. He couldn't make out exactly what they were saying. Ivor Johnson's voice was so low Edger couldn't hear him at all, but he knew when Ivor was talking because the others were quiet. Edger desperately wanted to be part of the drama. To be with them, contributing something. He always seemed to be on the outside of things. He put his head in his hands.

"Will things ever change?" he asked himself.

The conversation was suddenly over and they were moving back to the porch. Ivor and Duddy walked past Edger and went out the door. Pearl took the baby upstairs. Gabby came to the porch and picked up Royal's empties and put them in the case. She wiped the red plastic tablecloth with a damp cloth, making Edger lift his elbows. Then she emptied the ashtrays. Gabby seldom had a beer, but she opened one that night and took a big swig. She shook her head. "Life," she said. "How are you, Edger?"

"Okay," he replied. His head was busting again. He wanted to ask Gabby the really tough question and not waiting for his nerve, he barged ahead. "What's going on?"

Gabby raised her eyebrows. "Ivor's gone up to see Minnie. If she'll listen to anyone, it will be Ivor."

"Yeah," Edger replied. "People listen to Ivor."

"Someone has to talk some sense to that woman," Gabby declared and Edger nodded in agreement.

* * *

In the two minutes it took to walk to Duddy's place, Ivor Johnson and Duddy didn't speak. It had all been said at Gabby's. Duddy had used Ivor before in times of crisis. Ivor had intervened when Fudd got thrown in jail and when Pearl ran away. Years ago Minnie had caught Duddy with Emily Matthews and wanted to kill him. She might have, had it not been for Ivor. Over time, he got things simmered down and Emily Matthews moved down the shore, away from Whitehall. Minnie was happy about that and Duddy was relieved.

"Maybe it's best you go in yourself," Duddy said to Ivor. "Minnie's ready to bite my head off."

"Okay," Ivor said and walked up the steps.

Minnie was sitting at her kitchen table. There was a cloud of blue smoke above her and the ashtray was full of butts. As a rule Minnie wasn't a smoker. She thought tobacco a filthy habit that stunk up your house and fouled your fingers with a brown stain. Only when she was extremely upset did she light up. She'd been smoking a lot that week.

Ivor sat down across the table. Minnie looked at him but didn't say anything. Ivor folded his hands and waited. One, two, three minutes passed. Finally he said softly, "Everybody's mad or sad or upset, Minnie."

"And I suppose that's my fault, is it?"

Ivor didn't answer.

"Am I the one who went and got herself knocked up? Am I the one who doesn't have enough respect for her own mother to tell her who the father is, so I can get my hands on the son-of-a-bitch?"

Ivor knew how to handle Minnie. Getting into an argument over who might be right and who might be wrong never worked. Eventually Minnie would come around. After she blew off enough steam she would get down to the real problem. After a while she would tell Ivor the real trouble, which was never the trouble you thought, never the stuff on the surface. It was always the underneath stuff and you couldn't get underneath until Minnie was ready to let you go there.

They sat for half an hour. The kitchen clock ticking, Duddy outside walking back and forth, muttering to himself. He went up to Gabby's, had a beer and came back. Once he looked in the back door but all he saw was Ivor and Minnie sitting at the kitchen table. He went back for another beer. The clock struck nine then ticked past nine-fifteen. Minnie put out another cigarette. "I love my children, you know."

"I know," Ivor replied.

"But they're a big disappointment to me. My whole life is a disappointment to me."

"A lot of people have it worse, Minnie."

"Oh yeah?"

"Yeah. You got good kids, a good husband and a nice little house. That's a lot more than many people."

Minnie looked hard at Ivor Johnson. Her eyes were half closed and her lips pressed together. "Now, Mr. Big Shot. Let's look at what you just said. Start with the husband. That's what you said, wasn't it? A good husband? Duddy is a stray dog. He's a horny dimwit who never made enough money to support us and you know it. What was the other thing? A nice little house! The roof leaks, the toilet leaks, the floor is rotting out in Fudd's room, and there's so much cold air coming in around the windows you might as well be outside. And me married to a carpenter! What else? Ah, the kids. What did you call them, good kids?" Minnie's voice broke. "My son can't get a job. He's got a grade nine education, he's eighteen years old and reads comic books. My daughter's had a baby and doesn't have a husband or even a boyfriend. She won't say who the father is and you can't pin it on anybody because there is no likely suspect. Except —"

Minnie gripped Ivor's arm hard and he knew he was close to the core of the problem.

"Except what, Minnie?" Ivor asked.

"You know," she said as she put her hands over her face.

"My God! You don't think Duddy is the father?" Ivor asked.

"No, no. Not my husband, useless as he is. Duddy is not a monster who would touch his own daughter. Anybody else's daughter, yes, you can be sure of that, but not his own. Duddy is a simple-minded man but he wouldn't hurt Pearl."

"Then who?" Ivor asked.

Minnie sobbed, "I'm not so sure about my son." She blew into her wrinkled handkerchief.

So there it was. Out in the open. "You think Fudd and Pearl? No," Ivor Johnson said. "No, Minnie. I don't think so."

"Why won't she tell then? Why won't she tell me? Frankly, I wouldn't put it past Fudd. The doctor told me he's socially backward. He's never had a girlfriend. He pulls his wire all the time." She wept again and put her head down on the table.

Ivor let her cry.

Five minutes went by with no more words between them. When Minnie finally raised her head her eyes were red and her cat's-paw purple glasses were askew on her face. Ivor was staring at her.

"Everything you say about Fudd might be true, Minnie. But you've missed something. I might not put it past Fudd, but I'll guarantee you I could never believe it of Pearl. You've shortchanged your daughter. Pearl is not socially backward. She's smart and she probably won't tell you because she fears what you'll do to the father. When you fear Pearl's baby is a product of your children, you shortchange her. You should think about that."

"What if Fudd didn't give her a choice? He's strong and bull-headed. And if he did it, Pearl wouldn't tell on him. She's always protected him."

"Minnie, believe me. Fudd is not the father."

"How do you know?" she pleaded.

"Well, for one thing, Edger is tying himself up in knots over Pearl."

"Edger? Pearl detests him."

"Yup, so I've heard. My point is, there are guys who find Pearl very attractive. By the way, she doesn't detest Ledger."

Minnie lit another cigarette. "Better Ledger than Edger. He's almost as dumb as Fudd."

"No," Ivor replied, "Edger is not dumb. He's just a little different and shy. He's always been overshadowed by his brother. Edger is a good boy."

"And my son, is he a good boy?"

Ivor Johnson smiled. "Fudd needs a kick in the ass sometimes to get his brain working, but he's alright and your daughter is very much alright and..." Ivor took Minnie's hand. "She needs you, Minnie. It's a time in her life she needs you badly."

More tears rolled over the soft wrinkles on Minnie's cheek. "They've worn me out, Ivor, all of them. Worn this old woman out. I go uptown and clean houses, work my fingers to the bone and come home. Pearl's in her bedroom playing those damn cowboy records. Fudd's in his bedroom pulling himself. He doesn't even have enough brains to close the door. Duddy, he's off fishing or whoring somewhere. Nothing cooked for dinner, no food in the house and no money in the bank. They've worn me out. Worn this woman to the bone," she sighed.

"I'm going up to Gabby's and get us a couple of beer and I'm going to tell Pearl to come down in an hour."

Minnie nodded weakly.

* * *

The baby was asleep in Pearl's arms when she walked into the kitchen. Minnie and Ivor were at the table. There was an awkward moment between mother and daughter until Ivor said, "Let your mother hold the baby, Pearl."

A puffy-faced, tear-stained Minnie, hands shaking slightly, held her granddaughter for the first time. Her voice trembled.

"What are you going to call her? Have you decided yet?"

"I'm going to call her Minnie. Minnie Rhonda-Rae," Pearl whispered and Minnie broke in to such a loud cry it startled the poor infant who woke up with a wail. When Ivor slipped out the backdoor, the wailing of Minnie, Pearl and little Minnie Rhonda-Rae could be heard in unison all along the Snake, like three fire sirens in the night. Duddy was standing on Gabby's steps.

"Jesus, Ivor, what's going on down there?"

"It'll be fine, Duddy. You can go home soon, just give them a little time by themselves."

"You want a beer?" Duddy asked.

3

Tess Goodwin had twin boys out of wedlock on a cold winter night in 1934. She named them Earl and Lloyd but like so many things on the Snake, the names didn't stick. Somewhere along the way, Earl became Edger and Lloyd became Ledger.

They were twins in name only. Ledger was born big and healthy with bright eyes, as though he'd received all the nourishment. Edger was small and sickly. He cried a lot and clung to his mother, his tiny hands gripping her apron. As the boys developed, Ledger was taller and always seemed older. Many said smarter. Tess loved them both but worried more about Edger because he seemed less equipped to deal with the rigours of the world. His mother knew he had the bigger heart. He was the most giving but also the most needy. Edger was the one who had stayed close to her while Ledger explored the outside world. Tess knew when the time came, Edger would give all his heart to someone he loved and she feared for that too. In fact, she feared he already had.

Bruce Graham – Ivor Johnson's Neighbours

The next day Pearl moved back home and Minnie gave the baby a bath in the kitchen sink while Duddy tiptoed around, peeking over Minnie's shoulder and making faces at the infant until he finally scared her.

"See what you've done now," Minnie said. "Go get some wood for the stove."

While Minnie was bathing the baby, Edger kept walking back and forth in front of their house, wanting to knock on the front door. He had been in deep concentration and had pieced together most of the problem from bits and pieces of tidbits and talk. He was even more certain he was going to help Pearl, even if he made a fool of himself. That was the only thing he was scared of, making a fool of himself. But he was getting over his fear of that since he reasoned most people thought him a fool anyway.

If necessary, he would march in to Minnie's and reveal everything. But first he had to be certain – absolutely certain that he was right about everything. Ledger would be home from Halifax that day and, by God, they were going to have a little talk.

Just about the time he expected it, Mink Martin's old truck turned onto the Snake with Ledger at the wheel and a pale-looking Mink in the passenger's seat. Mink was having arse trouble and he had gone to Halifax to be scoped. They gave his arse a clean bill of health but ordered him to stop drinking. Mink suspected they were wrong about his arse and he told them so.

"Look at me," he said to Gabby. "Don't I look like death warmed over?"

"You always look like death warmed over," Gabby replied, which seemed to validate Mink's prognosis.

"I looked across the bay the other day and saw a cross on the cliffs. It's a sign," he said, affecting his best far-off gaze.

"That's where the rocks fell in," Gabby replied.

Mink sighed. He would get nowhere with this woman. He wondered if Tess was home.

Edger waited until things had settled down and Ledger had finished telling his mother about Halifax, the hospital, waiting for

Mink, meeting a good-looking nurse and visiting the trade school. Ledger had so many stories for only being gone a day, it took forever. One adventure after another until finally Edger couldn't stand it any longer and cut in.

"You want to go get some driftwood, that American lady is still around. She says she'll still pay for something really unusual."

"Nah, I'm going uptown."

Damn it. It was always hard to pin Ledger down. Maybe he should go uptown with him.

"Dinner will be ready in an hour," Tess yelled after them. Edger would be there on time. Ledger would not. She knew her boys.

She watched her sons from the window. Ledger had a confidence to his walk, a purposeful gait, shoulders straight, his wavy brown hair so perfectly combed it reflected the late afternoon sun. Next to his smooth glide, Edger seemed almost to stagger, walking all over the place. Edger seemed shorter than his brother because he hunched his shoulders and walked bent slightly forward, looking like he was bucking a strong headwind, his hair either falling in his face or standing straight up. Edger's arms swung in an uneven cadence as if mocking his brother's strong stride.

Tess sighed, wondering what would become of them. Had she prepared them for the slings and arrows of life? There was always the nagging doubt that she had been strong when she should have relented. When she should have accepted their father into the family. But she was strong then, strong and hurt and determined to make it on her own. She had them by herself and was raising them by herself. She bit her lip and for the thousandth time questioned the difference between too much strength and too much pride. She stood and watched her boys until they were out of sight, and then she set the table for two.

* * *

If Edger was going to get anything accomplished he had to get it started before they hit Main Street, where Ledger's friends would be hanging around the restaurants or the pool hall. It was only a ten-minute walk, so Edger had to hurry yet he wanted to be subtle.

"Ledger, can I asked you something?"

"Sure."

"Was it you that knocked up Pearl?"

"Me?"

"Yeah, you."

"Why are you asking?"

"Pearl's having a hard time by herself. Shouldn't the father be there with her to look after the child?" There, he had said it. He expected a curt and critical reply but all he got was silence.

"You've always thought Pearl was pretty hot," Ledger finally said. But he said it slowly, thoughtfully, trying to get to the bottom of Edger's inquiry.

"That's not the point, Ledger. My feelings are my feelings, but Pearl faces bringing up a baby by herself."

"Herself?" replied Ledger. "Look again. Pearl has more support than a husband could give her. Minnie and Duddy will dote on that baby. Then there's...."

"There's who? Fudd?" Edger asked. "So the kid has grandparents and a dumb uncle. Big deal! She needs a father. If you're the father you ought to step up to the plate."

Out of the corner of his eye he thought he saw his brother shiver.

"I got my life ahead of me. I'm going to Halifax in January and take a course in plumbing, get a good job. I can't do nothing for Pearl and she knows it."

"But what about Pearl's life?" Edger asked.

"I didn't ask her to get knocked up and I can't do nothing for her now.'

"Have you even seen the baby?" Edger asked.

This time Ledger did shiver noticeably and pulled up the collar on his windbreaker.

"Edger, why don't you marry Pearl and raise the baby? Then I'll be her uncle and bring her presents on her birthday and Christmas. Huh? What do you say? You're so concerned, why not step up to the plate yourself? I'll talk to Pearl. She'll tell Minnie you're the daddy and you're in. How about it?" Ledger was walking faster, leaving his brother behind. He'd had enough.

"Maybe I would if I could," Edger yelled after him, surprising himself. "Pearl wouldn't go along with it and nobody would believe it anyway."

Ledger stopped and turned. "Edger, I can't do anything for them and I don't want Tess to know. You keep your thoughts to yourself."

He walked across the street and Edger slowly walked back towards the Snake. He didn't fit in with Ledger's friends and besides, it would soon be suppertime.

Edger pushed the food around his plate and wondered if Tess knew she was a grandmother. He figured she'd have to know. Tess knew things that were unspoken, just like Ivor Johnson. His mother certainly understood him and his needs before he did. Edger wanted to push the conversation around to Pearl and her baby but he was mindful of Ledger's warning.

"Pearl moved back home today," he said.

There were just the two of them. Tess, sitting across the table had finished her dinner and was having her tea. After meals was the time they talked.

"You're very interested in Pearl and her baby, aren't you?"

Edger swallowed hard. Why the hell was his life always an open book? He wanted to deny it but he wasn't going to lie to his mother, not when he wanted to talk earnestly.

"Yes," he responded.

"Do you wish it was your baby?"

Her question caught him off guard. It was so direct it cut through Edger's defences, which he was prepared to let down for her, but not quite so quickly. He tried to play one-upmanship.

"How do you know it isn't mine?" he asked and immediately felt stupid for saying it.

"I don't think it's your baby and that's not what I asked. What I asked was, do you wish it was yours?"

Edger felt boxed into a corner and confessed. "Yes."

He suddenly wanted to be outside. Tess was making him uncomfortable. She was too close to his vulnerable ground. Too close too quickly. Edger was usually so comfortable with his mother but tonight he felt exposed.

"I just think it's hard on Pearl," he blurted.

"Edger, you're only nineteen years old. You don't have a job. You can't take on someone else's responsibility."

"Even if the baby is related to me?"

He didn't mean to say it, not like that. It just came out. Now it was out on the table. He had blabbed. Told on his brother, which he never, ever did. Now Tess knew. Edger kept his eyes on his plate. He waited, waited. When he finally looked up Tess had her eyes fixed on him.

"Even if the baby is your brother's?" she said softly.

"You know?" he asked.

"Yes, I know."

"Don't tell Ledger I told you."

"I knew already."

"What are you going to do about it?" he asked.

"About what?" Tess replied.

"About the baby," Edger said.

"Nothing."

"Nothing?" he said.

"Nothing," Tess repeated.

"Don't you think we should?"

"No," she replied. "I had you two by myself. I had help and Ledger will have to provide for the child. But that's between Ledger and Pearl, not you and me."

The boys had never learned who their father was but they knew money came to support them.

"You've got a funny way of looking at things. We grew up without a father and I'm against anybody doing that," he said.

"I gave you both plenty of love. I did the best I could and you didn't go without much."

"God, Tess. We're poor. We live on the Snake and you drive an old car. You're a hairdresser!"

"Look around you, Edger," she said with just a bit of hardness in her voice. "The floor is clean, you have good, clean sheets on your bed and you've got food on the table. You've got a lot more than many people and if you want more, go earn it. I did the best I could for you boys and I'll be damned if I'm apologizing at this point in my life."

Their conversation had gone badly. On some issues his mother would not bend. Tess believed in helping others but first she wanted clear evidence they were prepared to help themselves.

After dinner, Edger walked down the Snake. He was deep in thought. There was only one other person he could go to for advice.

4

When Pearl turned sixteen, Duddy made her a high-backed rocking chair out of willow. He fashioned it in their basement, shaping the long bows into the back and seat, weaving them together. He used stout pieces for the legs and fitted them with rockers he'd cut from bird's-eye maple. It was the only thing her father had ever made for her and Pearl loved it. The rocking chair, padded with calico cushions, sat by her bedroom window. It was her special place where she could sit and rock and look down the Snake past Gabby's to the second curve, just before Mink Martin's trailer. She would sit there at night with the lights off and watch people coming and going.

That's why she knew so much about Edger. She would watch him passing her house, staring up at her window. He looked up at her room every time he passed. She had been mad at him for so long it was more a routine than a true feeling. In her dark room, nestled under a quilt and rocking slowly, Pearl would let her true feelings seep out. She secretly acknowledged that when someone carries a torch for you for a long, long time it makes even a hard heart tender. Even a heart that was scared beyond belief by a spider. For months Pearl could feel the insect's legs dancing, scurrying across her spine, and the feeling so terrified her she fought the urge to throw up. She still hated spiders but the terror had gone and so was her hatred of Edger. The truth be told, Pearl felt a little sorry for Edger. He and his brother shared the same looks but they didn't work on Edger. They just didn't quite come together as well.

Pearl thought she loved Ledger at one time. She wasn't sure anymore. Wasn't sure about Ledger or anything else. She didn't even understand the things she did. Her treatment of Edger was the only constant in her life and even that was a sham. In public, Pearl played the role of forever unforgiving, but in her heart she had forgiven Edger long ago.

He was such a dummy. Did he think he could sneak into her yard night after night and climb a tree, for God's sake, without her knowing? She could hear him grunting as he stretched for the higher branches. She was certain she heard him breathing on certain nights when her window was open.

"All right, he wants a show, I'll give him one."

She took her blouse off once with the bedroom light on. She did it again, pretending it was Ledger watching her. One night after an argument with Minnie, Pearl stood with her back to the window and took everything off. That was the night Edger fell out of the tree. She heard the thud as he landed and Fudd running out of the house yelling, "Pervert! Pervert!"

"What is a pervert, Fudd?" Ivor Johnson asked him three days later in Gabby's porch and Fudd guessed it was someone who climbed trees and looked in windows. Everybody laughed and Fudd didn't call Edger a pervert after that.

Pearl was relieved Edger hadn't hurt himself. She knew he wouldn't be back up the tree, but she still sat some nights in the dark waiting for him.

Now, after one night of misadventure with Ledger, Pearl had company in her rocking chair. It was a wonderful place to feed the baby. She would sit by the window and the little package of life sucking for all it was worth gave Pearl immeasurable happiness. The baby filled her with such deep satisfaction that it overcame all her troubles. She could look at despair and smile. The bliss of the baby overcame the problems of no husband and no future. She didn't care. She had her baby. Ledger hadn't lied to her. He told her flat out that if she got pregnant he wouldn't be around. She let him take her anyway and it hurt and she didn't know why she did it. She risked everything, including breaking her mother's heart, knowing full well she would never belong to Ledger. The worst had happened but it was the best too. Minnie had cried at first and then got angry. Duddy fussed around Minnie until she shooed him away and nobody bothered to tell Fudd. When Pearl got big, Fudd just thought she was getting fat.

Except, of course, there was terrible tension. Minnie harboured suspicions concerning paternity and the turmoil in the house had grown with the expansion of Pearl's belly.

Edger was sitting in Ivor Johnson's kitchen trying to explain what he wanted to do. Except he couldn't put it in words that didn't sound crazy. He couldn't just come out and say he would step in and take Pearl off everybody's hands. The problem was, Pearl wouldn't go for it. Probably Minnie wouldn't either and even if they did, Edger had no means of support. Edger knew deep down he had no business trying to intervene in a matter that wasn't his business. He felt his face starting to burn as he fumbled through what he was trying to tell Ivor Johnson. On the third attempt, which was even more garbled, Ivor suddenly interjected, "Tell Pearl."

"Tell Pearl what?" Edger gasped.

"Tell her what you're trying to tell me."

"She'd laugh me out of the house."

"Maybe not," Ivor said. "There's a certain nobility to it. You coming to the rescue. Except maybe Pearl doesn't want or doesn't need to be rescued. But I think she'd be touched by you coming forward. You not being the father and all."

"How do you know I'm not the father?" Edger asked, a little indignant at the certainty of Ivor's statement.

"Hard to get a girl up the stump when you're up a tree," Ivor said and even Edger had to smile.

"Yeah," he replied. "It is."

Later, Edger went for a long walk along the shore. It was all hopeless. He should just go join the army, forget Pearl, forget everything. By four o'clock as the fog was rolling in, covering the shore in a milky mist, that was Edger's plan. A life in uniform, the infantry, a posting overseas maybe. In time he'd forget Pearl and everything and everybody on the Snake and that would be just fine.

By six o'clock, Edger decided since he was going away anyway, why not take one last shot at what he really wanted. Did he have the guts to face Pearl, who had hated him since she was twelve? Did he have the courage to tell her he loved her? He had the courage to join the army. He'd fight. He'd face bullets in battle and that didn't bother him, but facing Pearl took more courage. Why? Because she was just up the road, that's why. The war, when there was one, would be off somewhere, some time in the future but Pearl and her baby and her mother and father and brother were right up the road. Right there, right now. Edger felt there were land mines everywhere, ready to explode and blow him to smithereens. But if he was going away anyway, what the hell. If he left and didn't tell Pearl, he'd always regret it. If they all laughed at him, well, he would just never come back. He'd make a life somewhere else. He'd find someone else in time. Did he have the guts? He was going to jump in the cold water wasn't he? To save her baby, to save them both – wasn't he?

Edger took one admiring glance at his PF Flyers. They weren't new anymore.

At seven o'clock with a sizeable lump in his throat, Edger was walking towards Pearl's house. From her chair she could see him coming. She had watched him walk a million times and she detected there was something different in his stride – a directness. Edger with a purpose.

Before the baby was born, when she watched Ledger walk she would touch her breast and feel her womanhood stir. She didn't look at Ledger now, not at all. Didn't think of him either. Ledger was erased from her mind.

Edger turned into her driveway almost as if he was marching. He was coming to her back door. He was out of her sight but she heard him knock. She heard her mother open the door and Edger talking.

"Can I have a word with Pearl?" Edger asked Minnie.

"She's upstairs with the baby," Minnie replied.

Edger didn't wait to be invited in. He went by her and up the stairs, taking two steps at a time.

Well, if that isn't brazen, Minnie thought.

Pearl heard his footsteps and took a deep breath. He was at her bedroom door. It wasn't completely closed and when he knocked lightly it opened. Pearl covered her breast and snuggled the baby into her. She felt light-headed, as if all the air had suddenly been sucked out of the room.

"Can I talk to you, Pearl?"

Before she could reply, Edger had closed the door. Without hesitation he came and sat on her bed. He moved confidently as if he'd been in her room a thousand times. He locked his hands together and started talking.

"Pearl, I just want you to know that I know who the father of your baby is. I know and I wish it were me instead of him because I'd treat you better. I wouldn't let you bring up this child by yourself without a husband. I just want you to know that."

Pearl felt flushed. She could feel the burning on her face. Was that a tear travelling down her cheek? Was it real?

"I'm very sorry for the spider," Edger continued. "I never have apologized for that and I know –"

"It's all right, Edger," Pearl said softly. "It's all right and thank you."

She put her head down because she was scared she was going to cry and for some reason she didn't want to cry in front of him.

"If there is anything I can do."

"Thank you, Edger," and Pearl knew she was sobbing because real tears were rolling down her cheeks.

There was silence. A car went down the Snake and Pearl looked out her window. Edger sat very still. They were four feet apart and the breathing of the baby brought a rhythm to the dark room. He got up and came to her, bent down and kissed her on the cheek.

"I will do anything for you. Anything at anytime. If you ever need me for any reason to help you in any way, tomorrow, next week, next year, forever," he whispered and kissed her again on the cheek, saying softly in her ear, "forever."

Then he was gone. She didn't know exactly when he left. She didn't hear him go down the stairs. She tried to wipe away her tears to be certain she was even alone. In her entire life no one had ever said such things to her. Pearl cried for an hour.

5

Royal built a special fence at the back of his house to shelter his hybrid double teas. By his front steps he had planted new white miniatures with vivid, deep red climbers shooting up between them. In his side yard he had his two yellow bush roses, a type of grandiflora. He also had bush hybrid teas by the road and rugosa in the middle of his small front yard. In the spring he nourished his roses with bone meal, carefully working it into the ground.

Over the years he had learned from his mistakes. Despite what those American garden books tell you about keeping the crotch of the bushes just above the ground, Royal knew in Nova Scotia you can never plant a rose too deep. "Never too deep and never too much water" was his motto and he had the roses to prove it.

Ivor Johnson brought him his first rose bush from an old farm in Southampton. Royal watered and worked and nurtured it and the roses bloomed. He got more the next year and eventually joined the American Rose Society. He started passing the winter nights by his stove reading about roses. He imported roses from

Texas that died and roses from New York that flourished. Year after year, he tried new things. He dug up bushes and replanted them in different places. People began coming by on their Sunday afternoon drives just to look at his handiwork. Royal was proud of his roses.

Bad winters took their toll when the continual freezing and thawing of the soil practically heaved the bushes out of the ground. The boys on the street ran through some of his roses but Royal never got mad at the boys. His own son would be close to their age and he never got upset with them, no matter what they did.

Despite his roses, at times there was an ache in him, deep in the roots of the man himself. He couldn't quite find the centre of the pain but it caused a numbness in his very core. When autumn came with its cold October nights and the roses withered and died, the ache always got worse. The Matthews woman had moved away in the autumn too. She left suddenly in the midst of a scandal, with Minnie marching down to her house and shouting at her from the street.

He missed the Matthews woman, although he really hardly knew her. She was the one woman whose smell Royal remembered. Although they'd never been close, he nurtured her memory like a rose. She and Duddy? Royal could never understand women. Here he was across the street, alone and available and she took after Duddy. Dear befuddled Duddy who would do anything for anybody, but who had a wife and family. Royal was, well, right there and she didn't notice. He knew he was no Valentino. Tall and thin, with glasses and going bald. No Gary Cooper either. She had been the first woman to light a fire in him in a long, long time. The first since his wife had gone.

Royal was a regular at Gabby's. He came nightly after thumbing through the latest gardening magazine or rose catalogue. Didn't matter if Gabby was home or not. Someone was usually there – Ivor, Duddy or Mink or somebody.

Bruce Graham — Ivor Johnson's Neighbours

Royal lived on a very fixed income but still contributed to the wood stove they'd purchased for Gabby's porch to make it cozy in the winter. They endured long winters and the stove that Ivor got in Amherst had been a good investment.

Royal had once considered Gabby or Tess as possible mates who might want to share his life. Both women were attractive but there was something in Tess that told you to keep your distance and Gabby, with her frizzy auburn hair and nice figure, was appealing but she was like a sister. She had told him bluntly that's how he should see her and he followed her advice.

The truth was, Royal had only had one real love in his life. It was his custom to go down to the shore once or twice a week and just look out over the water. He was still waiting. He had been waiting for years, knowing better of course, yet still expecting them to come over the horizon, Jonathan waving wildly at him and Gloria smiling from the boat. It would have been such a different life if they'd come back.

It was only a day trip across the bay on his father-in-law's fishing boat. They had just disappeared — vanished. The search lasted for days with never a trace except for a few pieces of debris bobbing on the choppy tide. Finally there was a memorial service and Royal didn't want to go because he didn't believe it could end like that. There must be more. His son was seven, his wife twenty-nine.

Even now in some corner of his little house he'd come across something of theirs. A little spoon in the drawer with New York on it that he had bought for her when he worked on the ships. It caused his heart to twist in his chest and left him gasping. Once in the basement, after he thought all of Jonathan's clothes were put away in the trunk, he found his son's striped shirt, the short-sleeved pullover with three buttons on the front. It had been on a hook under an old coat all these years. Royal had taken the shirt off the hook and covered his face with it and cried and cried. After that he didn't go down in his basement and turn things over. If it had been there awhile, it stayed where it was, just in case. Who needed that gut-wrenching experience?

Royal was an early riser. In the summer he would be outdoors as the sun climbed in the eastern sky, its first beams lovingly touching his roses. Sometimes he'd turn on the radio, open the kitchen window and listen to cowboy songs. He loved the Sons of the Pioneers and Hank Williams. Minnie complained, barking across the street that he was waking the dead, so he kept the radio low, worked and smelled his roses. At night he'd slip down through Ivor Johnson's backyard to Gabby's house and hope somebody would be there. He'd been alone all day.

6

abby and Royal had something in common. Both their spouses had disappeared. At least in Royal's case, it was accidental. But in Gabby's situation, Richard's disappearance had been planned and deliberate. She'd come home and his clothes were gone. The closet cleaned out, his shaving things, rubber boots and tools had been taken. She'd never seen him again. Two years later a letter came from a lawyer in Saint John. They divorced and Gabby got the house.

Richard's departure hadn't exactly broken her heart. It was more a relief. She'd hoped his leaving was permanent, that he wouldn't have second thoughts or feel sorry for her and decide to come back. She didn't feel sorry for herself, and as the years passed she questioned whether she was the type of woman who could really love someone. Love and marriage weren't made for everyone and, over time, Gabby came to the conclusion that she was a good woman but not a particularly loving one. Not in the way you should be if you're going to have a husband. Very early on in her marriage she realized the awful truth. She didn't love

Richard. Why had she married him? That was the question that always troubled her. It left in her a mistrust of her own instincts. She supposed in the long run, it didn't much matter. Life went on.

She cooked uptown at Burke's Restaurant, the morning shift. Nothing difficult – bacon and eggs, pancakes, toast and coffee by the buckets. She was home by three. Sometimes, if it was Friday or Saturday night, she made treats for the back porch people. She liked having people around. Sometimes it would just be Royal or Ivor and they'd listen to *Boston Blackie* on the radio or a Red Sox game. Sometimes the porch would be full and her house would ring with laughter and loud talking.

Gabby liked to travel. She made annual visits to Ruth's place in Ontario. Ruth was her older sister who had left home at sixteen and never came back. She didn't talk about it. Their father and mother had died within a year of each other but Ruth didn't attend either funeral. She had married a farmer who owned sheep and cattle. They also owned a big home, a new station wagon, a half-ton truck and always treated Gabby to restaurant meals and movies. Ruth certainly had the money to come home; she just didn't.

Gabby always wanted to ask Ruth about it, but a little voice inside her cautioned it was forbidden territory. Ruth was still the big sister. She was sixteen when Gabby was twelve. Ruth had her own room. Gabby shared a room with her other sisters. Shingles would come off the roof in a high wind and you had to snuggle down and put the covers right over your head. Some nights there were noises Gabby didn't understand at the time. They would hear Ruth crying at night. Sometimes very late, they heard footsteps because the floor in the old house creaked. One night, it was her mother yelling at the top of her voice. She remembered the words that cut the winter chill, her mother sounding animal-like, a despairing shrillness in her tone.

"Leave that child alone."

Then Ruth was gone and nobody took her room because her mother nailed the door closed with three-inch nails, hundreds of them. When Gabby left two years later, the door was still nailed tight.

At times she felt the need to talk about things that happened when they were young, but she couldn't approach Ruth and she repressed the need to try.

Gabby went other places besides her sister's. There were plates on her living room wall from Niagara Falls, Montreal and Florida. Vacation was a special time. Once she and Tess had gone to Boston together but there was edginess between them. Gabby was much more the free spirit, who had to do a selling job to get Tess to try things. Tess wanted to see the Red Sox and do some shopping, but she wasn't fussy on strange foods or tramping around Harvard Square to look at "weirdos."

Tess was more guarded than Gabby. "I have my boys to think about. If something happened to me...well. I'm not prepared to take the chances you take."

Gabby thought, Why not say it. I have nobody so I'm expendable. She kept her mouth shut but found travelling with Tess more of an ordeal than she expected.

When they got home, Tess learned both her boys had been in trouble. Ledger, in court charged with mischief and Edger having problems at school. Tess never went away again. Gabby kept going. She had told herself long ago, despite the stings and slings and arrows, life was short and you might just as well go through it with a smile on your face. There would be time enough for brooding when the worms were crawling through you. Gabby had a practical side.

* * *

Mink Martin didn't have much of a mirror except for the little one he'd walked on and cracked. It was good enough to shave with once a week but it wasn't big enough. He wanted to examine himself front and back. Since he'd come home from Halifax, he expected the mysterious pains to get worse and boils to break out all over his body. He couldn't feel anything and an examination of some sort was called for. They'd been telling him for years he didn't eat properly. The fact was, he didn't eat at all until he was hungry and that wasn't often. Nothing a can of something – beans, Irish stew or soup – couldn't cure. His doctor said leafy green vegetables were needed but Mink had never had time for that rabbit stuff. It got in the way of his drinking, which usually started around noon. In the evenings when he went over to Gabby's, Mink was already well underway. Usually he'd fall asleep on her table. Mink only ate well when Gabby fed him which, fortunately for him, was often.

Mink was a veteran. He had been overseas in the Great War and every November, Mink would shake the moths out of his Legion jacket, pin on his medals and go uptown for the ceremonies. His infantry company had been assigned to a British regiment with the stupidest officers possible who blundered through four years of war, sipping sherry by the fire while their men shivered in muddy, rat-infested trenches.

Most of the war was a blur. He felt he'd spent four years face down in the mud. The guns had deafened him. The smoke had been so thick that if you stumbled during a charge and got up dizzy, you didn't know which direction to run. Once Mink found himself running alongside someone. He couldn't see much through the mist and just assumed it was another Canadian. It was a young German about his age. They were side by side, running in the same direction. They looked at each other, trying to make sense of things. The German, breathless and wide-eyed, staring at Mink as if they were caught in some hideous time warp. He wanted to say something to the German but of course he didn't. They both stopped, breathless and weary, looking at each other until the German ran off in the opposite direction. Mink didn't know if he was running to his side or away from it. Mink didn't run. He just sat down on the ground and closed his eyes.

The French always baffled him. They were sometimes helpful and sometimes hostile. Their women had hairy legs and were so pious around priests but so free at other times. His only experience with women was during the war. Willing women. Mass at nine and frolicking in bed by ten, sneaking away from their sleeping families to meet the soldiers.

At the end of the war, Mink got drunk and punched an officer in the face. He would have been thrown in the guardhouse, but there was so much confusion, nobody wanted to do anything but celebrate and they let him slip away.

"Go on, nobody knows who you are anyway. Go on, get lost," a sergeant bellowed.

He didn't find his regiment for a week and didn't remember where he'd been, except there was an old lady and a candle and she was leading him up some stairs. That's all he remembered of his last leave in Paris.

And then home. Suddenly. So different. Home with his hearing damaged and his eyes watery from the gas. He couldn't adjust. Every night he thought he was still in the war. He would wake up screaming. It had ended too fast. He wasn't ready. Or he was past being ready.

He worked in a lumber mill loading lumber when a ship came in but he was never very strong. He finally got a small pension. He lived on that, the flatfish he caught, the dulse he picked and the clams he dug.

Ivor Johnson took him places. Uptown for a pair of boots or up to Amherst once in a while. On a Sunday afternoon sometimes, Ivor took him down the shore. Mink liked that until they got too close to where he grew up. He'd repay Ivor with flatfish or by leaving beets and turnip on Ivor's back steps.

Mink was sixty-three and he still had bad dreams. They were the things he couldn't remember when he was awake. Blurred images of men running through the smoke and a canopy of large shells whizzing overhead with deafening noise, body parts, arms and legs, flying through the air. Once, a man's torso struck him as he was advancing and it made him retch. Everything at once: fire, smoke, shells, men dying and himself on his knee getting sick.

He fell over, off his haunches and realized he'd messed himself too. He started to laugh then. It was funny. He'd shit himself and it made him laugh. They'd sent him on leave after that and his hearing partially came back. He was sent up to the front again. His first day back and he saw his captain's head blown off.

Mink had always been poor. He had grown up in East Advocate. He and his brothers slept on old straw mattresses. There was only one room with a big wood stove in the centre and a barrel of rainwater in the corner. His mother and father slept up in the crawlspace underneath the roof. They had a dirt floor and plenty to eat in the winter as long as you liked rabbit and deer meat. They didn't see fruit except a few apples. His father was a harsh man who worked in the woods and put his boys to work at an early age. At fourteen, Mink was swinging an axe ten hours a day. When his hands blistered he'd break the ice and stick them in the cold water of a brook until there was no feeling in his fingers. Then he'd curl them around his axe and go back to work.

His father had cuffed him hard once in front of the other men. Mink had said nothing, just picked up his axe and walked away. When he got to a deep gully he threw the axe as far as he could, watching the handle rotate end over end down the deep ravine. He walked in the freezing cold until somebody gave him a drive. He kept going until he reached Halifax. It was 1915. They were looking for volunteers. Eight months later he was in France and the woods of East Advocate seemed far, far away.

He'd lost touch with his family except for one brother who used to visit occasionally. He hadn't even seen him in years and expected he was dead. Mink's life hadn't been much to start with and it hadn't got much better. He never bothered with electric lights. His was the only place on the Snake without running water. He still had his outhouse and he couldn't see the need for indoor stuff.

Gabby and Tess brought him stew or biscuits and homemade soup. They offered to clean up the place for him but Mink declined.

He had taken a liking to Ledger and let Ledger drive the old truck. Mink's truck was a vintage Ford. Mink was an authority on motor vehicles and owned various parts to various makes and models. But Mink's pride and joy – his most valuable possession – was his hubcap collection. Mink collected many things but hubcaps were his speciality.

People in town thought of Mink as a hermit. He didn't know that and wouldn't have believed it anyway. What way was there to live except the way he lived? Tobacco, whiskey, sugar, beans, and firewood. What else did a man need? Mink Martin lived the way he wanted to. The only way he knew. He didn't have a philosophy of life because he didn't need one.

7

On special days like Christmas or Easter, Tess would invite Mink over for dinner. He'd dress as respectably as he could and try not to drink too much ahead of time. She would invite Ivor Johnson, Royal and Gabby too. Like Gabby, Tess was a fabulous cook. Everybody agreed on that.

She was also an excellent housekeeper. You could eat off her floors. That was the key to good housekeeping in Whitehall, eating off the floor. Not that anyone actually did but if they did, they didn't have to worry about germs.

Tess always looked trim and neat. Her dark hair had a classic touch of silver at the temples and was never askew. That would be bad advertising. She had worked at Barb's Beauty Parlour for years and the women of the town trusted her hands to make them look younger and prettier. If she succeeded in their eyes they gave her a tip. Tess was Barb's best stylist. Even Barb admitted it. People said she should open her own place and Barb feared she would. But the years passed, and Tess became a fixture at the beauty parlour on the little street behind the drugstore.

Tess was fifty-two, still attractive and more than one man, including of course Duddy, had made advances. If you could call Duddy's outstretched, trembling hand an advance. Tess had slapped it away and told him to behave or she'd tell Minnie. He never tried again.

"If your backside hasn't been brushed by the wandering hand of that man, you must live in another county," Tess told Gabby. She was not fat by any means, but her shape was beginning to take on the middle-aged plumpness that rounds out curves and tells a woman she is no longer the young thing she once was. Tess was more distinctive looking than pretty. The grey temples and raven hair highlighted her slightly protruding green eyes, which gave her an expression of mild surprise. She was attractive and distinguished enough to turn a head or two.

Like every house on the Snake there were secrets hovering over Tess's domain. The identity of the boys' father had always been a mystery. Nineteen years ago when they were born, it was the topic to wag tongues, but it became one of those things the moss of time grew over. Occasionally in the years since, there were guessing games as to whether there was a man in Tess's life. She was seen with Ivor or Royal but there was never anything definitive. People just gossiped anyway. Who needed validity?

Tess went to church Sundays with her boys. She sometimes went to dances Saturday night with one of her girlfriends. No man ever took her home. Maybe it was because of the incident that had made Tess famous.

Years ago when the boys were small, she had shot a man. He was a drifter working on a farm outside of town, helping bring in the hay. He broke into Tess's house on a late summer night in 1937. She heard the breaking glass and met him halfway up the stairs. He was unarmed. She wasn't. The small 410 shotgun tore the muscle off his right calf but he still made it to her front yard before collapsing.

There was an inquiry. It was in all the newspapers and Tess received letters of support from as far away as Quebec and Manitoba. "You have a right to defend your children."

With no will to prosecute, the matter was dropped but it wasn't the end of the story. The burglar's name was Hathaway. He was from over the bay some place and had no home and no next of kin. During his hospital stay he became a ward of the town. They needed a place for him to convalesce before his trial. A local woman named Norma, who ran a boarding house, agreed to take him in if he was handcuffed to the bed to protect her and her boarders.

Things happened. Norma found Hathaway was not without charm. Eventually he went to jail and she wrote him regularly. When he was released, they married. They still lived just outside of town and were seen some Saturday nights coming in for their groceries. Hathaway still walked with a bit of a limp and people often asked Tess if she ever ran into him.

"Wouldn't know him if I did," she declared. "And I want to keep it that way."

Tess was an independent woman.

Tess's reputation with a gun didn't deter Duddy. He was afraid of her but fear mingled with lust is a powerful force. Duddy was afraid of Gabby too and more afraid of Minnie. Duddy lived with fear. After Minnie had caught him with Mrs. Matthews, she threw him on the kitchen floor and kicked him, but it was the drop down the cellar steps that did most of the damage. That, and the stick of hardwood that caught him under the eye and caused him to receive several stitches. Ivor Johnson took him to the hospital where they kept him overnight – for his own safety.

Since then, Duddy's passion had cooled and the world's most unlikely Casanova had more or less gone into retirement. When he found a willing woman Duddy couldn't help himself. His secret weapon was that he could make women laugh. Sometimes they laughed because Duddy was so funny looking. He was like a puppet, with arms and legs seemingly attached to strings somewhere above his head. No wonder he brushed so many bottoms; his hands were always in motion. When he was worried, mostly around Minnie, he would pace back and forth making faces. Duddy had a face that could curl up like a rubber doormat.

Duddy was what they called a half-assed carpenter. He didn't take on big stuff like building houses or barns but if you needed a new set of steps Duddy was your man. Need a new platform for your clothesline? Call Duddy. There was never much work and never much money. Minnie cleaned houses and did the washing at the hotel, so between them they survived.

When Minnie closed her legs after Fudd was born she unleashed that passionate half-assed carpenter on the landscape of Cumberland County. But Duddy was never the threat more sinister men were. Duddy took no for an answer, if not constantly, frequently. But there was a highly likeable side to Duddy and that was enough to get him in trouble. The stories about Duddy were numerous.

Once in the spring, Duddy was parked at the beach with Marlene Rafuse. Passion has a way of holding one's attention even when the tide is creeping in. Marlene's heavy breathing blocked the lapping of seawater. Intensity and preoccupation are not always good. Duddy and Marlene should have noticed the odour of petroleum as the ocean surrounded the gas tank. Love is blind and sometimes dumb too. Duddy didn't bother to look; he was preoccupied. Had he just cleaned the steam off the windows!

Lucky for Duddy it was Marlene's car, bad luck for Marlene that it actually belonged to her husband. Duddy didn't think about ownership at first of course. He didn't know if the perspiration pouring out of him was from the bumping and grinding they had been doing or the fact that the engine had gone dead and Marlene had gone white. The water was almost to the windows. She tried and tried to start the engine, believing that by erratically slapping the steering wheel, the dash and Duddy it would somehow help. There was not even a sputter. Duddy tried to open the door but the water was so high it wouldn't budge. Marlene was becoming hysterical.

In a panic they abandoned the vehicle by climbing through the windows and wading in the waist-high seawater. They stood on shore and shivered in the moonlight as less and less of Marlene's husband's car stayed visible and more and more of Marlene was in a state of frenzy. Crying one minute and jumping up and down the next, she swore at Duddy using such a high grade of profanity that even Duddy was shocked. Such language from a respectable woman was undignified.

He helped her off the beach and into the bushes at the edge of the woods where they huddled and shivered. Marlene alternately cried and swore. Duddy understood they had a lot to worry about. Marlene's husband was a big strapping man known to have a bad temper. And there was his almost-new car slowly being engulfed by the salt water of the Minas Basin.

"What the hell am I going to do?" she wailed. "He'll kill me, kill both of us. God, look, look, look the car is drowning!"

In normal circumstances with women other than his wife, it was Duddy's inclination to pacify them. In a less urgent situation, he would have slowly rubbed Marlene's shoulders, whispering "Now, now." But there was no time for such niceties. Besides, the poor woman was beyond the point of pacification. Duddy was thinking, and thinking hard. He didn't waste his brain on what he saw as the humdrum, day-to-day aspects of life. He saved his grey matter for when it really counted. There was nothing he could do about the car so he went on to the next step. This man who had built so many steps was not concentrating on the present, but on the future. The car might be done for but he and Marlene were still alive.

"It's God's revenge," she moaned while they crouched in the bushes.

"God had nothing to do with it," Duddy replied.

"Yes! Yes, He has. Who made the tide come in and who covered the car with water? It's God's revenge on a Christian woman who has always worked for the church, who has been faithful in prayer. Me!" she screamed as though she walked through a nightmare.

"Out here on the cold beach letting you... Oh my God, it's His revenge."

An idea bloomed in Duddy's mostly unused mind at that moment, but first he had to quiet her down. "Marlene, the tide comes in, the tide goes out. Day after day. The water would be here whether we were here or not. Don't blame God. Tell me about your church."

She looked at him in one startling second as if he were a mad man.

"You crazy bastard," she screamed and ran out of the bushes, down to the beach. Duddy sighed, shivered and ran after her so he could explain his plan.

Two hours later, Marlene Rafuse called the police to report her car had been stolen from the parking lot of the Baptist Church where she was setting tables for tomorrow night's ham and potato scallop dinner. The car was recovered the next morning.

"Kids out for a joy ride," the police chief said. "Damn young people today. No respect."

Marlene got royal shit for leaving the keys in the vehicle. "But who," she pleaded, "would steal a car at a church?" People agreed there were some low scoundrels in the world.

Minnie told the entire story to Duddy while nursing him back to health from a severe case of pneumonia. Police never caught the culprits. The only clue left behind was an unexplained pair of woman's panties. The insurance settled eventually and Marlene's husband bought himself a new Chevy sedan. It was a long time before he let her drive it.

Besides thinking his way out of tight situations, Duddy had some other good points. He helped the needy. He took apples and flounder to the down-and-outers. Duddy knew some folks had it hard. Without deer meat and flatfish there would be no food on the table. Duddy helped as best he could.

Duddy's charity started a few years earlier when he was doing a job next door to a large family with several children and a still attractive mother. He saw the need. He brought apples and potatoes. He even gave the guy a lift to town and brought some of Fudd and Pearl's old clothes to the youngsters. The family was grateful. The mother rubbed her hands on her apron as she did when she was sincere. Duddy tried to take advantage of course, which ruined the moment and he left a little less of a saint but she still waved goodbye when he drove away.

He was a saint on one occasion. Coming through Halfway River early one morning, Duddy came upon a house fire. He was credited with saving a family of four. Minnie made him a pumpkin pie as a reward and smiled at him all day. Duddy was in her good books and he wasted no time taking advantage of his hero status. That's when Minnie relinquished her vow of celibacy and took her hero husband to bed.

That was Duddy: a brush with death one minute and brushing your backside the next. Duddy was predictable.

8

If Duddy was a half-assed carpenter, Fudd would have to be classified as a quarter-assed carpenter and even that was only on a good day. Once Duddy got a job in town putting new shutters on a house. The owner was a cat lover and she wanted feline figures on each shutter. Duddy traced the figures, cut them out with his jig saw and left Fudd to put them up while he went up to Five Islands to price another job. When he got back, Fudd had nailed half the cats hanging upside down.

Fudd wasn't stupid in the normal sense of the word. He just didn't notice things. Once on a Monday, he skipped school and went fishing, totally oblivious to the fact that it was the beginning of final exams.

Fudd dropped out after grade nine and Duddy knew his son wasn't going to get very far from the Snake. "Best to take him in with me and try to teach him something." But teaching wasn't one of Duddy's skills and Fudd wasn't a quick learner.

Fudd had erotic problems too that worried Minnie. There had been stains on his bed sheets since he was thirteen and it became a point of contention between Minnie and Duddy as to who should talk to him. Duddy tried explaining the facts of life but they were mostly unexplainable. Fudd didn't have a clue what his father was jabbering about. Finally Dr. Hill took on the task, but after the facts of life lesson, the stains increased dramatically, as if Fudd had been given a license to whip the lizard as much as he wanted.

The escalation of events caused Minnie to use her last weapon — threats of blindness and insanity. She told Fudd at the kitchen table that the asylum was full of people who got into bad practices. Fudd said nothing, just lowered his head until his face was almost in his Cornflakes.

The last Halloween had been a particularly low point for Fudd. Most boys might soap a few windows or drape a stolen clothesline across the road to expand and snap when caught by unsuspecting motorists. Fudd had come home in such a deplorable condition that Minnie was first enraged, then troubled to the point of crying and then laughing, when the humour of it finally hit her. Fudd wasn't happy with her rage and he didn't like his mother crying, but he damn well didn't like her laughing either.

It had been noted that Fudd often came out the worst in things. On Halloween he and Ledger decided to turn over a few outhouses so they picked Ned Smith's as a good place to start. Ned's outhouse was larger than most. In good weather, he liked to take the newspaper and spend enough time out there to get through the sports pages, which meant he needed a good-sized window, high enough off the ground to provide privacy, yet big enough so he would have light to read by. Ned was a man who liked his pleasures.

Because of the size of the rather opulent outhouse, it took all the strength Fudd and Ledger could muster to topple it. They braced themselves at the back and pushed and heaved until the building slowly lifted off the ground. They let their hands walk down the back wall to get more leverage and heaved again. It almost toppled. One more time and it would go.

Fudd had on the new jacket Minnie had just bought him at Resnicks' fall sale. To him it was beautiful. Black corduroy with thin, vertical gold stripes. As he pushed, Fudd's outstretched arm was right in front of his face. He couldn't help admiring the soft corduroy with the almost invisible metallic strips while listening to Ledger's whispered commands.

"Push, push!"

Between the jacket, the commands and the pushing Fudd didn't notice the nail. It protruded three inches below his left arm. When the substantial structure finally toppled, his sleeve caught in the nail, propelling poor Fudd off his feet and hurling him headfirst into the vacant hole where the outhouse had been. Fudd squirmed, let out a cry and was immediately sorry he did. He bobbed around before finding his footing at the bottom of the pit. He was waist deep in the shit and slime.

The outhouse had crashed down with a terrible noise that alerted Ned Smith's dog. The lights came on and Ned was at the door. Ledger was already flying through the fields while Fudd was still trying to scamper out of the shit hole. It got worse. At the end of the field behind Ned's house was a high wooden fence, a fence Ned had put up to keep the deer from coming into his yard and eating his apples. Ledger, always the good athlete, scaled the fence like quicksilver. By the time Fudd got to the fence, Ned's dog was at his heels. The aroma wafting off Fudd heightened the dog's animal instinct for rotten meat. With a great grunt, Fudd got to the top of the fence and jumped into the darkness – straight into the middle of the biggest bunch of burdock in Whitehall.

Ledger was waiting at the edge of the woods when Fudd arrived, covered in human waste with bits of toilet paper fluttering off his shoulders like small white wings. Burdock covered his hair and he smelled like the stinkhole he'd just climbed out of.

"What the hell happened to you?" Ledger asked, rapidly backing away. He already knew the answer, but he wanted to hear the firsthand account from Fudd.

"Shit!" Fudd gasped with shock and exasperation, totally missing the irony of his comment.

Minnie wouldn't let him in the house. She made him strip naked and hose himself down. Unfortunately, Pearl's friends from town picked that minute to drive into the yard, their headlights catching the shit-stained body of a naked man running for cover.

Pearl was upstairs getting ready. She saw the car lights and looked out the window just in time to see her brother's bare buff and burdocked head race around the corner of the house. Her friends peeled out of the driveway, squealing tires, and Pearl was too humiliated to go anywhere. She spent Halloween slowly rocking in her willow chair.

Fudd spent most of the evening in the bathtub.

Fudd had a voice you didn't want to listen to very long. It had such an unusual pitch it got your attention at first, then shortly drove you crazy. It had an unnatural, high scratchiness.

"His balls never dropped," Mink Martin said, and people nodded in agreement as if Mink was the unquestioned expert on dropping balls.

Minnie had a different theory on Fudd's voice. It went back to when Fudd was five. He and Lumpy Brown got some of Duddy's chewing tobacco and put big plugs in their mouths. Once the strong juice started going down his throat, Lumpy spit out the wad and went into the bushes to get sick. To prove he was superior, Fudd kept chewing. The juice made him gag and in trying to catch his breath, he swallowed the entire wad – lock, stock and plug. There was no running into the bushes for Fudd. He got sick right on the road. On his hands and knees he was gagging and vomiting and stopping traffic. Minnie said his voice was never the same after that. She blamed it on the tobacco burning her son's voice box.

So Fudd was a quarter-assed carpenter, a prolific masturbator, and an eighteen-year-old virgin with a squeaky voice. He was short of stature, with Minnie's blocky square shoulders but none of Duddy's rural charm. Fudd walked with his arms dangling at his sides and his head pitched slightly forward, as if he were about to fall on his face.

The one thing Fudd had going for him was muscle. The only thing he had stuck with since childhood was bodybuilding. He had sent away for "The Atlas Man Muscle Course" when he was ten. Unlike most customers, Fudd had remained loyal to Charles Atlas. He was as uncoordinated as Duddy, but unlike his father, Fudd had a physique of chiselled stone. The biceps bulged in his short arms and his stomach rippled. That was why Fudd, unlike anybody else on the Snake, walked around in short sleeves in mid-winter. Fudd had a physique.

Ledger would never admit it but he was envious. He thought the muscles were totally wasted on Fudd. Secretly, Ledger tried to duplicate the same physique but he could never develop the bulging biceps or the washboard stomach that Fudd had built. He finally gave up. It was too chancy being caught by Edger or his mother and they might tell somebody that he was trying to look like Fudd. Besides, Ledger rationalized, he was doing great the way he was. He would stand in front of the mirror, shirtless and do his best pose. Ahhhh...he was just fine.

If Ledger had been the type to take himself under the Whitehall Bridge and really think about things, a few conclusions might have come to him. But Ledger had little time for deep thinking. The only "deep" he was interested in was getting "deep" between Nancy Johnson's legs and the sooner the better.

Unlike the hapless Edger and the inept Fudd, Ledger had lost his virginity early. He was fifteen and hired to pile wood for Peggy Upshaw. She was a widow in her thirties who took more than a casual interest in Ledger's wood piling ability. She was interested in the human body, she said, because she sketched and wanted Ledger to pose for her. She showed him a book with several male models in various stages of undress.

"Would you be too shy to take your clothes off for me?"

He laughed and said he'd be happy to. When the wood was piled, Ledger went to Peggy's bedroom, "where the light was better."

He took off his clothes and Peggy sketched. Once the novelty of being naked wore off, Ledger could feel himself starting to get an erection. He did everything to stop it, finding the best remedy was imagining himself plunging into cold water. When he stopped thinking of cold water, the erection began again and Peggy started to laugh. Then she seduced him.

Ledger came back for more, twice, three, four times, until Peggy said they should stop. She never let him into her house again. He never saw the finished sketch either. When they'd meet by chance uptown, Peggy always gave him a knowing little smile that made something inside him stir.

Ledger learned when he was sixteen that there was a great difference between a willing, experienced woman and a not-so-willing, inexperienced sixteen-year-old. With his background, Ledger just assumed he would have no trouble. He was totally wrong and his next attempts at increasing his sexual range and variety failed miserably. It was often a question of penetration. The wet willingness of Peggy Upshaw turned into something dry and taut.

The reason Ledger wasn't fingered as the father of Pearl's baby was not a mystery. Their entire romance was over before it was a romance. One night after a dance and a Sunday drive to Diligent River in Mink Martin's truck, Ledger turned onto a dirt road and became most diligent himself. Pearl thought it was love, that her prayers had been answered. She tried to restrain herself when Ledger didn't call. She didn't confront him until she was sure she was pregnant. They went for a long walk on the shore and Ledger made it all very clear. She was nothing special and he would not take responsibility for the baby. He would help financially but only when he got on his feet. A future together was out of the question. His abruptness was easier to take than evasion or a half-hearted commitment. At least Pearl knew.

Once the crying was over, Pearl would live with the pain. Ivor Johnson helped her. Pearl never knew exactly why she went to him. She guessed she just followed the example of her father.

Ivor listened, nodded and said a firm no when she asked if there was anything that he could do to bring Ledger on side.

"There are people, including me, Royal and Gabby, who can help you, Pearl." He laid things out for her. What would happen and how it would happen. Ivor Johnson knew from day one who the father was. But he was a man who could keep his mouth shut.

Ledger kept his mouth shut too. There was no bragging to his buddies about his conquest of Pearl, partly because it was no big deal for him. Pearl was known to be loose. She wasn't, but as with many young women of meagre circumstance, the frustration of rejected boys turns to fabrication, which unfortunately doesn't often translate into truth. Life is never fair. Even if Ledger were suspected of being the father, he would probably be excused. Ledger was excused from much. There were even guys, in an effort to be in his inner circle, who were ready to take the blame for him.

Ledger looked at pro sports as a career. He was a good hockey player and considered trying out for the Amherst Ramblers, a team that could be a stepping stone to the NHL. Easier maybe than making the majors in baseball, at which he also excelled. He decided he could play semi-pro sports in Halifax. By taking the plumbing course he would have something to fall back on. He didn't want to look down drains the rest of his life. But owning a small plumbing company wouldn't be so bad.

He would make enough to look after Tess, provide for her in her old age. Now there was the baby too. Ledger hoped Pearl would get married. She wasn't bad looking, slightly plump and taller than most guys, but she had a pretty face. It was harder for a woman with a child to catch a guy. Not impossible but more difficult.

Maybe Edger would step up to the plate. Ledger knew of no other brother who would do such a thing. But Edger just might, considering the load of hot coals he carried for Pearl. Would Pearl go for it? Probably not. Would Minnie allow it? Maybe, just to get her daughter married.

Ledger would not abandon the kid. He just wanted to put some distance between himself and all of them until the baby was two or three and there wasn't so much drooling and bawling. He could skip that diaper stage, but he did want to have a real good look at his daughter just to see if there was any resemblance.

Ledger had his built-in defences. It was a good thing he was going to make enough money to look after Tess, because it wasn't certain Edger was going to be able to look after himself, let alone anybody else. Edger had somehow detached himself from the world. He was in a fog. He had no plans. He didn't give a thought for tomorrow. Ledger couldn't understand it. His brother didn't seem to want to get away, to get the hell out of here. He seemed content with the same people he had known all his life, the same dumpy little street, the same dull little town.

Not Ledger. He was going to make his mark in the world. Ledger would come back with a new car. He didn't know the make or model but he knew it would be long and black, with high tail fins and plenty of chrome. Ledger would be the one who made it. Ledger had confidence in Ledger.

9

Minnie believed in Minnie, but not because she wanted to. She believed she was the most misunderstood woman in Cumberland County. If Minnie were a piece of furniture, people would see her as an upright chair: a straight back with solid arms when she really longed to be a recliner. Except she couldn't recline, she just couldn't. Her parents had rammed the straight back down her spine permanently. Straight-backed themselves and hard workers too. Church every Sunday, lodge workers, abstainers from strong drink, abstainers from fornication and anything else that spelled fun.

Minnie followed their example. Except in times of total desperation, she frowned on foul language; she had taken the lye soap to Fudd more than once and Duddy too, for that matter. Minnie marched the straight and narrow with a rigid view of life. Not that she wanted too. She'd like to relax, she told herself, but when you really thought about it, what choice did she have? With a family like hers, what was the alternative? Minnie was the moral compass and it was a tiring, thankless job. The kitchen sink was where she cried. Her hands in warm dishwater equalized the hot tears streaming down her face.

Minnie would have loved to have a real confidant, someone to share her troubles. Tess maybe, but Minnie had trouble getting close to people. She never remembered being hugged by her mother or patted on the head by her father. Theirs wasn't a family of loving bonds.

Both her parents thoroughly disapproved of Duddy. Her father called him a jackass.

Her mother's response as she remembered it was "Even you, Minnie, can do better than that."

She hadn't shed a tear when they died, even in the double blow of death. They were found by neighbours – purple, blue and bloated on their bed, their hands on the family Bible. On her mother's chest was the poison bottle.

They had gone together. Her father had tumours. The doctors said he was riddled with them. They were causing him a lot of pain and when he heard he had only a matter of months or a year at the most, he took things into his own hands.

And her mother? She wasn't dying of anything but repressed freedom. Minnie guessed her father told her to take the poison with him and she willingly obeyed. Stupid woman.

No, Minnie never shed a tear for her parents yet she was perceptive enough to understand that many of the tears at the kitchen sink in subsequent years were because of them. You cry now, you cry later. Tears are tears and delayed tears are just as wet.

Minnie was rife with multiple levels of mistrust that caused much of her anxiety.

She didn't trust her husband. That was easy to understand. She didn't trust her son because – well, Minnie wouldn't admit it, didn't want to say it even to herself, to let loose in her conscious mind that Fudd was slow. In her day they would have called him half-witted but that was untrue and unkind.

"Oh God, please let me know it isn't so. That he just appears to be dim-witted but really isn't."

All the mistrust in Minnie made her doubt Pearl as well, when in fact Pearl gave her no reason. At least until the one indiscretion that led to pregnancy and doomed any hope of rebuilding the bond between mother and daughter. When Pearl refused to reveal the identity of her child's father, it hurt Minnie because it reminded her of her own mother. Then it infuriated her so much, it unearthed a dark gloom in her soul. The years of layering despair rose to the surface. The vileness of the human soul was so bad and so black anything might happen. Her thoughts churned as she recalled all those things her mother told her were possible. In her mind's eye, Minnie could see her masturbating, dim-witted son and her daughter copulating like frenzied animals. It was almost more than she could bear.

Minnie had fought the gloom. She had to in order to go on, but the picture and the veiled images remained. Coupled with the hurt and the anger, that was enough for her to drive Pearl from the house.

Pearl rushed up the road and cried in Gabby's arms. Minnie did the dishes and added to the water in the sink. Duddy in despair shuttled back and forth between the two houses, having a nip on the way. Then he finally knocked on Ivor Johnson's door.

Ivor had the touch. He was the only person who could move Minnie away from a fixed position. It's difficult to shift a moral compass. There wasn't anybody on the Snake who could dig in their heels deeper than Minnie.

Fifteen years ago, her lodge was having an appreciation dinner and Minnie brought three pies, only to be told by Marge MacDonald she was supposed to bring salads, not pies. Minnie said no, she certainly was not supposed to bring salads. That started it. She and Marge got into a bit of a donnybrook right in front of their lodge sisters and some paying dinner guests. Fifteen years later, Minnie and Marge were still lodge sisters but they never spoke another word to each other. Over the years, various members felt the call to attempt reconciliation. All failed to bring the disputants together.

Her argument with Marge was one of the few occasions when Minnie permitted some latitude in her pristine language. Marge MacDonald was always "That damn woman!" Otherwise, except when she was really upset at Duddy, or Royal had his radio so loud it would wake the dead, Minnie's vocabulary was quite proper.

Lately, Minnie felt a change. She knew the moral compass was wearing down. She felt the needle moving away from magnetic north. She could tell by her relationship with Duddy. She was upset with her husband often but not as often as a few years ago. She was beginning to let little things slide, maybe because Duddy himself was slowing down. Minnie was relieved. She knew he had broken all his marriage vows but she had never given serious thought to leaving him. Leaving her husband would prove her parents right, and Minnie would not permit even the fantasy of them smirking from beyond the grave. Besides she would not, could not, break her vows. If Minnie pledged to do something, or even casually suggested it, it would get done.

The straight back chair was reliable. So was Ivor Johnson.

* * *

When Ivor Johnson was born in 1906 his father was away fishing, so the task of naming him fell upon his mother. Mrs. Johnson was a well-read woman but her interests did not include weaponry or sporting guns. If that had not been the case, she would never have named her nine-pound baby boy Ivor. Had she known about shotguns, Mrs. Johnson might have been perceptive enough to understand such a nomenclature would quickly have produced a nickname like Shotgun. There was hardly a house in her community that didn't have an Iver Johnson Shotgun. Even if her son's name had a slightly different spelling, it didn't matter. The Iver Johnson Arms and Cycle Works Company had been in existence since 1871. If you bought a shotgun from the Sears, Roebuck catalogue, you didn't get a Sears, Roebuck shotgun, you got an Iver

Johnson shotgun. So it was natural for Ivor Johnson, early on in his life, to get the nickname Shotgun.

A few close friends called him Hammer, another relationship to the shotgun. The motto adopted by the Iver Johnson Arms and Cycle Works Company in 1904 was "Hammer the Hammer." Ivor would get at least a couple of Christmas cards each year with a short message starting "Dear Hammer."

Nobody on the Snake ever called Ivor Johnson Hammer or Shotgun.

People in town speculated Ivor was wealthy, at least by the meagre standards on the Snake. People said he had invested wisely, bought and sold when times were right. When he was in his late thirties he'd sold his lobster boat, traps and everything and bought lumber and blueberry land. A few years later, he sold all that property to an American with deep pockets. Of course it was only speculation. Ivor didn't flash a wad of bills around. He didn't drive a flashy truck or take trips to far away places. Ivor didn't have a grand house or great plans. He lived a quiet and unassuming life.

He was a man you could put the touch on if things were really bad. Again it was all rumour, the loose talk of the barbershop or beauty parlour. The kind of idle chatter below the cloud of cigarette smoke from men making the corner pocket at Sam MacClary's pool hall. Rumours maybe, but there were witnesses too. People who would swear Ivor had helped a woman in Riverside send her daughter to Teachers College or that he had donated enough for an operation for Bobby Giles to get his neck straight. Was it true, or was it just the chatty breeze that sweeps the streets of all small towns? Only Ivor knew and he wasn't talking. But when you were down on your luck you could take a chance. You might swallow your pride and knock on his door.

"Ivor, I'm strapped. The wife is sick, the kids got no food. Can you stand me a loan until I get back on my feet?"

People came away with the cash. The only condition was pay it back when you can and ...

"Keep this between us. Okay?"

"Sure Ivor, if you say so."

A secret transaction is often so secret the borrower forgets. Ivor never tried to retrieve unpaid loans. Of course there were those he flatly refused. If you came reeking of whiskey you got nothing. Two downshore deadlies out of money and looking for another bottle knocked one night. They were quarrelsome guys, trying to look sober through bloodshot eyes. They asked first and then demanded in slurry sentences that a loan was necessary.

"Boys, best you go home and sleep it off," said Ivor.

The deadlies thought of making a stand and pressing the point, but one look at Ivor's barrel chest and huge arms and they backed off. Their intoxicated minds worked well enough to decide against it. Ivor was not a man to trifle with. Stories of his strength were almost as common as stories of his wealth and philanthropy.

Gabby had seen it when they brought the wood stove for her porch. Royal, Duddy and Ledger struggled to get it out of Ivor's truck while he went home to get some strapping. They left it at the bottom of her steps until they got more help carrying it into her house. Ivor came back in a few moments and picked up the stove by himself, his bear-like arms straining under the weight. He carried it up the steps and across the porch to the new hearth he'd built. She never forgot the look on Duddy's face when he came back and the stove was in place.

Gabby would wonder sometimes what it would be like to have arms that strong around her. She and Ivor had been alone many a night sitting on her porch. He had never made an improper advance or even hinted he was having an impure thought. Gabby wasn't a bad looker, she told herself. She still had a figure, even more so than Tess, since Gabby never had children. She wasn't even a little broad in the beam. No schoolgirl, but not dried up either, yet Ivor never once tried anything even resembling a pass.

"Ivor's not the kind of man who needs someone," Tess had told her a few years ago.

Gabby guessed she was right. She knew he would help her if she ever needed him and just having him next door was a comfort.

Yet still, late at night under the warmth of her bedcovers, Gabby wondered sometimes if she was really like Ivor – a person who didn't need anybody. It was not that she was in love with Ivor Johnson, or even that she had what you would call a crush on him. Gabby remembered her marriage and had no desire for a permanent relationship but still, there were times when she felt she had much to give. She could think of no one other than Ivor Johnson suitable for receiving what she might offer. It was not something she dwelled on. Why bother? Gabby looked in the mirror, bounced her frizzy hair a couple of times and went on with her life.

Ivor Johnson had a wife once. That was another mystery. What happened to her? She'd gone off soon after they were married; ran away some said with a travelling salesman, but that's what they always said about wives who ran away. If all those stories about travelling salesmen had been true, those in that commercial occupation would have found it unsafe to travel the highways and byways of Cumberland County.

Ivor didn't talk about his wife but there was something mysterious behind those grey eyes. Gabby thought it was something resembling a deep scar.

"What does he do all day?" Gabby wondered.

There were times when, even in summer, Ivor didn't venture out of his house until evening when he sauntered over to her porch for a beer. What did he do with himself all the time? Royal had his roses and Mink a small garden. At least they puttered around outside. But Ivor seemed so sedentary. A few years ago he built a garage for his truck with a top floor for storage and Gabby was amazed how fast it went up. He worked on it from six o'clock in the morning until after dark and it was done in a few days. Yet he seldom put his truck in the garage. What had he stored overhead? He never seemed to carry anything in or out of the garage. The man was a mystery and you couldn't get a thing out of him.

"What did you do all day, Ivor?"

"Nothing much."

He'd been in the war but didn't talk about that either. He hadn't been overseas but did some kind of training.

Ivor was a volunteer fireman. He dove in the water and hauled a man out of a submerged car once. The newspaper wanted to put his picture in the paper but Ivor wouldn't go for it. "Too flashy," he said. "Best keep a low profile."

Saving lives or building garages, whatever Ivor Johnson did he did quietly. They approached Ivor to run for town council.

"There isn't one councillor from Whitehall. Let your name stand."

He refused.

He did help with things. He spearheaded the drive for the Fraser family when they lost their roof in a hurricane. Ivor organized dinners, dances and raised seven hundred dollars. The mill donated the lumber and they had enough for a new roof. That was as high profile as Ivor Johnson ever got. It was the only committee he ever chaired.

Ivor liked to deer hunt but he hadn't brought home a deer in years. He went off to the woods early in the season, walked all day but never shot anything. When Royal went with him, Royal always got a deer. Royal told Gabby, "Ivor had lots of chances, but he didn't take a shot. He just likes being in the woods. I got enough meat for both of us anyway. And you too."

Since Gabby was a small girl she nurtured the idea houses could talk. They spoke to her by their appearance. The shady mansions under majestic elms that she'd seen outside of Boston made a statement, as did the sleek suburban bungalows of Halifax with their wide driveways. The little houses on her street spoke volumes. Each advertised their ownership and told something of the occupants. When she looked across her yard to Ivor's little white house with its grey trim it always sent her the same message: "Do not disturb." She knew this was because it was so neat and well-painted. Nothing looked out of place. Some houses shouted at her, "Look at me here under the trees." Ivor Johnson's house whispered, "I am quiet."

It was such a different view from the other side of her house with Mink's hovel and the shore behind it. Some moonlit nights when she looked out her window, silver beams danced across the full tide, a beautiful view of the shore spoiled by Mink's jungle of cardboard, tarpaper, rusted car parts and weather-beaten boards. She thought it strange the things that co-exist, the ugly and the beautiful together in the same picture. If there was a truer statement of life, she didn't know it.

Over the years, people had tried to persuade Mink to clean up. The town had threatened him with eviction but then the Legion intervened. "The man is a veteran with an outstanding war record." Gabby, Tess and Minnie had approached Mink and were permitted to conduct a "one time only" Saturday clean up, as long as nothing was thrown away but simply organized. His place did looked better for a while. A day or two, a week or two and then the junk just crept back in.

Cleaning up Mink's place was, to the best of Gabby's recollection, the one neighbourhood chore in which Ivor Johnson had refused to participate.

"Mink's happy," Ivor said. "How many people do you know who are really happy?"

"But his place," Gabby replied.

"It won't bother you if you don't let it."

Gabby looked out her window and smiled. It didn't bother her anymore. She wouldn't let it. The irony made her smile too.

"How can I have the neatest man in the world on one side of me and the messiest on the other? Only on the Snake."

10

On the second day of June, 1953, Princess Elizabeth was crowned Queen of England and all her dominions. It was a fine sunny day, so Ivor and Royal were sitting on Royal's front steps listening to the coronation on the radio. It was all pomp and ceremony; Her Highness in Westminster Abbey was flanked by the Bishop of Durham and the Bishop of Bath. Royal was nodding in approval. He had been brought up in a house that believed in the monarchy.

"She could be Queen a long time. Twenty-six now, she could live out the century," Royal declared.

"You never know," Ivor replied and Royal nodded again.

"That's right," Royal said, wanting to continue. "You never know. Things change, people always coming and going, living and dying."

On the Snake, nobody much had come or gone in a long time. It had been fourteen years since Minnie and Duddy had moved onto their street and they were the newest inhabitants. Snake Road was one of those places where people lived out their lives. Even after they died, their kin stayed put. That's the way it had always been.

That's why the news was so remarkable. Both Ivor and Royal remembered exactly what they were doing when they heard about the schoolteacher. Tess heard it first at the centre of the town's information and communication system, the beauty parlour. She told Ledger who told Mink, who came up the road and sat on Royal's front steps right after the young queen was crowned and told Ivor and Royal.

"New people moving in," Mink said. Ivor and Royal could tell he wasn't happy. "A schoolteacher and his family from somewhere in Cape Breton. They're going to build next to me. God damn it. You know what that means? I'm going to have to haul that truck off the field because it's their property. I won't have storage anymore. That's my overflow area."

"Build? Next to you? Nothing personal, Mink, but have they seen your place?" Royal asked. "Must be going to put up a hell of a fence."

"Very funny," Mink snorted. "I'm the one who'll be putting up a fence. You think I want neighbours sticking their noses into my yard?"

"You're right," Royal said. "That's no place for a nose."

Mink put a plug of tobacco in his mouth and was lost in thought. "Little brats stealing my stuff," he grumbled. "Who sold them that field anyway?" he demanded. "Who owns it?"

Since nobody knew, it was impossible for Mink to vilify any particular individual so he vilified the entire human race.

"Personally, I'm delighted," Gabby told Ivor that night. "It will make Mink clean up his place and it will bring some new blood to our street. They're both good things," Gabby continued. "A schoolteacher. Imagine a schoolteacher living down here with us."

"Yes, but why?" asked Royal. "Of all the places to live, why come down here and build a house in a vacant field on the Snake next to Mink Martin? Do they have a death wish or something?"

"There's nothing wrong with our street," Gabby replied. "Why not here? It's as good as any place else and they're on the shore."

Royal shook his head. "I don't know. You look at Mink's place and you have to ask yourself who would build next to that?"

"You got a point," Ivor said.

They learned a lot in the next few days. For one thing the schoolteacher wasn't a him but a her. Claudia Abbott and her sixteen-year-old daughter, Melissa, would be the new citizens of the Snake. Mink learned something sooner than anyone. He was going to be in for trouble. Claudia was his worst nightmare. She had frosted hair and Mink didn't like any woman with frosted hair. She had freckles on her face and arms too and he didn't like freckles. She was taller than him and that made him uncomfortable. She was strident and from their very first meeting she gave him a list of things to consider.

1. His place needed to be more presentable.
2. She wanted the junk removed from her property within a week.
3. She had read all the town bylaws and would be meeting with the mayor shortly regarding unsightly premises.
4. She was not living next to a garbage dump.

Well! Mink was so flustered by her verbal bombardment that he couldn't speak and it took four beers at Gabby's to unlock his jaw. He hated that woman. "And she called my stuff junk." That was the final blow. The callous creature had no sense of value. That junk, as she called it, consisted of the better part of a '49 De Soto – minus the seats and floor – in addition to a hay baler with the big wheels, plus the block and tackle from the tern schooner *Stewart T. Salter*. Then there was the old wire cage Melvin Smeltzer used for his hunting dogs, two tractor wheels, the sink from the Masonic Hall and Hattie Trueman's old dresser drawers. Mink had picked the dresser up at an auction twenty years ago but never brought it in from the rain and snow. So now it had two noticeable warps or bulges, much like Hattie herself, God rest her soul.

"And she calls it junk," Mink muttered.

Ivor, Edger, Royal and Duddy pitched in and the field was cleaned up in an afternoon. Mink wasn't much help. He couldn't lift much with his bad arse and besides he'd spent most of the day uptown trying to determine who had done the dastardly deed of selling his storage field to this dreadful woman. When Gabby invited Claudia Abbott to dinner, Mink refused to step in Gabby's yard.

"Mink's boycotting you," Royal said.

"That should save on the beer supply," Gabby retorted.

Then things happened fast. Calvin MacAloney came with his bulldozer and dug a big hole for the new basement. The Henwood brothers came with hammers and saws and the Abbott house began to take shape. To make things worse, for Mink anyway, it was going to be two stories. As Mink said, "even worser," Claudia cut down the alders and scrub spruce in the back of what was Mink's storage field, so she could have a clear view of the shore. "That will just let the wind blow around my place, make it harder to heat all winter. Put up my costs. What does Miss Moneybags care?"

Every day Mink walked back and forth watching the construction with his jaw set and steam coming out of his nostrils.

He was hatching a plan. This was war and Mink was on the counterattack. Old and sick as he was, his bad arse was overshadowed by his bad disposition. Then Mink was pounding and hammering himself. The ringing hammers of the Henwood brothers combined with the bang-bang-bang beat of Mink's echoed across the inner harbour to the other bank and Riverside, where people pulled back their curtains and wondered what was going on with "them crazy Whitehallers."

Mink knew about battles. He had different war dreams now. He was still running through the artillery smoke and gas of a German attack. He had lost his way again and someone was running along next to him. He could see the familiar form in the fog, hear the breathing and the feet of the German lad striking the battered down ground. They had run together through decades.

They were friends now, accustomed to each other. But then Mink saw the runner's feet. The foggy form had women's shoes, silky legs, and a dress. He felt the tremor. It's her! That strident, dreadful, hateful, awful bitch. His new neighbour, running with him and she had a rifle. A German rifle and she was pointing it and —

Mink shivered violently and woke himself. He was soaked, his underwear cool and clammy. He wanted the German boy back instead of this new enemy.

Mink hired Ledger to drive stakes in the ground with a heavy maul. Then he made a frame, covered it with sixteen-foot boards and wove baling wire through them. He pounded for three days, using more nails and spikes than the two Henwood brothers combined. Then he put in guy wires for stability. As a final touch, he covered the entire creation with chicken wire.

The first time Claudia Abbott saw Mink's fence was on her return from a week in Cape Breton. She stared speechless, her mouth agape. On the chicken wire over the boards, posts and stakes, Mink had affixed his large and versatile collection of automotive hubcaps dating back over the century. Everything that had ever rolled on the wheels of a Ford or Chevy, Dodge or De Soto from 1923 onward was on the fence. There were the flashy types, a Buick, a few Studebakers and Packards too. Mink only held back on his prized caps from the Studebaker Lark. Those hubs were still hanging on the wall in Mink's cluttered living room.

"Junk indeed!"

There weren't words to describe the showdown. Claudia Abbott's vocabulary was somewhat more diversified than Mink's. Some of what she said Mink didn't understand. Within twenty-four hours of seeing "the artless eyesore next to my new house," Claudia had the mayor and most of the town council on her property. She gave them a firsthand demonstration of her feelings towards the hobby of hubcap collecting.

If all were revealed to Claudia Abbott, she would have seen that some of the elected representatives, if not entirely on Mink's side, at least had some appreciation of his collection.

"I don't think we can issue an order to tear it down," the mayor said. "I mean it's, ah, it's his property and he's claiming artistic license."

"There is nothing, absolutely nothing, artistic about it," Claudia sputtered. "I've studied art, I've taught art and I can tell you that this, this – "

She didn't get a chance to finish because Mink let out his mangy old German shepherd and most of the councillors jumped in their cars.

Mink's fence was the subject of an emergency town council meeting. Even by that time it was making news across Nova Scotia. "It's all because of one nosy reporter," one councillor complained. One story in one newspaper and the fence was famous. People were driving by and taking pictures. Children got out of their cars and posed in front of the sixteen-foot high Hubcap Wall, as it was called. A photographer from *National Geographic* was photographing the unique rock formations along the Minas Basin shore and even he took several shots.

"He said he was going to send them to his magazine," Mink said with pride. The story spread and so did the fame of Mink's fence.

All his life, Mink Martin had been a man in the background. But unlike Ivor Johnson, Mink could handle a little notoriety. For Claudia it was a nightmare. Her house was going up, her daughter was arriving soon and it was all too much. Claudia broke down at Gabby's table and cried her heart out from sheer mortification. Gabby was touched and also alarmed. Her newly found friend was already debating selling the unfinished house and moving somewhere else.

"She can't break her teaching contract, that's the only thing keeping her here," Gabby told Ivor. "Can't you help her?"

Ivor mulled it over for five long minutes looking out Gabby's window toward the shore. It was dusk and the tide was coming in, the water a dark intruder on the sand and mud. Gabby wasn't sure if Ivor actually saw the small army of sand birds rising and darting in one direction then the other, resembling a loose curtain that had suddenly been flung open to the wind. The clock ticked and Ivor remained lost in concentration.

Gabby waited. Over the years she had become accustomed to his quiet spells. Ivor could make some people uncomfortable the way he could slide out of a conversation. Gabby ran her fingers through her frizzy auburn hair. They were sitting next to each other at her table. She could hear his breathing. Ivor was never very talkative and when he was deep in thought it was best to leave him alone. Gabby went and got herself a coffee and sat down again. She looked across her lawn and the adjoining field to the shore. It was one of her favourite views. From her back porch you couldn't quite see Mink's place as you could from her living room windows. Long shadows were creeping across her lawn. "Purple fingers of the night," her mother used to call them.

Her mother! God, that woman carried a load. How different her life was. Gabby had no children, no dependents, an easy job, and an easy life. Was that why she chose to live alone, she suddenly wondered, because of her mother? It scared her sometimes how little things, long buried and she thought lost forever, would suddenly pop into her mind, revealing something about her she would rather not think about. Who chooses their life anyway? Aren't we all victims of circumstance? Why was she living this life? Why was she sitting here with Ivor Johnson, contemplating her existence?

Gabby felt a shiver go through her. The flowing and swaying curtain of seabirds was farther out on the black water. The first rays of the moon put dipping splotches of silver on the rolling waves. She watched the birds until they were half hidden and finally swallowed up by the darkness. She was used to Ivor. She waited and said nothing.

"She'll have to come halfway," he finally said.

"Halfway?" Gabby replied. "What does that mean?"

"It means compromise," Ivor Johnson said.

"You'll help her then? Talk to her and to Mink, do what you can?"

"Yes, if she wants me to. But don't expect miracles. Both parties are dug in and that means both sides have got to do some undigging."

"I'll tell her you'll talk to him too. She's desperate and desperately embarrassed. She feels she's the laughingstock of the town."

"She is," Ivor said and took a swig of beer.

The meeting between Ivor Johnson and Claudia Abbott was set for Springhill, a half-hour's drive from town. It was Claudia's idea to hold it away from prying eyes. She wasn't even sure Springhill was far enough, but how far could she expect someone to go? She had met Ivor Johnson only a couple of times and didn't really know him. Gabby said that if anyone would have influence with Mink, it would be Ivor.

They met in a dingy little restaurant with faded linoleum on the floor and a too rapidly flickering neon sign that advertised breakfast, except the B was burnt out so reakfast flashed crazily, as if the neon was in a final frenzy of output before expiring.

When she got there, Ivor was sitting along the wall at a table for two. The wall light directly above him gave his head and shoulders an angelic halo. Did he pick this table on purpose she wondered and hoped this broad-faced man with the grey eyes and sandy hair tinged with silver would be her guardian angel. Claudia Abbott was a woman who got right to the point.

"Let me lay my cards on the table, Mr. Johnson. I cannot live with that hideous monstrosity next to my house. I can force the matter in court, which I may have to do. But to be frank, my lawyer tells me I might not win. At least it isn't an open and shut case and then there are the legal costs. I'm building a new home and the expense of that, well...."

"Spend your money wisely," Ivor Johnson interrupted. He said it with such quiet force and assurance Claudia momentarily shut up and watched him take a sip of his coffee.

"What do you mean exactly?" she asked after catching her breath.

"I mean you and Mink are in a feud. There are two ways to end a feud. They don't let you fight it out on the street anymore, so you fight through the courts or sue for peace on a personal level. You would be better suing for peace."

Before Claudia could respond, he continued, "If Mink were to take down the fence, that would make it look like you won. Right?"

"I guess so."

"Then sue for peace. Make Mink an offer. Give him something in exchange for him taking down the fence."

"You mean give him money?"

"More than money. Make him see you're not his enemy. You've come in here and challenged him, got his back up. Reverse things. A little money? Yes, it would be less than the courts will cost you. A little pampering too wouldn't hurt. I know Mink. Have your carpenters build him a little shed for his hubcaps, like a little museum where he can show them off and just to seal the deal, maybe cook him a meal once in a while."

"Have that dirty, drunken reprobate at my table!"

"No," Ivor replied. "He wouldn't be comfortable at your table. Just maybe once a week, wrap up a little something good for him."

"Mr. Johnson, making me pay to build a shed or a museum as you call it, and cooking for him. This all sounds like I'm in the wrong here and I'm not."

"No, you're not." There was something very reassuring in Ivor Johnson's voice. "But this isn't about right and wrong. If you're waiting to be right those hubcaps will be facing you a long time. Don't think of right or wrong. It's Mink's street, not yours. Not yet anyway. Personally, I think you're both wrong but that's not important. You have to get past who's right and who's wrong. Stick to the important thing. Getting this over with and getting that fence down."

"I don't think that will work, even if I agreed," Claudia replied.

"It will work," he said, smiling. "Mink is terribly scared his hubcaps will get stolen. That's his worst fear. Offer him what he wants, security for his collection. I'll talk to Mink. He can be reasonable in short spurts when he's sober."

"Is he ever sober?" Claudia asked.

"In the mornings mostly," Ivor replied.

"I've moved next door to a madman. I think he's dangerous as well as a degenerate." Claudia looked at her coffee and shook her head.

"Mink is alright. He'd never hurt you. Like all of us, he's just set in his ways. Except Mink is set a little deeper than most people. He's the deepest rut in the road."

For the first time since she entered the restaurant, Claudia gave a faint smile.

So Ivor Johnson was the go-between, the arbitrator between hubcap collector and experienced educator. It wasn't an easy job. Negotiations ran over two weeks with no settlement in sight. The progress made one day was often lost the next.

Among the unresolved issues at the end of two weeks were:

1. The size of the hubcap museum.
2. Who pays for the museum's appropriate sign that distinguishes it from a shed.
3. The amount of financial compensation from Claudia.
4. What constitutes a meal and does it include gravy.
5. An apology from Mink for calling Claudia a bitch nine times and something even worse at least three times.
6. An apology from Claudia for calling Mink a total degenerate, lacking in all morals and gentlemanly behaviour.

"I'll show you my gentleman," Mink roared, grabbing his crotch and jumping up and down on the street in front of his hovel. That would have constituted number seven on the list of unresolved disputes, but there was so much more that needed to be forgiven.

Ivor was patient. Gabby was encouraging. Royal would nod and add a few suggestions. Claudia Abbott swallowed a bucket of pride. With a look of complete satisfaction on his soot-streaked face, Mink Martin finally took down his fence, board by board. All the while he sang dirty ditties and Claudia could only cover her ears.

Claudia paid Ledger and Edger to clean up Mink's yard, and she paid Royal to plant a hedge where the hubcap fence had been. Late one night she slipped over to Ivor Johnson's and gave him a hug and a bottle of wine.

There was peace again on the Snake.

Then at the end of summer, there was also something else on the Snake.

The first time Claudia Abbot's daughter swayed up the road, it was as if Ledger and Fudd's eyes were burned by the sun, their retinas damaged beyond repair. They were just the most obvious responses. Royal pulled back his curtains for a peek at Miss Swaying Hips. Duddy too, when Minnie wasn't looking. He stood at the window and scratched his unshaven chin at the wonder of what he saw.

Melissa Abbott was one of those rare young women who totally bypassed that gangling, hormonal transition between girl and woman, that period of pimples and small bumps on the front of sweaters. The time of cramps and chills and sweaty palms and lack of confidence – well, Melissa Abbott missed all that. She just turned the page and stepped into the body of a beautiful woman as if it were a pair of coveralls that carried all the prime equipment for a totally successful life. She stepped into a body complete with curves, hips, developed, firm breasts, straight shoulders, clear complexion, and a graceful elegance that belied her years and her experience.

"I know why Claudia left Cape Breton," Gabby declared after catching her first glimpse of Melissa. "My God, that girl could get a lot of men in trouble and I bet that's what happened up there."

Gabby looked at Ivor, who said nothing, so she added, "Claudia told me she made the decision to leave quickly, almost overnight and when I look at her daughter, I know why."

It was all speculation of course, but Gabby was rapidly convincing herself if not Ivor. He just smiled. "I wonder how long it will be before that Ledger is all over her," Gabby continued.

Ledger had the same idea. He was ready to dump What's Her Name when he saw Melissa. But this prize was so special he decided that for once he had to be on the safe side. He better practice his best approach, polish it up in the mirror a few times just to get it down smoothly.

Ledger had already changed his mind about plumbing. Instead, he was going to be a paratrooper. Why settle for drains and plugged toilets when he could be jumping out of planes, wearing a uniform and travelling to exotic lands? Ledger was certain Melissa would be impressed. How could she not be impressed? If she had any imagination she could see him with the brass buttons of the paratroopers. God, life was grand.

But here's the strange thing. Melissa didn't take to Ledger. There was something in her internal radar that reported to her early warning system this guy was trouble. So even Ledger's best pitch, oozing all the charm he could muster, did not impress her.

For the first time in his life when he really tried, Ledger had hit the wall. The shocking rejection took twenty-four hours to really sink in and it sent him back to the mirror in his bathroom. With the door closed, he replayed his pitch. How could she? Blind, stupid, impossible. How could she not see what she was missing?

And what was worse, much worse, Melissa's warning system read Fudd as harmless and one she could befriend. When Fudd started walking her to school, the hurt tore at Ledger so badly he had no choice but to start a slander campaign on Miss Big Boobs. What was a guy to do?

Royal got a great charge out of Fudd and Melissa walking by his house every morning. "And here's the best part," he told Ivor and Gabby. "That girl doesn't know that Fudd quit school two years ago. He told her he's in high school, and he just says goodbye to her and goes around the corner like he's going in the other door. God Almighty. Have you ever heard anything like it? The kids all think she's so stuck up they won't tell her about Fudd."

When Melissa finally found out about Fudd it didn't make any difference. She kept letting him walk her to school. They were a strange looking pair. There was Melissa, turning every head in town. Even the old geezers on their front steps stopped biting down on their wads of tobacco to watch the swaying of her hips and the bobbing of her long blond ponytail while her firm breasts stayed perfectly still. There was Fudd next to her, short sleeves even in the coldest days, bulging biceps, arms dangling in front of him, shoulders rounded, head tilted forward.

A beautiful princess with her Cro-Magnon cave dweller.

"Fudd's a buffer for her," Ivor said.

"A buffer for what?" Gabby asked.

"Her surroundings, the newness of this place. A buffer for guys like Ledger."

"Poor Fudd," Royal replied. "I like the kid. He's harmless enough but, boy, he's going to be hurt when she gets used to it here."

The months rolled by, winter came and the strange thing was, Melissa and Fudd were still keeping company. Every morning Fudd was waiting at the end of her driveway. He couldn't meet her at noon or after school because Duddy was mad as it was, having to wait around until nine o'clock every morning before Fudd would get in his truck and go off to a job. "I might just as well drive the two of you," Duddy said.

"No thanks, we like to walk," Fudd replied.

Duddy grumbled and wondered to himself, No thanks? When the devil did Fudd start becoming so polite?

It was true. Politeness was the first sign of a change in Fudd. Over the months there were more major renovations on the quarter-assed carpenter. The most noticeable thing was that Fudd started walking upright. Only on the Snake could a hundred million years of evolution, bringing Cro-Magnon man to Homo Erectus, take place in a matter of months. People watched and wondered at Fudd's transformation to a more advanced form of humanoid. Fudd's head was no longer slumped forward as if he were watching his ankles; his arms no longer hung lifeless at his side. Fudd had form and walked with erect purpose. Whatever that girl was doing to her son, it put pride in Minnie's heart and she said a prayer for Melissa Abbott. Fudd was praying for Melissa too, but in a slightly different way.

The only young man who didn't lust after Melissa Abbot was Edger. He only had eyes for Pearl and Pearl knew it. In her way, she loved him for it. Edger still walked past Pearl's window every night. She sat in the dark feeding her baby and watching him. The streetlight caught him at just the right time, as he was looking up.

Since Edger's surprise visit and startling announcement in her bedroom, Pearl had done a lot of soul searching. She had been rotten to him all through their teenage years. Part of it was real and part of it was just a way of keeping the creep away from her. But she didn't think of Edger like that anymore. As Rhonda-Rae grew and the child's father remained at a distance, something replaced Pearl's need for him. She didn't miss Ledger at all. The hurt he had inflicted was gone. There was something else. She couldn't define it, but it was there and it was real. It had to do with Edger. An overwhelming appreciation perhaps and a deep-seated thankfulness that at least one person in this entire world had come forward and said he was on her side. When Edger had left her bedroom that night he didn't know the impact he had made. Neither did Pearl at the time. Like that seed inside her that turned into a beautiful daughter, Edger's seed had turned into a warmth.

At first it was just a flicker, the flame from a tiny emotional match but the fire was feeding on something. It was growing and Pearl could feel the heat. It was turning into a furnace. Pearl knew the next move was up to her. Edger had probably embarrassed himself beyond belief because he was so terribly shy. He would not repeat the performance. It was Pearl's turn and she was ready.

Her only reluctance was her mother. The two of them were almost back on an even keel after the most trying time a mother and daughter can endure. The unexpected and unwanted pregnancy combined with dark suspicions over the father's identity had created turmoil for both of them. A mother's demand to know and a daughter's refusal to tell had healed, but it had left them leery of each other. Their threats and screams, with Duddy scurrying around trying to escape the crossfire, had worn them all down. Pearl retreated to Gabby's to get away from her mother and get her rest, while Minnie retreated to the warm water of her sink.

The two women had always had a tumultuous relationship. They didn't see eye to eye on many things. Pearl protected Fudd, sometimes too much, Minnie thought. Pearl also interfered with the way Minnie wanted to bring him up. Their personalities were different, as were their tastes. They didn't even resemble each other physically as mothers and daughters often do. Minnie was short and stocky, well packed in her small frame. Pearl was a head taller and her stockiness more evenly distributed. Minnie had light brown hair while Pearl's was so dark brown it was almost black. She parted it in the middle so it framed a pretty face with a slightly upturned nose. Her hair came together in a widow's peak, adding to a look of intelligence. Pearl's skin was as white as ivory, Minnie's slightly darker.

When they were bickering sometimes Minnie wondered where this strong, opinionated woman came from. She knew. Minnie both despaired of Pearl and was proud of her too. Although just as stubborn as her mother, there was still something that told Minnie Pearl was stronger than her and not just because Minnie was worn down. There was something else – unreadable – but it was there and it said, "Despite the baby, this daughter will land on her feet."

There was one incident that helped heal the mother-daughter relationship but it had cost Minnie dearly within her own family. When Pearl was seven months pregnant she had to go to the hospital in Amherst for some tests. It was a stormy night and since Pearl might be there for a while, Minnie arranged for her to stay with her great-uncle, Fred McAllen.

"Of course she can stay. Stay as long as she likes," Fred replied.

"One night will be all she needs," Minnie said and thanked him.

So Pearl showed up at her great-great-Uncle Fred's. However, Fred's wife was away nursing her mother back to health in Fredericton. He hadn't bothered to say anything about that.

Well, Pearl thought, I guess it's all right.

But it wasn't. Around midnight Pearl suddenly felt the mattress sink. When she opened her eyes, Uncle Fred, in his red long johns, was crawling under the covers with her.

"And me seven months along," Pearl told her astonished mother the next day. "And him with his children in the house. I told him if he didn't get out I'd scream so loud it would wake the dead."

"Don't wake the children," Uncle Fred said. Seeing the look in Pearl's eyes that advertised the rock hard determination of his distant niece Minnie, Uncle Fred retreated. Pearl put a chair against the door, got dressed down to her hat and coat and stayed on top of the bedcovers with her boots on for the remainder of the night.

Well, there was hell to pay for great-great-Uncle Fred. Minnie got on the phone to her sisters. One sister called a cousin, who called a nephew and within a week there was a family council, which by that time unfortunately included Fred and his embarrassed, very angry little wife, Flo. The council was really unofficial and disorganized but after a fearful set to, it found that Fred was innocent and Pearl was only looking for attention.

Minnie, who wasn't invited to the council, hit the roof. The telephone wires were burning up and the result was Minnie no longer spoke to or sent Christmas cards to the rest of her family. "Bunch of ingrates anyway," said Minnie. Her gumdrop Christmas cakes, a holiday favourite in the homes of many a cousin, were not forthcoming that year, causing even more hostility in all the branches of the family tree.

The regrettable event was the first stepping stone of reconciliation and reunion for Pearl and Minnie. Minnie's belief in her daughter's story forged the first step on the path back to each other. Minnie never wavered in her belief that Pearl was telling the truth. She had reason to believe Pearl. Thinking back over the years, she remembered a few things she'd forgotten about Uncle Fred.

Minnie still made as many Christmas gumdrop cakes as ever and while she still supplied her sisters, she simply didn't send them to her other relatives. Instead, every house on the Snake was the recipient of a delicious cake on Christmas Eve.

As Royal said, "It's an ill wind that doesn't blow some good gumdrops somewhere."

11

It was during the Christmas season that Minnie got the idea of a makeover. She'd been listening to her radio and someone was talking about "Creating a new look for yourself" as a good way to start the new year. A total makeover included hair, skin, nails, eyes and clothes. Now Minnie was not an extravagant woman. Anything but, and that may have been part of her life-long problem. She had been in a rut since she was eleven and for some unexplained reason she suddenly, miraculously realized it.

Minnie dropped what she was doing and ran into the bathroom and stood in front of the mirror. She took a long, long look at herself and burst out crying. Not that she was surprised by what she saw. Only later did she understand that while she had been crying in the sink all these years, she was repressing the impulse to cry at the mirror. The urge had been there. Been there for years in fact, but Minnie just buried the feelings at the sink. Now she was facing up to all manner of things. All those impulses needed to be met head on and addressed.

She stopped crying and suddenly got very angry, scolding herself for her weakness. She took a really deep look into her face and studied the ravages time had made. The little lines around her mouth and eyes that Duddy and pain had put there. She investigated the thin streaks of grey in her hair that disappointment had painted. She looked at her rough hands, callused fingers and broken nails. Minnie was not stylish. She had worn her hair in a bun since she'd been married. It was a woman's way of saying, "I'm taken and dedicated to all things that are domestically important."

"It's not that I want to look attractive," she told herself. "I want to look different. I've looked dedicated long enough."

With typical determination, she marched to the telephone and made an appointment with Tess. The time had come.

While Minnie was downstairs deciding on a new direction in the looks department, Pearl was upstairs deciding about a different kind of makeover. She was wondering how she was going to approach Edger. There was a new urgency. Pearl could see plenty from her window. Melissa brought new competition to the neighbourhood. That Abbott girl might be taking an interest in Edger.

This new girl, whom Pearl had never met, had such a profound impact on her brother it had shocked the entire family. Fudd was saying "thank you" and "please" at meals whenever Pearl passed the peas or pork chops. Manners? And he wasn't walking around like a drooling primate anymore. He was dressing better too, shaving every day and talking of going to trade school. If that busty sixteen-year-old turned her attention on Edger, Pearl knew she would be in trouble.

As for Melissa, she believed there was goodness in everyone and her keen instincts told her the ones worth saving. She was practising for her life's work, to be a missionary. She had already seen the face of Satan. Gabby's guess was right. Claudia had left Cape Breton because her daughter got involved with a married man. A married man who had touched Claudia's child and her child had responded willingly.

Melissa never wanted sex again. It hurt her physically and spiritually. It ruptured her hymen and her conscience. There were other hurts as well, such as the grief she caused her mother and the man's family. To assuage her guilt, Melissa knocked on the young Mountie's door and told his astounded wife the entire sordid story. That made everything worse. Claudia had sent her to their priest, who talked to her over several evenings. Before long he was putting his hand on Melissa's leg and Melissa terminated her visits.

Her mother resigned on a Tuesday, and Melissa went to her aunt's in Glace Bay until Claudia found a place far away from North Sydney.

Melissa would never fall again, she told herself. She would never – never, ever – give in to the flesh again. She would leave lust to others and concentrate on making the world a better place. Fudd was her first attempt at a worthier world and he was a willing subject. He wanted her control. Of course he wanted other things too. He wanted to touch Melissa and when he tried, she slapped his hand and told him if he ever did that again, she would never speak to him. Fudd never tried again. Better to be a slave to this goddess than be cast into the darkness forever.

Fudd believed without question everything Melissa told him. Minnie had tried to drum into Fudd's head since he was a small boy that he should walk the straight and narrow. It had gone in one ear and out the other. But when Melissa said the spirit was more important than the flesh, that was it: the truth and nothing but the truth. Fudd even stopped getting an erection on their way up Whitehall in the mornings. If Melissa wanted him to get a trade, he'd go to trade school. If she wanted him to make something of his life, he would make something of it. Anything. Anything at all, just in case down the road, she might relent and let him touch her. Who knows where it could end?

Pearl felt she was right in her suspicions of Melissa. With Fudd standing straight and on his way to a better life, Melissa was casting around for a new subject and easygoing Edger, with his broad smile and open face, looked like a natural choice. If she succeeded with as many as possible, the experience would only help her when she went to where her services were even more drastically needed, whether it be darkest Africa, the sub-continent, India or China. Melissa Abbott was ready to give her life to the Lord, to be his vessel in helping the misguided in need of redirection. Fudd was her first. Edger would be her second. Melissa was on a roll.

It was more than Pearl could bear when she saw Edger and Melissa walking by and Edger, for the first time, didn't look up at Pearl's window. He had been as constant as the tides. Suddenly the tide was turning.

Pearl knew she had been hiding away too long. That afternoon she dressed Rhonda-Rae in the wee tartan outfit Tess had given her at the baby shower. Wednesday afternoon the stores were closed and so was the beauty parlour. Tess would be home. It was her house cleaning and washing time. When Edger came home at four o'clock Pearl was sitting in his living room having tea with his mother. The baby was asleep beside her. Pearl looked radiant. Edger had never seen her so beautiful. There was a stirring in Edger. It was a physical movement of body parts, a rearrangement of organs. Everything internal tingled as Pearl smiled at him.

"Hello, Edger. Want to see the baby?"

He couldn't remember Pearl ever smiling at him. It was like feeling the sun on his face for the first time. Oh, the blessings of the world. Edger felt he was running naked through waist-high wildflowers. Their aroma was intoxicating, the sunshine was warming and exciting him. In fact, Edger felt flushed and his knees seemed to be giving out. He sat down quickly next to Pearl. He smelled peppermint somewhere and thought he was going to pass out.

Tess, smiling to herself, went to the kitchen to get more tea. She had known for a long time where her son's heart was but she wondered why she wasn't more concerned about the situation. She was a woman who trusted her instincts and her instincts weren't flashing any warning signs.

Pearl and Edger sat in silence for a while, Rhonda-Rae gurgling softly in Edger's arms. "You have a nice way with her," Pearl said as she watched them.

"I'd like to give her a present," Edger said. "Maybe make her something."

"Oh yeah? Like what?"

"I don't have any ideas. What's she going to need?"

Pearl hesitated. It was on the tip of her tongue, burning there as if she had taken a penny out of boiling water and placed it in her mouth. "A father," she said softly, bowing her head. She could tell he nearly jumped off the couch. Funny how you can see things without actually viewing them.

They were silent again. When she finally found the courage to look at him, he was flushed, his cheeks covered with a rosy patina. She didn't understand that at that moment, a great emotional war was being waged inside Edger. He desperately wanted to respond to her comment. He wanted to jump up and say, "I'm your man!"

But a lifetime of insecurity stopped him. Not by much, mind you. He was close to boiling over and repeating his pledge to Pearl, but he wouldn't here. There was too much of his brother in his mother's living room, too much of his mother and of him — and his past. Edger could only make such a stand on territory that was emotionally neutral. His home, his mother's home, wasn't such a place.

When the silence got so uncomfortable that he had to say something, he spoke up. "Maybe I could build her a dollhouse."

Pearl looked at him and smiled, "It will be a while before she could use it."

"It will be a while before I can finish it. I've never built one before, but I've got some money saved and I can buy my nails at Ralph's."

He paused and lapsed into silence again. He had worked at Ralph McFadden's store since he was eleven. Edger always showed up right after a big snowstorm to shovel Ralph's driveway. Twenty cents if he did a good job, and Edger always did a good job. He stacked shelves Saturday mornings. At Christmas, Ralph and his wife always gave him a box of chocolates.

Edger had plenty of things in his head. He didn't need to talk all the time but he sensed the silence made Pearl uncomfortable. He was right. His quiet spells forced her to do the talking and alone in her room with Rhonda-Rae, Pearl could think of plenty of things to say but they dissolved as soon as she needed to say them. Pearl regretted saying anything about Rhonda-Rae needing a father.

God, how desperate I must sound, she thought. That's not the way she wanted to sound because that wasn't the way she was. She wanted to sound as strong as she felt, as strong as she needed to be. Her child didn't need a father, not like some children needed a father. Pearl could go it alone. She could and would so why did she say something so fundamentally stupid. Goddamn it! Why, Why, Why? God, I'm so stupid, she berated herself silently.

She started gritting her teeth, as she did when she was extremely upset with herself, but she stopped when she realized she was making a noise.

Edger looked at her. He had been talking to himself in an orderly monologue, outlining the possible details for the dollhouse: the height, width, physical dimensions, the number of rooms.

"You know, Dad can build me a dollhouse," she said, wanting to salvage some middle ground of independence. "It's nice of you to offer, but...."

"What's wrong, Pearl? Do you think I can't built a really good dollhouse?"

"No, no. I'm sure you can." She was slipping back again, giving him the upper hand. "But I can build one myself, if I want one," she blurted out and it was her turn to flush as he watched her with a broadening smile.

"Whatever it takes, we can do it together," he said softly and left the room.

His words lingered. She would sit in her room and repeat them in the darkness, with Rhonda-Rae nestled at her breast.

Whatever it takes, we can do it together, she thought. Yes, she said to herself, yes, maybe we can.

* * *

Tess, humming softly to herself, purposefully lingered in the kitchen, leaving Edger and Pearl alone in the living room. That's what her son wanted and, she suspected, that's what Pearl wanted too. Tess glanced at a photo she had tacked to her pantry wall. The photo of her boys when they were young showed two freckled-faced rascals, smiling scamps with front teeth missing. They were alike, yet so different. That had always been the way it was. Then and now.

Ledger was going off to join the army. But Edger had no such plans to leave. Pearl was why.

Tess knew what was going to happen yet she was at peace with herself. There was something about Edger. Underneath that shy exterior, there was something very substantial and trustworthy, something that was missing in her other son. Twins, so close yet so far apart. Tess knew Pearl was a good mother. She had a certain stability that even a mistake, a big mistake like getting pregnant, wouldn't eradicate. Pearl had a great many of her mother's attributes and despite Minnie's rough edges, Tess figured that was a good thing.

Meanwhile, down the road, Minnie was going through *The Ladies' Home Journal* in preparation for Friday, her big day. She had already laid away a new dress at Resnicks. It was one of the newer styles, higher and exposing a little more leg. "These dresses should be cheaper, since they don't have as much material," she commented. The sales ladies all agreed, nodding in unison as they always did, but the price stayed the same.

That was life. People often agreed with her, Minnie noticed, but so what? It didn't change anything. Duddy always agreed with every word she said, and then went out and did as he pleased. Minnie knew she shared some of the responsibility for her husband's failings. His passions and needs and moans and groans had sickened her to the point she eventually refused his advances. She knew it was wrong and she had gradually let down the gate in an effort to keep Duddy contained. It wasn't just the sex she didn't care for, it was the awful noises Duddy made. The howling and baying. She knew he could be heard all over the house. Pearl and Fudd were listening to their parents fornicating like animals in the forest. It was disgusting.

But there was something going on inside Minnie. She could feel it as much as you could feel the tide lapping at your toes when you're barefoot on the beach. The excitement of the coming makeover was turning on something inside her. Not sexual, surely, but an inner warmth that made her nipples hard. "Now what does that mean?" Everything perplexed Minnie lately. Sometimes she looked at Duddy and wanted to punch him right in the nose with all the strength she could muster. The next minute she wanted to kiss his wrinkled, bewildered, twitchy face. She really did love him. Sometimes.

Minnie had no idea what the makeover would do, if anything. She wasn't really looking for results in the sense most people would. She just wanted to bring herself to a higher plane. For once in her life she wanted to stand above the crowd, above her dreary existence of dishes and duty. Minnie was tired of being Minnie. Friday was a secret. Only Tess knew. Minnie would tell no one else.

* * *

Pearl felt she had made progress. Edger walked her back to her house and they lingered at the front door until Rhonda-Rae got fussy. "Edger, do me a favour. Take me for a walk tonight down by the shore. I need to get out more."

They walked and Edger, despite his bravado in her bedroom months earlier, was very shy. He was tentative, uncertain of what to do with his arms. The prize he had sought for so long was by his side and he didn't know how to handle it. Pearl could feel his discomfort and she knew she would have to take the initiative. She stopped and put her arms around Edger. They kissed three times and it felt good but Pearl was alarmed. She could feel Edger's heart racing.

My God, she silently warned herself, don't kill him. They lingered and walked back to the Snake and kissed again at her door. Pearl felt something else besides Edger's heart. She felt happiness.

That's why the next day it was a shock to see Edger walk back up the Snake with Melissa Abbott. Pearl jumped out of her chair. If her glare could kill poor Melissa, the chesty, budding missionary in training would have been slaughtered right there on the road. Pearl was so upset her milk wouldn't flow. She fumed and paced. With Rhonda-Rae in her arms, she walked back and forth across the bedroom floor.

That afternoon, like gunfighters of the old west, Pearl and Melissa faced off on Snake Road. Pearl was standing on the street in front of her house waiting for Melissa. There was no introduction, no welcome to the neighbourhood. The discussion started with a fuming Pearl pointing her finger at Melissa.

"You stay away from Edger."

Melissa gulped, surprised by the sudden attack. But she might just as well get used to it. She knew the heathen of far-off lands would often resent her. This was just another practice, she told herself. That's why her response so startled Pearl.

Pearl was ready to fight for her man if she had to, and she was not opposed to punching out Miss Big Boobs with a good right hook. Pearl was prepared for nasty words and name-calling. If it got dirty, even for hair pulling. She had already rehearsed a few arrows of her own for her verbal sling, although "big-boobed bitch" was out of the question because with Pearl still nursing, her breasts were as big as Melissa's.

To Pearl's rude command concerning Edger, Melissa replied, "Edger is a very nice young man who has strengths he's not using. If I can assist him in his effort to fully develop his potential, then that's what I'm going to do. Period."

Pearl had absolutely no defense for that. What the hell was this silly girl talking about? She sounded like a middle-aged schoolteacher, not a sixteen-year-old. Edger was almost four years older than Melissa and here she was calling him, "A very nice young man."

Pearl opened her mouth to say something but no words came out. Just a long "Ahhhh...."

Melissa smiled, "I hope we can be friends. I'm sure I can learn so much from you." She was walking away while Pearl still had her mouth open.

By the time Melissa had rounded the second curve on Snake Road, she was confident. She knew she could battle the Philistines and come away victorious. Virtue was its own reward and every step Melissa took brought her closer to her personal nirvana. It was her way of protecting herself. By wrapping herself in good work and helping others she could fight off her own personal demons. She could make up for the past. The awful experience with the young Mountie, with his wife crying at her front door. Her mother's anguished tears. The awful scandal, the shameful embarrassment. All of it had been so bad. Her transgression had resulted in uprooting their life and moving to this one-horse town that made North Sydney look like a metropolis.

Melissa was surprised by Pearl's frontal assault. It was, she thought, typical of these people. They were the weirdest she'd ever seen. That crazy Mink with his junk and hubcaps and mangy, very scary dog. He would wolf whistle as she walked by. Gabby seemed nice but still, letting all those people on her back porch to drink beer? That Duddy, if he isn't nuts who is, she thought to herself. He winks at me when I pass his house and Royal peeks through his curtains. I can almost hear them drooling. It doesn't matter. I'll always live among the heathen but I will never be one of them.

This is just another test and I'm passing it with flying colours, she assured herself.

As for Pearl, left speechless on the street, there was no victory. She went back upstairs, shut her door and tried to write down exactly what Melissa had said, word for word. Pearl's head ached and each remembered word cut through the cords in the back of her neck like a buzz saw. Pearl felt peril. She had made a forthright decision to make Edger, for better or for worse, her man. That decision had taken time and had turned Pearl's thinking totally around. But, like her mother, once a decision was made, that was that. Suddenly she was in danger of losing him before she really had him. She wanted Edger far more than she ever wanted his brother. She loved Ledger for a month but never expected to spend her life with him. He was never within her grasp. But Edger was reachable and Pearl was not going to lose, if not first prize, then certainly second.

Minnie found what she was looking for on page thirty-seven in a three-year-old issue of the *Saturday Evening Post*. It was perfect. She cut it out and took it over to Tess for a professional opinion.

"Wow!" was Tess's first word. "This is what you want?"

"What wrong with it?" Minnie asked rather defensively.

"Nothing. Nothing at all," Tess replied. "It's just so different and it makes a ... well, such a statement.

"A statement's good, isn't it?"

"Yes," Tess said, looking at Minnie directly. "It's very good. What does Duddy think?"

"Duddy doesn't think. He hasn't in years. Duddy will see it when it's done and I don't think he'll even notice."

"Oh, he'll notice alright," Tess laughed. "Even Duddy will notice this."

12

Duddy not only noticed, he was dumbstruck. He was left as speechless as his daughter had been two days earlier in her showdown with Melissa. The day of the makeover, Duddy had dropped into Gabby's to have a beer with Royal and Ivor Johnson. When his stomach started growling he knew it was suppertime. Duddy walked into his kitchen hoping for the aroma of corned beef and cabbage mixed with the sweet fragrance of a hot apple pie. The only aroma that hit his nostrils was a strange, sweet perfume and standing there looking at him was a stranger. Who is it? Minnie? Not Minnie, at least not his Minnie. Somebody else's Minnie. A younger, slick-looking Minnie. The bun was gone. Her hair was bobbed in a pixie cut, ragged across the forehead like saw teeth. The colour was different too. Not a radical change but the brown had a silky sheen to it and there were streaks of a lighter gold. The lips were definitely bigger and redder. And – and – and her eyebrows were....

Duddy felt perspiration trickle under his arms as he tried to study her eyebrows by squinting both eyes almost closed. What were they? Arched? By God, they were! Arched like the Gothic doors on an ancient cathedral. It was more than poor Duddy could take in all at once. He wanted to ask questions but it all alarmed him so much, he suddenly felt the need to urinate. It was unnerving, the way Minnie just stared at him without saying a word. The half smile on her face frightened him. She was standing by the sink drinking a glass of something. There was nothing on the stove for supper, no sign of any preparation of a meal. She was dressed to go out, wearing a dress he'd never seen before. Duddy felt he was on the verge of some new discovery in his life that meant big trouble.

He took an unsteady step towards his newly made-over wife. His eyes, big as saucers, tried to determine how her eyebrows could arch at such an angle when they hadn't just a few hours ago. Only this morning he'd left her. It was unfair that a husband had to come home to face a barely recognizable wife. He wished Minnie wouldn't keep staring at him without saying anything. He was bothered by the slight smile that pushed the corners of her much bigger lips upward. There was something else too. This made-over Minnie had a sleek figure; the girlish curves of her youth had suddenly come back. Duddy opened his mouth and closed it again. Then he opened it again and said, "Did you make a pie?"

Minnie hadn't been expecting much. All her life she had been a woman of few expectations. Otherwise she wouldn't have married Duddy in the first place. "I want you to take me out to dinner. Let's go to the Ottawa House."

"That will cost a fortune," Duddy replied, never taking his eyes off her eyebrows except to occasionally dart a quick glance down to her new slim waist. "What's the occasion?" he asked.

"The occasion is, I've put up with you for thirty years. That's all the occasion I need. Come on."

Duddy didn't argue because he thought it must be their anniversary. They were halfway to the Ottawa House before he remembered they were married in the autumn, at the start of deer season. They had honeymooned at his hunting camp where Minnie had sharpened his skinning knife and helped him haul a big buck out of the woods.

All the way down Whitehall he kept sneaking peeks at Minnie. She looked twenty years younger and that made him even more uncomfortable. What was going on? As Minnie was getting out of the truck, Duddy said, "You look nice. How come we're doing this?"

"You ever heard the expression, all dressed up and no place to go?" Minnie said.

Yup, he'd heard it and decided he'd just have soup and they might get out for under five dollars.

Minnie ordered for both of them without asking him. She had the full roast beef dinner, just about the most expensive thing on the menu. And to add insult to Duddy's wallet, she even ordered an appetizer of shrimp cocktail. Jesus, he thought to himself, this woman thinks money grows on trees. But he didn't complain out loud, not with Minnie all dolled up with new hair and new lips and those arched eyebrows that gave her a cunning look. It crossed his mind that maybe Minnie was going to murder him and this was their final meal together, a final, fatal celebration of sorts. A token perhaps for all the shit she'd endured. Maybe she planned to poison him at bedtime, put deadly powder in his tea.

Duddy had the fish and it was very good. He relaxed a bit and tested Minnie by ordering a whiskey sour. Minnie didn't complain and shocked him by ordering one herself. Now Duddy knew something was up for sure. Minnie might have one beer a year. She never drank strong liquor. Something was wrong. Duddy wondered if he could sleep at all. Would he dare? If he closed his eyes would it be for the last time?

When he paid the bill and they walked back to the truck Minnie suggested they sit for a while and watch the water. The tide was full. Slips of moonlight were dancing on the waves. Duddy sat and waited. What was coming? Oh God, this is going to be bad. A sense of dread washed over him. Waves of remorse flooded his consciousness. After a few minutes of silence, Minnie reached over and took his hand. It was sweaty. All of Duddy was sweaty, as tiny rivulets of salty perspiration ran from several parts of him. Duddy felt he was immersed in the water he was watching.

He understood then. She was leaving him. Oh God, he'd been such a rotten husband. Minnie had put up with so much, no wonder she wanted out. He put his free hand to his face and started to weep. "I'm sorry, Minnie, I haven't been a better husband to you," he wheezed. He felt full of grief as he waited for the announcement of abandonment that she was about to drop on him. Minnie put her hand on his shoulder, reached around his neck, brought him to her and for the first time in thirty years they kissed in the moonlight. Duddy wished he'd had two whiskey sours.

Other reactions to Minnie's makeover were much more positive. Pearl thought her mother looked wonderful and the two women embraced in the kitchen. Fudd kept circling Minnie, trying to figure out where his old mother was buried underneath this new one. Finally he turned to his sister.

"God, Pearl, if they can make Mom look good, there's hope for you."

Pearl, who could be frank and sharp with others, was always extremely tolerant of her brother. She told him it was one of the nicest things he had ever said about her, which made Fudd frown. The truth was, the seed was already planted. The following Monday, Pearl was off to Barb's Beauty Parlour so Tess could work her magic again.

Monday night Minnie and Pearl stood on their front steps as Lyle Canning, the town photographer, took several photographs.

Royal came across the street and told them they looked like sisters, and Minnie was ready to burst with pride.

Edger thought he would burst with love. He watched Minnie and Pearl pose and as usual around Pearl, he could feel his heart beat faster.

* * *

In early May of 1954, the Englishman Roger Bannister broke the four-minute mile. He ran faster than any man had ever run and everybody was talking about the fastest man on earth. Royal didn't believe a word of it. "It's one of them put-up newspaper stories, that's what it is." Royal had a very low opinion of newspapers generally. He thought most things in the papers were made up. "Some of those things in foreign countries, how do we know they're true?" Royal was pretty certain newspapers were responsible for most wars, droughts, famines and plagues. "Who benefits?" he asked one night on the porch, holding up the Halifax paper and striking it with his pointed, soil-stained finger.

No one argued with him and he left to get his truck and take a rosebush to a friend. An inebriated Mink went with him because he thought they were going somewhere special.

"I'm going fifteen miles an hour," said Royal. "See, no one can run that fast."

"Yeah, but you're driving," slurred Mink who had just fallen against the window and bumped his head. "So sure, you're going faster than him, 'cause he was running, not driving."

"What?" Royal asked.

"That guy running, you'd be going faster," Mink said, trying to roll down the window.

"Faster than what?" Royal asked.

"Faster in a truck."

"Mink, if I'm going the same speed as him, it isn't going to make any difference."

"Bullshit," Mink slurred and spit a gob of phlegm onto the window, thinking he'd already rolled it down. "However long it takes you to go a mile, it's going to take him longer. He has to run, only makes sense."

After smearing the phlegm over the window with his sleeve, Mink took out his tobacco and tried to roll a cigarette. He was hiccuping badly by this time, and with every hiccup, more of the loose tobacco fell into his lap and onto the seat between them. Royal looked at the wide arch across Mink's window and the tobacco on the seat and realized he'd have to clean the truck. He decided not to probe Mink's logic further. You probe Mink too much and you just might start thinking like him.

Later, back on the porch, the argument began about whether two runners going the mile and running at exactly the same speed in opposite directions, would pass each other at exactly the half-mile mark. "Life is never that simple," Ivor said while Duddy and Gabby said it would have to be true.

Royal just shook his head. "It's them damn newspapers. That guy Bannister probably never even ran. It's all horseshit."

"Royal, people have been trying to break the four-minute mile for a long time. They've come very close, so it was only a matter of time," Gabby said.

"Yeah. Well, like who? Just who came close? Did you ever talk to anybody that came close or did you just read it in the papers?"

Gabby shook her head and wished she had known just one person who had come close.

Royal's mistrust of newspapers started when his wife and child disappeared. The stories often had minor inaccuracies and sometimes they were worse than minor. It made him fume that people could get things so mixed up. His wife, son and father-in-law not coming home was the only newsworthy event to which Royal had ever been connected. He needed to fume in those days, to blame somebody for his grief. His first and last experience with newspapers had left a very bad taste in his mouth.

The next day there was a photograph of Roger Bannister at the finish line on the front page of the *Halifax Herald*, just as the string was about to break. Roger was the picture of pure agony, a lanky man with his mouth agape who had, incredibly, exerted himself for three minutes, fifty-eight and eight-tenths seconds. He was gasping with his head thrown back as his hungry lungs grabbed all the oxygen they could find. He wasn't a handsome man, certainly not in that state of exhaustion, but neither was Royal in his natural state. Bannister crossed that finish line physically fatigued with his hair and body covered in sweat, the same state Royal got in when he forgot the time and burned his back, working shirtless on his roses in the sun. He would arise from his knees covered in sweat like Roger Bannister.

Royal took the newspaper into his bathroom and shut the door. He looked at himself in the mirror and then he looked at the newspaper. He pushed his head back in the same position as Bannister's was in the photo. Yes, there was a similarity. They could be brothers. Royal was older certainly, but there was a strong resemblance. They were both men who covered themselves in sweat, yet one was famous and one was unfamous, or whatever that word was supposed to be. They called Bannister the fastest man on earth. Do something the best on earth and you'll be famous, he told himself. Anything.

Not wanting to be seen, Royal took his truck up to the top of Kirk Hill and used his odometer to measure off a mile. He set his watch and drove the distance. How fast did you have to run to be the fastest man in the world?

Because he was afraid of being spied upon, he sat in his truck a long time and looked for any movement. Finally he got out and started to run. At least a quarter of the way, he told himself. As he ran his legs ached, he was gasping, his lungs burning. Slower and slower he ran down the bumpy road that crossed the wide-open, barren fields. "Almost three minutes. Damn," he gasped, doubled over with pain and retching. If he could run a mile, which he couldn't, it would take him twelve minutes. Roger Bannister didn't have to worry. Royal definitely wasn't in the race.

He drove home with the empty feeling he got sometimes – as if there was nothing left in him, as if he was simply hollow on the inside.

He had protested to Ivor, Mink and all of them that he didn't believe the papers, but he knew better. He had narrowed his life to roses. Flowers consumed him because they drew him away; they were challenging yet predictable. They bloomed, had fragrance and roots that spread through the ground. Some had stems that could prick you and draw blood. Yet there was the pay off – the personality, the colour and the beauty. He loved them for what they had given him but he resented them for keeping him small. Everything else seemed untouchable, unmatched, like the rest of reality was behind some invisible screen that blocked his view. He hated Roger Bannister. He resented the fame. He wanted to propel himself above his meagre circumstances to grab something that would make him stand out as a worthy member of the human race. He believed his desires were themselves worthy and that justified the resentment that burned in him whenever he thought of Bannister or anyone else who rose above the crowd. They were just his feelings anyway, he told himself, not his flowers. While he nurtured his roses, he had learned to treat his feelings with contempt. It was his way of dealing with the disillusionment in his life. He had become skilled at burying things, covering them up so they remained out of sight like the roots of his beautiful roses.

13

For a few days, Minnie's makeover was of course the talk of Whitehall. More than one person stood with mouth agape trying to see the old Minnie through this vision who lived on the Snake: the housewife, Duddy's other half and the mother of Fudd and Pearl. As for Duddy, he was home for meals promptly. One day, out of the blue, he brought Minnie flowers, a bouquet of day lilies and forget-me-nots that he'd picked out of an old garden on the side of Woods Mountain. He had never before, in thirty years of not-so-wedded-bliss, brought her flowers.

It was a whirlwind for Minnie. She would never admit how much she loved the attention. Here was a woman who had stood in the background all her life, even when recognition was richly deserved. Once a year when her lodge put on its turkey supper, all her lodge sisters came out of the kitchen to take a bow from appreciative diners. Minnie usually had her hands in soapy water and didn't bother. The success of the dinner was reward enough, she always said.

A hardworking, no-nonsense kind of woman was Minnie, at least until recently. Until that mysterious thing tugged at the mental ripcord inside her. The parachute opened so swiftly at first it scared her, then it made her brave.

She and Duddy started doing it again. The long abstinence was over. Minnie at forty-eight had come alive and it felt wonderful.

Even the death of her older sister didn't sideline Minnie for long. Minnie had hardly known the woman and had never liked her husband. That sister was Mrs. Herbie Rafuse, the wife of Rabbit Rafuse who was a distant cousin of Marlene Rafuse, who had her car stolen at the Baptist church.

Rabbit earned his name because of all the children he fathered, fourteen by Mrs. Herbie and all of them hellions. Even in her forties Mrs. Herbie was still pumping them out, one a year. As a result, when she was in her fifties she still had a mess of unruly kids. At sixty-four she just got the last one out the door when the older ones starting coming home again. Two daughters, divorced with kids, parked themselves in Rabbit's house, smoking a pack a day with no jobs. Mrs. Herbie just up and died.

"Who could blame her?" said Minnie.

Rabbit's children were the other reason Minnie had never been close to Mrs. Herbie, whose name was Alice. Minnie had a mother's natural love for children, but she had the practical mind to know trouble when she saw it and Rabbit's brood was trouble with a capital T. Alice had come to visit once with four of her runny-nosed tikes hanging off her skirt. That was years ago but Minnie never forgot it. In half an hour, they'd broken three of her ornaments and one of her favourite teacups.

Worse than the children was Rabbit himself. He was a no-good bum, a drinker and a slacker. The idea of having her sister and her husband to dinner or down for an evening was something Minnie never even considered.

But then Alice died and that was different. Minnie had to pitch in. Relatives – more slackers – were coming from New Brunswick. The slightly cross-eyed cousin who always made Minnie uncomfortable would be there. An overbearing, elderly aunt from Moncton was coming on the train.

"She never misses a family funeral," Minnie told Tess. "She has to come. She sees herself as the one designated to deliver the gossip about the dearly departed just as they're going in the ground. The woman is a menace. The one thing that scares me about dying is going before her."

But Aunt Maude had no intention of staying home. She was arriving and Jessica, Minnie's domineering, snobby, bossy, prudish sister, gave Duddy the job of driving to Amherst and delivering Aunt Maude to her home in Port Greville. Jessica's house was the command centre for funeral operations. Let there be no doubt about it, Jessica was in charge of everything.

"Jessica couldn't stand her when Alice was alive, but now it's on with the big show. You watch, you just watch. She'll probably boo-hoo at the funeral. My sister is such a hypocrite," she told Duddy.

"You want to go to bed, dear, take some of the pressure off?" asked Duddy.

"No, I don't want to go to bed," Minnie said indignantly. Then she ran over and kissed him on the cheek and thanked him for last night. Duddy beamed and walked down to Gabby's for a beer.

Then the day before the arrival of Aunt Maude in Amherst, Duddy came down with the flu. Minnie knew he wasn't faking. Duddy did a lot of things, but the only time he stayed in bed during the day was when he was ill and besides he had a temperature of a hundred and one.

There was no way, not in a hundred years, that Minnie was going to phone up Jessica and tell her they couldn't do their part in getting ready for the final farewell of Mrs. Herbie. Duddy was supposed to pick up Aunt Maude but if he couldn't, Minnie could. She wasn't going to have that busybody Jessica hanging up the phone, shaking that big head of hers saying something like, "Well, Minnie just let us down," or "Too bad you can't count on anybody." Minnie was a woman who could be counted on.

Several of the highway workers swore the old grey truck was airborne when it hit the gravel. Otherwise, it would have gone right in the hole they were fixing instead of sailing over it. The foreman wasn't certain because he was running for his life. Nobody got the license plate.

"That damn thing came out of nowhere," the foreman told his wife that night while checking to see if his insurance was paid up. "The scary thing was," he said, "two hours later it was coming at us again from the opposite direction. It still didn't look like anybody was driving, but one of my boys swore that the second time there was an old lady in the passenger's seat and she looked just scared shitless."

Then there were the two cars in the parking lot at the train station. Minnie wanted to tell somebody but she was in a hurry. She left a nice note with her license number.

The problem was that Duddy's truck was too high for her. She couldn't see enough and, to be truthful, Minnie hardly ever drove. The last time she operated a motor vehicle was ten years earlier when Duddy let her back out of their driveway. She rolled across the street, running over Royal's yellow hybrid.

The only answer for Minnie was to go as fast as possible so things would get out of her way. Look at those nice men working on the highway, had they not cooperated?

Trying to peer over the steering wheel had already given her a pain in the neck by the time she arrived in Amherst.

Here's another pain in the neck, Minnie thought as she veered into the station.

Aunt Maude was not the type of woman to have a naturally happy disposition. She had a grim demeanour, but it did make her somewhat glad to see Minnie, rather than the alternative. Aunt Maude detested Duddy. He was the only man in half a century to make a pass at her.

The old lecher, she thought, I let him have a piece of my mind.

It was three years ago on her last trip to Nova Scotia. Duddy picked her up in Amherst, when another long-suffering sister of Minnie's renounced her earthly bonds. Maude was sixty-one at the time and so shocked that Duddy's hand was on her leg that she couldn't speak. Trauma can do that. It can leave you totally speechless. Without a word, she struck Duddy so hard he went off the road at Maccan, just in front of the Studebaker dealership. His truck had to be hauled out of the ditch. The embarrassment of it all. When Duddy lost control and left the road, Maude's dress went right up over her waist. She knew Duddy had seen her bloomers. The old lecher! It was another sign her mind was slipping that she had forgotten to tell Jessica to send someone else to fetch her.

But her last trip to Cumberland County was mild compared to what she was experiencing with Minnie, who sat below, if not behind, the wheel.

Twice Maude fought the urge to throw up. She was too scared to open her mouth for fear her overpriced breakfast on the train would come flying out of her. Before they had reached the outskirts of Amherst, Minnie had sideswiped a dog and nearly run down a pedestrian. The dog yelped, shaking itself all over. The pedestrian just shook her fist.

Knocking the mirror off the mail truck made an awful racket. Maude was scared by then, but not totally terrified until she saw the cow. Fear, like trauma, can do strange things to the human psyche. The moment the cow meandered onto the road, Maude regretted she was not a vegetarian. She tried to speak but what came out was garbled. She wondered if she was having a stroke and didn't know whether to wish for one or not. She didn't open her eyes for another twenty minutes. When she finally found the courage to peek, farms and fields were flying by in a blur of green and white.

"Death will be quick," she murmured to herself. She wanted to pee and vomit at the same time. She knew if one thing let go, everything would. She closed her eyes again and prayed.

It was the first time in two months the chief of the volunteer fire department in the village of Southampton had the pumper out of the station. He drove it once in a while, as he put it, "to blow the cobwebs out of 'er." He stopped by the river to top up the water level in the tank. Being an exemplary driver, he always looked in the rear view mirror before pulling off to the side of the road. He saw an old grey truck but it was well back of him. What he couldn't tell from his mirror was its rate of speed. The chief pulled over, jumped down from the cab and was swept around in a whirlwind. He could not see the two hands on the wheel nor the chalk-white passenger. There was no opportunity for observation. When he regained his equilibrium he was alone, face down on the stretch of road with a ringing in his ears. He got to his feet and fought the dizziness. He was not even certain there had been a vehicle. Maybe he'd had a bad spell. Had he suffered a stroke? Trauma can do strange things.

During the first few moments of their trip together and after two major frights, Maude had tried to engage Minnie in conversation. Minnie apologized but said she couldn't talk and drive at the same time. Maude closed her eyes and waited for death.

Thirty-five minutes later they were in Port Greville. There was no dignity left in Aunt Maude. She toppled out of the truck like a bag of laundry. Minnie just wiped her forehead. Aunt Maude was delivered.

Maude, almost hysterical, had to be put to bed. By the time Jessica came down the stairs, Minnie had finished her cup of tea and was gone. In fact, at the very moment Jessica's foot alighted on the last step of her staircase, a gaggle of geese at a nearby farm, accustomed to crossing the road several times a day, were squawking, wildly flapping and running for their lives.

Aunt Maude was barely able to make the funeral. She was propped up by a second cousin who was hard of hearing and a skinny nephew she didn't know. When she saw Minnie enter the church, those nearby said Maude uttered the worst profanities they'd ever heard from a woman.

Minnie and Fudd arrived together. Fudd had a new smart-looking tie, a gift Melissa had given him for being accepted in trade school. Fudd was going to be a plumber.

Mrs. Herbie, surrounded by flowers, looked serene in her coffin. Minnie thought there was just the hint of a smile on her face, as if she was saying to the world, "I've escaped. So long, suckers." Twelve of her fourteen children were there. Of the absentees, one was up north working and the other was doing time in the Amherst jail.

Rabbit had the smell of liquor on his breath and he needed a shave, but Rabbit always needed a shave and always smelled of liquor. To everyone's relief, he was able to stand up at the appropriate times and didn't nod off during the prayers.

It was at the graveside that Aunt Maude suddenly came to life. Just as a smiling Mrs. Herbie was going into the ground, Maude found the strength to whisper, not too softly, to those around her, "She had another child you know. Bertha is really her child, not her sister."

Jessica spun around to stare at her sister, Bertha Brown, who was really her niece. "But Mother and Father?" Jessica gasped and Maude nodded.

"They covered for her and raised Bertha as their own."

Wildfire has nothing on the speed of a juicy tidbit about the dearly departed. By the time the mourners left the cemetery, everyone knew Mrs. Herbie had fifteen children, not fourteen as supposed. It was hoped Mrs. Herbie's other children would be spared the news, at least for a while. But there was so much chatter about them, even the dull ones picked up enough bits and pieces of the information to figure it out.

The only person who didn't know was Bertha Brown. She just thought she was lucky Mrs. Herbie had given her the brooch she'd won at a draw in Moncton, plus her almost new cigarette roller with the long papers that made six smokes at a time. Bertha Brown drove home from the funeral, hardly caring what so many people were whispering about. It was enough to remember the kindness of her sister.

The aftermath of Minnie's drive from Amherst to Port Greville concerned the Royal Canadian Mounted Police. Due to the incessant number of complaints suddenly received from citizens of Wharton, Diligent River, Wards Brook, Port Greville, and the farms and villages in between, immediate action had to be taken. Reports of vehicles travelling at excessive speed, the one hit and run of a pet pig named Oscar, prompted extra RCMP patrols. Sixteen speeders and four drunken drivers were charged over the next month. The police also seized three loads of illegal moose meat and a dozen barrels of moonshine from the back of an old truck being driven by a man who was totally nude.

The crackdown ended then and life went back to normal. Oscar the pig was eaten and his sibling, Norman, was adopted as the family pet, meaning he was spared the trip to the slaughterhouse. Like his brother before him, Norman was allowed to roam back and forth between the house and the barn, crossing the road several times a day. He lived to a ripe old age.

14

While Mrs. Herbie was going in the ground, Ivor Johnson was washing his truck. The day of the funeral marked ten years exactly since Ivor had sold his fishing boat, a day he always remembered. For him it concluded twenty-four years as a fisherman. He always thought about fishing on that anniversary. He had done well but there had been heartache too. He wasn't a man to show emotion but that didn't mean he didn't have feelings. Most things didn't ruffle him, but it didn't mean he didn't care.

There had been that time they had searched all day and night for the crew of *The Mary-Anne*. Only bits and pieces were found at dawn. Charred boards and some clothing were recovered. It wasn't until the second day they found the body of one of the three men on board. They brought him ashore to the very house where Mrs. Herbie Rafuse had been laid out for viewing. Ivor Johnson volunteered to take the body to the funeral parlour in town, ten miles away. He tied up his boat, borrowed a car and they put the body in the backseat. Since the deceased was too long to lay down in a dignified manner, they sat his body upright as if he was just taking a ride. That didn't seem quite proper so they covered him with an old blanket.

The road along the shore was rough and the car bounced along until the blanket covering the dead fisherman slipped down over his shoulders and finally fell to his waist. It might have occurred to someone else to stop and cover the body but to Ivor, the guy wasn't going anywhere, was he? Ivor hadn't had any sleep in over twenty-four hours. It was all he could do to stay awake, so when he saw the hitchhiker he stopped and picked him up, just to have someone to talk with.

The hitchhiker, Dexter Hatfield, had just walked out of the woods after a long early morning trek rabbit hunting. It was Dexter's routine to thumb a ride home.

Dexter and Ivor were making small talk about the weather and rabbit hunting and Dexter wondered about the guy in the backseat. Why was he sitting in the back, anyway? Must be carsick. Dexter didn't want to turn around and stare as that would be impolite. Dexter had good manners and being a gregarious fellow, he was inclined to include backseat passengers in his conversations. Dexter usually did this by slowly adjusting himself, putting his arm on top of the car seat, so he could half turn to include the occupant of the backseat. Still, in his talk there was no response. Quiet fellow, Dexter thought. Can't get a word out of him.

Finally, Dexter, who had a strong streak of curiosity as well as good manners, couldn't stand it anymore. He did an about turn to the backseat, while making a strong point about the best way to prepare rabbit stew. The passenger was ghostly white and wet. He stared back at Dexter with open, lifeless eyes and bits of seaweed sticking out of his hair. Dexter turned ghost white himself but refused to believe what he saw. He did a full about to look again. The situation was surreal. Ivor was talking away about adding pepper to rabbit stew and how long rabbits should be hung before cooking, and in the backseat was, if not a dead passenger, certainly a very sick one.

Dexter felt fear. It passed through his mind he might be sitting next to a murderer, a madman driving the countryside collecting bodies. He looked to see if his door handle had been removed to prevent his escape. But that was silly, he told himself. The best thing to do was find out who was driving. He introduced himself and was a little less shaken to learn Ivor's name.

"And who is this gentlemen in the backseat? Don't believe I know him either."

"It's Harry Little from Fox River," said Ivor.

Dexter looked at the backseat again for double confirmation. "Is he alright? He doesn't look well."

"He's as well as can be expected," Ivor revealed. "He drowned two days ago."

"Oh," said Dexter. "You can drop me off here."

Dexter opened the door and said, "Bye now" before Ivor could even stop the car.

The last Ivor saw of Dexter Hatfield, he was rolling into the ditch. Ivor Johnson and Harry Little drove off, with Ivor thinking, What a strange fellow.

For the next year Dexter Hatfield had bad dreams. They were always the same. He was in a car with dead men in the backseat. They were smoking, offering him cigarettes and candy, asking if he wanted to come back and sit with them. Dexter rabbit hunted the rest of his life. He never hitchhiked again.

* * *

The two sons of Mrs. Herbie who weren't at the funeral were Melvin in the north, one of the smart ones, and Leroy, who was in jail and wasn't one of the smart ones. Melvin had become a cartographer.

"He always liked to draw," Mrs. Herbie used to say of Melvin. Mrs. Herbie had been particularly proud of Melvin because he was the only child who had taken her advice to make something of himself. A flower, she thought, among the thorns.

Mrs. Herbie's other children weren't necessarily bad. They just hadn't reached the potential she hoped they were capable of. Yet she really knew better. The fact was, many had reached their potential, but that wasn't a very high watermark.

But at least none of her children had disgraced her the way her sister's son had. She was the one sister who hadn't shown her face at the funeral, hadn't been seen since "The Disgrace."

Stealing, as her Leroy did, was one thing, and the bootlegging and intoxication of another offspring could be forgiven. Fighting and deer jacking charges didn't carry shiploads of shame to your doorsteps. Mrs. Herbie didn't have much to be happy about, but she derived a certain satisfaction that the crimes of her children were at least on a higher level of lawlessness. Her nephew was in jail for something outrageous. His crime was so repugnant Mrs. Herbie couldn't drink milk without thinking of it.

Cousin Joe was a deviant, a behaviour that exhibited itself when he was exposed to alcohol or Holsteins. Joe was in jail for bestiality, having been caught having sexual intercourse with a cow in Hap Morrisey's barn. It was the talk of the county.

Joe's lawyer pleaded for leniency, saying Joe needed professional help. Because it was his first offence, the judge spared Joe a term at Dorchester Penitentiary and gave him six months at the county jail in Amherst.

The jail-keeper was a good-natured type who liked to be called Warden, which was a fairly big title for having all of seven prisoners. The warden ran a pretty relaxed institution. Cell doors were seldom locked and inmates had the freedom of the whole jail. After all, nobody there was considered dangerous, just light-fingered or frisky or made crazy by alcohol.

The warden appreciated practical jokes. He believed in breaking the ice early in a new inmate's sentence. The day Joe arrived, the warden walked by his cell and threw a handful of hay on the floor.

"What's this?" Joe asked.

"Lunch," replied the warden.

"Lunch?" Joe said, puzzled.

"Yes," said the warden. "If it's good enough for your girl friend, it's good enough for you."

At which the entire place – the warden, his wife, the assistant janitor, the janitor, and all seven inmates – broke out in uproarious laughter. The joke was actually an initiation ritual for all animal pokers at the Amherst jail.

It was a dismal time for Joe. He wanted to kill himself. A visiting clergyman suggested Joe needed to find someone who might provide work and stability. Joe searched through friends and family. His friends had deserted him and the fact he finally settled on his Uncle Duddy may bear witness to the limited branches on his family tree.

"Dear Uncle Dud," the letter started. Minnie read it, because she read all Duddy's mail, her new eyebrows arched almost to her hairline, giving her the appearance of a woman who was all face and no forehead. A look that still rather scared Duddy.

"He wants to come here and live with us. Oh Lord, that pervert wants to be under our roof."

"He's your kin," Duddy replied. "Besides, I need an assistant with Fudd going off to be a toilet plunger."

"I wish you wouldn't call him that. You hurt his feelings. That girl put this in his head and what's wrong with him having a real trade with papers?"

"A real trade is carpentry," Duddy scowled. He'd done everything to get Fudd into the carpentry field, but Fudd didn't want to be building front porches and clothesline platforms. Duddy told him he could build more but Fudd had a good comeback.

"You always told me I never had no talent. Now you tell me I got talent."

"What's with all this talent shit? They teach you, you learn. I can't teach you 'cause I don't know. It's got nothing to do with talent. Fancy-Nancy-Miss-Big-Boobs been usin' that talent word on you."

"I can do better with a wrench than I can with a hammer," Fudd replied.

"No you can't," Duddy responded.

"Yes I can," Fudd countered.

"No you can't."

"Yes I can. I took an aptitude test."

"You took a what?" Duddy asked.

"An aptitude test," Fudd said.

Fudd had the upper hand since Duddy didn't have a clue what an aptitude test was.

"What's an – " Duddy struggled.

"Aptitude test. It tells you what you're good at."

Duddy used to despair over Fudd before Miss-Big-Boobs got her hands on him. Now he was using new words and taking appetite tests. Duddy didn't know this son, who was going off to be a toilet plunger, anymore.

"Melissa gave me the test. It was in a *Popular Mechanics* magazine she found at the drugstore and I'm better off, as far as life expectancy goes, being a plumber."

Duddy was getting a headache but he had to ask, "Life expectancy?"

"Yeah, I think that's what it was. I'll check but I think that's what it said."

Fudd never did get back to him. But he was going and Joe wanted their help, and Duddy didn't mind nearly as much as Minnie.

"We don't have any cows," Duddy said on his way out the door.

"God forgive us," Minnie prayed. For Joe's request was a plea for help and it fell on a woman who took her responsibilities seriously at a time in her life when she needed less, not more, responsibility.

Bruce Graham — Ivor Johnson's Neighbours

Duddy was walking up the road to Gabby's instead of cutting through Ivor's backyard because he saw Melissa coming his way. He nodded and let out a low wolf whistle. Melissa just rolled her eyes and took a deep breath. She knew this strange little man with the contorting face and looping walk was Fudd's father.

That explains a lot, she told herself. Where do they come from? She looked away and noticed Royal peeking at her from behind his curtains. There is a reason I'm here. There is a plan for me. If there ever was a training ground for my life's work, it's here on this strange street.

* * *

Royal was the type of man who liked to fiddle around in his kitchen. He was not a great chef, but he was not afraid to try any recipe, no matter how challenging. So when the doctor told him to stop drinking beer, Royal decided to make moonshine because the doctor hadn't said anything about that. Technically, it wasn't moonshine but a complicated home brew that had the taste of whiskey and the aroma of lemon gin. It fooled you because the smell was nothing like the taste. In fact, the smell, for most people, was considerably more pleasant.

Royal figured it was a way to have a little liquor in the house and maybe augment his small income. After all, there were only three bootleggers in Whitehall and two of them were slowing down because of age and infirmity. The third was out of business because he drank some of his product and had gone blind. He eventually got most of his sight back but his experience scared away his customers.

Royal would be meticulous in following the recipe and with sanitary conditions he would have success. If it weren't for one small oversight he would have achieved his goal. There was nothing wrong with the recipe Royal copied from a bootlegger down the shore named Captain Spry. Unfortunately, he wasn't wearing his glasses at the time he was taking down the specific measurements, and he incorrectly wrote a cup and a quarter of corn sugar per gallon, instead of a quarter cup.

There was quite an investment getting into the major league moonshine business. More expenses than Royal expected, what with tubing, vials and carboys and big pots for cooking. There was work too. Bottles that had to be collected and cleaned, and yeast and disinfectant and big mixing spoons to be purchased plus a variety of other essentials to get the brew just right.

Royal had already come up with a good name for his product: Royal's Regal Whiskey. He wanted labels too, but Ivor Johnson advised him against anything that would identify the manufacturer.

"Maybe just the initials," Royal said. "R.R.W."

"Royal, how long do you think it would take for the Mounties to catch on to that?"

So Royal skipped the labels, although he dreamed of his own brand somewhere down the road. In fact, Royal was thinking big. He saw an entire line of products: Royal's Premium Brand Kentucky Scotch Whiskey, Royal's Northern Comfort, Royal's Nova Scotia Charm. Royal was looking ahead and Hiram Walker had better watch out.

He decided the best place to establish his operation was in his basement, where he would install a small stove and build storage and bottling facilities. Ivor, who had failed to convince Royal to sell rose bushes rather than whiskey, came over a couple of nights to install the stove and build bins and shelving. Royal figured three months would be enough for ageing, which meant in the winter his whiskey would be ready, just when folks needed a nip against the chill.

Everybody showed up to help. While it was cooking most didn't stay as the stuff smelled awful. Instead, people retreated to Gabby's but the aroma filled the whole street. Driving down the Snake, people rolled up their windows in an attempt to block the foul odour. Melissa Abbott held her nose walking home from choir recital.

Royal only smelled profits. He slept soundly as his brew bubbled away, transforming into the Elixir of the Gods.

Except the sugar mix was wrong and six nights later the Gods rebelled with an awful explosion. Ivor, Minnie, Duddy, Gabby, Tess, Ledger, and Edger all heard it. Ledger was packing his suitcase. He was leaving in the morning for basic training. He'd been over to Gabby's porch for a farewell toast with his mother, Mink and the others. The army was very much on Ledger's mind at that moment which explains why, when he heard the explosion, his first thought was heavy artillery.

They said later that the fortunate thing was no one was walking past Royal's house when his basement windows blew, spraying shards of glass across the street. One stray dog, digging in the garbage, had to be taken to the vet but otherwise there were no injuries outside the house except for Royal's cat Tippy, who suffered psychological damage. The exploding bottles were mostly contained to the basement, where they took out the side of Royal's furnace and destroyed his water heater. When the fire department arrived, the basement walls and floor were covered in a gooey brown film that stuck to the boots of the fire fighters.

Hours later when the sun came out, the basement looked like the tomb of an ancient emperor. Embedded in the walls and ceiling, thousands of small shards of glass reflected rays of gold and green. As Mink observed, "They cast the disaster in a totally different light."

When the explosion shook his house, Royal ran down to his basement in his bare feet. Steam and smoke filled the air, water sprayed from busted pipes and a pungent layer of raw sugar and sticky resin covered the floor, walls and ceiling. Both of Royal's feet were bleeding. The water heater was spewing the last of the hot water, which added to the dangerously slippery, yet sticky floor.

Ivor turned off the water and took Royal to the hospital.

Tippy was on the back fence, howling. The cat got his name because he used to wander to Gabby's where Mink would give him a little beer in a saucer. Tippy would zigzag back home, unsteady but ready for any feline that crossed his path. After the explosion, Tippy never came back to the house. They would see him sometimes at the back of Royal's yard. He would let out a mad hiss and run off if anyone approached. Tippy took his food only at night and stayed outside even during the coldest winter.

Royal lost more than his cat. He required a new water heater and the repairs to his furnace and basement cost him five hundred dollars. That ended his ambition to be a liquor baron. The people at Hiram Walker could relax.

Ledger went up to the hospital in the morning to say goodbye to Royal. The insurance man had already been to the basement and Royal had the bad news. He was not covered. There was defeat in his eyes. "All that work and money, all gone, all my whiskey gone, my basement ruined." Then he stopped and looked at Ledger.

"Good luck, Ledger, with your jumping out of planes. God, don't forget your parachute."

"Goodbye, Royal. Sorry I can't help you clean up."

Royal had plenty of help with the cleanup. Ivor, Edger, Duddy, Fudd, and Mink Martin were all in the basement. Mink was wondering if he could scrape the goop off the walls and put it in Mason jars.

Gabby, Tess and Minnie could hardly pull their feet off the sticky floor so they left to make soup and sandwiches. They also pampered Royal when he came home from the hospital, once the shards of glass were picked out of his feet.

That night at Gabby's, Tess asked Ivor Johnson, "What was he trying to do?"

"Make moonshine," Ivor answered.

"He doesn't even like moonshine," Tess replied.

"No, but he wanted his name on something. He wanted his mark on something that people would enjoy."

"But he's got his roses," Tess continued.

"Roses belong to the world," Ivor replied. "They aren't in bottles. A bottle is similar to the cover of a book. It shows you're apt and able at something. That's what Royal wanted. He wanted a label, I guess, a personal identification marker. In a way, most folks want the same thing."

"You don't," she said.

Ivor smiled. "No, not me," he replied.

The porch was crowded that night but only one person noticed when Tess took a little step and kissed Ivor Johnson on the cheek. "I'm glad you live close," she said and walked into Gabby's kitchen.

15

On the train going to basic training, Ledger wondered how he had missed the mark with Melissa. She had been impervious to his charms and that had never happened before. It made his last weeks at home unsettling. Nothing could be permanent anyway when you knew you were leaving, but losing the final conquest of your growing-up years had left a mark of failure on him. Melissa should have been his final triumph of adolescence – Melissa with the magnificent breasts and swinging walk. She moved like music. She had timing and rhythm. Her sway set steel drums pounding in Ledger's head that went beyond conquest; fires burned within him, scorching the very fibres of his manhood. Melissa Abbott, the final conquest of his youth and he had failed, failed, failed.

Other things were eating at him too. Ledger didn't want to admit it but the guilt about Pearl and his child was growing in him like a tumour. Pearl had taken up with Edger. She was smiling and Edger was smiling and Edger was holding the baby and something inside Ledger twisted like a knife. He wanted Pearl sometimes, or maybe he didn't really want her but he wanted the happiness she and his brother represented.

Then there was his child. Ledger tried to block out all conscious thoughts of her. His attempt to squeeze her out of his life left him numb.

There was also his mother. He complained to Tess about Edger not having a job, not having a plan for the future and fooling around with that baby and Pearl when he should be planning for his life. Tess just turned him off.

"Edger will find himself," she said.

"But aren't you worried about him?"

"No, not really. I'm more worried about you jumping out of airplanes. Edger is on solid ground."

The question of his father had flared up again and their talks had turned harsh. "When are you going to tell us who our father is?"

"You know when. When you're twenty-one."

"That's not good enough. I have to put something down on my army papers when I get to basic training. A family history, medical stuff."

"Put down he was killed in combat."

"Was he?"

"No, he wasn't. Put down he was healthy — is healthy. Put down whatever you like."

"So he's still alive then?"

"Yes, he's still alive."

"What's his name? I need a name."

"Make one up."

"I did that when I enlisted."

Tess sighed, "Use the same name then."

"Don't you think you've done us a real disservice keeping him from us all these years? You robbed us of our father."

It had become a familiar theme in their arguments. Edger never mentioned his father. Ledger often did. Yet of the two boys, Edger seemed the one who would have benefited most from a man in the family. For Ledger, a father would have meant competition. Maybe that was what was missing. Someone to spoil with. Ledger was spoiling for a fight, seething underneath, and the opponent was missing. He had bullied Edger when they were young. Ivor Johnson caught them in a fistfight when they were ten, down at the swimming hole at Dyas's Brook, with Edger getting the worst of it. When Ledger wouldn't stop, Ivor threw him in the water. Ledger got out enraged, but the look in Ivor's eyes kept him at bay.

"I ever see you beating on your brother again, I'm going to beat on you," Ivor said and walked away without another word. But the stage had been set. Edger had a defender across the street and that fact alone rebalanced things between the brothers.

As his train chugged along through the New Brunswick and Quebec countryside, Ledger thought about that day at the swimming hole and how he wanted to kill Ivor Johnson. It never seemed to make any difference to Ivor. He didn't treat Ledger any differently. He had taught them both how to drive when they were twelve. Ledger remembered rushing home to tell his mother he had driven Ivor's truck all the way down the Snake. Ivor had taken them fishing and camping. There were no grudges.

Ledger and Edger had become closer in recent years. There was less acrimony between them. They stopped bickering and lived in the same house in different worlds with different friends. Twins, but very different. Ledger knew he was the lucky one. He was the one who would go places, the one with the natural charm and intelligence. Edger wasn't slow really, he just took his time figuring out things that came swiftly, instinctively, to Ledger. Ledger didn't waste precious time thinking. His decisions were quick, made with instantaneous certainty.

He had picked the paratroopers solely to impress Melissa. He had never even considered such a career until Fudd said he was going to be a paratrooper. Ledger a plumber and Fudd a paratrooper? That would never do. He wasn't coming home with a wrench in his hand to find Fudd in a uniform with brass buttons. Fudd couldn't make the grade in the paratroopers and that gave Ledger some comfort, but it wasn't enough to relieve the rejection of him and the acceptance of Fudd by Melissa Abbott. Ledger pressed his head back into the seat. At that moment he hated the world.

* * *

Royal was carried down to Gabby's that night by Ivor, Duddy, Mink and Edger, like a potentate transported through the streets of his ancient kingdom. Most of the residents of the Snake were there and Royal, the exalted guest of honour, with his feet bandaged, his complexion pale, his comb-over askew, received an ovation upon arriving. He was placed on a chair with his feet up and given a beer.

Earlier in the evening, Melissa had read Fudd selected poems of Shelley, and Fudd closed his eyes as instructed and listened with his eternal soul.

Melissa had helped him fill out his application for trade school. She had advised him and finally typed out a résumé, telling Fudd he must be more assertive about his experiences and good qualities.

"You have carpentry experience and you are taking your grade ten by correspondence. That shows ambition, Fudd. That's very, very important."

Fudd nodded, not even hearing the words. He was close enough to smell her and at times like that nothing else was important. Fudd hated the thought of trade school because it meant being away from her, but Melissa had impressed upon him the obvious benefits of self-improvement. He tried hard to keep up with her thinking. It could be confusing, but Fudd was so awestruck that if

Melissa Abbott told him to take the deep dive off the steep cliffs of Wasson's Bluff, Fudd would be airborne.

He had tried to touch her again. Nothing fresh, just on her arm. She had been gentle but firm. They were friends of a higher order than people who dated, who just wanted a physical relationship. Fudd wasn't articulate enough to explain to her that's exactly what he wanted – that physical relationship. Finally, after weeks of fantasies and wild and wet dreams, he confessed. Melissa, this time taking his hand, went on about that higher plane stuff. She told him he had to work to reach it but he was definitely on his way. The plane Fudd thought he was on was the one driving him crazy.

Fudd would have been insanely jealous had Melissa fallen for somebody else. But she didn't. Even that smoothy Ledger couldn't sway her. Fudd remembered Ledger walking home with them. He watched as Ledger kept smiling at Melissa, telling her how pretty she was and what great hair she had. She was cold. God, Ledger was so cool. So confident, Fudd was getting turned on. He was certain if he was a girl, he'd fall for Ledger.

Then, shortly after that, Fudd had the awful night. He was participating in his usual masturbatory practice, the one ritual Melissa hadn't broken, only because she didn't know of it. Fudd was near his climax when the image of Melissa disappeared and the handsome face of Ledger was before him as he ejaculated. Fudd shot up like a bolt of lightning, ready to fight the curse of homosexuality.

Fudd had told Melissa much about himself but not everything. He didn't want to be totally diminished in her eyes. Now he was a homo. God, if he had ever wanted that woman to love him like he loved her, she couldn't. Not like he was now. Fudd didn't understand the obvious conflict in his desire for Melissa and what he feared as his emerging homosexuality. The contradiction didn't bother him. He had never heard of bi-sexuality. In fact, he didn't know much about homosexuality. Except he was one of them and he loved Melissa.

Bruce Graham – Ivor Johnson's Neighbours

Trade school, being gaga for Melissa, homosexuality – it was all too much for the muscle-bound, masturbating, quarter-assed carpenter who was soon going off to be a plumber, and was already a fruit. Fudd beat his fists on his forehead and cursed silently.

* * *

Back on Gabby's porch, Royal was being treated like a king. The noise level went up with the amount of beer consumed and, for once, even Claudia Abbott had two.

Claudia seldom came to these nightly gatherings in Gabby's enclosed porch but she was getting tired of her sterile surroundings. She already wished she had put more colour on her walls. Maybe she should have picked a more cheerful floor for her kitchen. Her house was hospital white and light blue, antiseptic in atmosphere and very quiet in mood. Melissa usually had her nose in a book, reading the Bible more and more. Claudia wondered if it was normal to a have a seventeen-year-old who talked of becoming a missionary, who read the Bible and spent too much time with that nincompoop Fudd. At least she didn't worry about Melissa getting carried away again, or falling in love again. Certainly not with Fudd.

Gabby was talking to Claudia and the beer was going to Claudia's head. She was only half listening. Her eyes roamed the room and stopped on Ivor Johnson, who was leaning by the window at the other end of the porch talking to Tess.

As a newcomer, Claudia could see things, sense things the others couldn't detect through the haze of friendship and years of living close to each other. Claudia thought a lot of Gabby. She liked Gabby's outgoing manner, the way she shrugged off problems and seemed to squeeze a cup of happiness out of every hour.

Tess, she felt, was uncomfortable in her own skin. Claudia didn't know why, but she felt that her very presence was somehow a threat to Tess.

Minnie seemed to be nice. Since her makeover she seemed much more relaxed. Duddy was a dingbat. You could certainly see where Fudd got it. She thought Royal might have had a screw loose somewhere. More than anyone, it was Mink Martin who was wearing down Claudia's once high standards. Mink got his old dog to bay at the moon, by baying himself first to get the animal started. Once the dog caught on, he wouldn't stop.

Even the fragile peace over the fence was disruptive. Mink had gone from swearing at her to showing up at her door with dead rabbits.

"What do you expect me to do with those?" she said with all the kindness she could muster.

"Cook 'em," Mink replied.

"They've still got the fur on them."

"Of course they have the fur on them. You expect them to run around through the snow naked, for Christ's sake?"

He cleaned them and Claudia got a recipe from Gabby and made rabbit stew. Melissa refused to touch it. Mink was back a week later with more rabbits and this time she didn't tell Melissa what they were having for supper.

One day Mink yelled over the fence, "You're a goddamn good cook."

Claudia went in the house and smiled. She must be getting a little accustomed to the Snake. That night she showed up at Gabby's porch.

While Gabby was collecting empties and emptying ashtrays, Claudia watched Ivor Johnson. He was the enigma on the street. She noticed things about him. He wore expensive shoes and a very expensive wristwatch. He didn't seem to do anything. While Duddy chased women and Royal grew roses and Tess and Gabby held jobs, Ivor just was. He had the complexion of a man who spent his time outdoors, but he was seldom seen outside. He had a barrel chest and large, muscular arms. He seemed like a man who was fit and trustworthy. Since her experience in North Sydney, trustworthiness was high on Claudia's list of priorities.

Bruce Graham – Ivor Johnson's Neighbours

Ivor Johnson and Tess were standing a little away from the others. Claudia was the only one to witness Tess's tender kiss. She wondered if they were lovers and what it would be like to have Ivor Johnson's arms around her. She knew it was time to go home.

* * *

In the first twenty-four hours of Ledger's basic training, he decided he didn't like the military. People yelled at him. He had to get up early and although he expected a little bit of that, the army carried it much too far. Also, some of the other recruits thought they were the cat's meow. If there was going to be a top dog in the outfit, it was going to be Ledger. If not, he was gone.

Despite all the newness and the many things he had to learn, Ledger had Melissa very much on his mind. Night after night, tired as he was, he tried to write to her. He wanted just the right tone, not too aggressive, not too meek. He wasn't begging, that's for damn sure. He wanted a polite but firm inquiry into the reasons why she did not find him as irresistible as other women did. Of course he wasn't going to use those words exactly, but that's what he wanted to say, sort of. What he really wanted to say was "Are you blind or stupid or what?" He wasn't going to use those words either. It had to come off just right, a firm inquiry, yet letting her know he cared without actually saying so. He'd know when his letter was perfect.

But perfection can be elusive. He couldn't find the right mixture of humility and firmness, coupled with caring and consideration. His letters took a strident tone or, when he read them back, they sounded like a weak-kneed, bitter complaint. Night after night, Ledger would crumple the unfinished letter in a little ball and put it in his mouth. He'd get it nice and wet and then he'd spit it in the waste paper basket. He gave himself ten points if the spitball went in. The paper tasted awful but he didn't care. It kept him awake for one more try. At the end of a week he had accumulated hundreds of points but no letter. Sometimes he didn't get by an opening sentence, other times he got a few paragraphs on paper.

"Dearest Melissa, Since I arrived in boot camp you have been very much on my mind. I find it difficult to understand...."

"Dear Melissa, I arrived at Camp Borden for my basic training last Monday. All is going very well here and I expect to be jumping in a month or two, once I go through training in hand-to-hand combat and firearms. When I come home I want to see you. Frankly, I fail to understand your reluctance to go out with me...."

"My Dear Melissa, Since I arrived here you have been very much on my mind. I would like to know one thing. Why? Why do you turn your nose up at me for that stupid Fudd?"

"Dearest Melissa, I hope this letter finds you and your mother in good spirits and good health. I also hope Fudd is well...."

"Dear Melissa, OK, Abbott, I want to know the truth. Why are you putting out for Fudd? Are you trying to give birth to an idiot? I've been nice. I asked you once, twice, three times. When I come home I'm taking you, see...."

Finally, still not satisfied, he sent off a letter that began, *"Dear Melissa, I hope you are well and so is everybody else. Since I arrived here they shaved my hair all off, making me look like a monk. I will send you a picture once I have one taken. Please just answer one question for me. Why don't you like me? Did I do something to offend you?"*

A month later he received a polite reply. Melissa was not upset with him in any way and she liked him just fine. There was not a sign of encouragement anywhere, not a dangling participle of a promise, not a hint of hope hidden behind her looping letters and neat sentences. It was formal, flat and to a great extent, concerned Fudd's spiritual growth and preparations for trade school, and Melissa's plans for the future and the books she was reading, a biography of Pearl S. Buck and *The Robe*.

Ledger looked in the mirror on the rare occasion when nobody else was around. He examined under his chin and both sides of his face. Was there some defect he didn't see? No, there wasn't. He was as handsome as ever except his hair was stubble, but the rest of him was fine. Chiselled chin, high cheekbones, blue eyes, broad forehead. What the hell was the matter with her?

Training was difficult. Many had already dropped out. A few had been kicked out and others had been injured. However, Ledger faced the challenges with a new bitterness that filled him with ferocity. He grunted and pulled himself through the hurdles and practised drills, marching and marksmanship while seething inside. He would show her, by God. He would show her.

The base commander held a dance for the recruits at the midway point of their basic training. The dance was the first exposure to girls for the recruits since arriving in boot camp. Most acted like caged animals about to be let out of their pens. There was much bravado and wild exaggeration concerning the manliness that would be displayed and physical exploits that would take place, given half a chance. The dance offered Ledger the opportunity he'd been waiting for. It was a test to see if he still had the old charm, the smooth moves, the old gitchy-goo that propelled him to popularity among the fluttering hearts of female high school students.

The truth was, Ledger had been shaken. Try as he might, he no longer stood on the broad pedestal of adolescent self-assurance. The dance only made things worse. To begin with, he was stiff and clumsy. The loosey-goosey grooves that made his jive the hit of high school had been replaced by a regimental stiffness. One girl left the floor the second time he stepped on her foot. When he tried to be suave to a pretty auburn-haired girl, she told him he needed new lines.

"Where ya from, anyways? You army guys are all the same."

She smelled of fresh straw and sounded like a hillbilly. It didn't get any better as the night wore on. During the last dance, a skinny girl with buckteeth, a girl he wouldn't have looked at six months earlier, told him he was shy.

"Shy? What the hell do you mean, shy?"

"Don't be mad," she replied. "If you want, I'll see you again."

He went to his bunk and put the pillow over his head. He tried to hold his breath until he expired. The charisma he'd crafted to a fine art had vanished like the air from a leaking tire.

"Dear Melissa, Thank you for wrecking my life, you bitch. I hope you and Fudd have a house full of idiots and I hope he gives you the crabs...."

It was another month before Ledger actually did a jump. Even with all the training and lectures, when he was actually airborne, the viciousness of the wind surprised him. His arms and legs were being torn from his body. There was a different experience every second and many things to remember. Once the chute filled with air Ledger was snapped upward in a lunge that knocked the breath out of him. All the time a checklist was running through his mind. What to do if you were dropping into water or on a high voltage line. There were procedures to follow, positions to remember, important things to contend with. Despite everything, at three thousand feet above the ground, Melissa Abbott came into Ledger's mind and for a fraction of a second, he forgot where he was.

"Dear Melissa, Today I almost killed myself thanks to you...."

* * *

While Ledger was undergoing his rigorous training, Fudd was undergoing rigorous self-improvement. While Ledger was learning to march, Fudd was learning to walk. He would go back and forth across Melissa's living room by the hour with a book balanced on his head.

"Good posture is so important and you're doing so well."

Fudd was also deep into poetry from Burns to Byron, from Swinburne to Shelley to Robert Browning.

"What is he buzzing in my ears? Now that I come to die."

He liked the love sonnets best, as read by Melissa when they lay on the floor together. Fudd watched the regular heaving of her chest. She led him through Marlowe and Dickens and Robert Louis Stevenson too. She explained the complexities of the Bible and what she knew of Freud and nature and the difference between deciduous and coniferous trees, how plants reproduce and why Baptists don't believe in dancing.

Ledger was merely jumping out of airplanes but Fudd was hurtling into new worlds. Much of the information whirled by him at such a speed he couldn't take it in, but part, a small fraction, stayed with him.

In his last weeks before trade school, Fudd learned enough to hurl little gems of newly acquired knowledge across the kitchen table at his increasingly nervous father. When Hank Williams came on the radio, he told Duddy, "That music comes out of the Appalachia and is really not indicative of our culture here in Canada."

"Eat your vegetables," Minnie replied.

He could never rock his mother with his learning, but his father would twitch and Pearl would roll her eyes and look at him, wishing he didn't spend so much time under the spell of Miss Big Boobs.

16

Pearl was rolling her eyes a lot. Things had changed at home. Right after Minnie's makeover there were just little hints of things to come. A dirty plate left in the sink, Fudd's bed not made, Duddy's shirt not pressed. Minnie wasn't so fastidious anymore. The dishes finally piled up in the sink until Pearl or – perish the thought – Duddy did them. Pearl didn't really mind the extra duty because her mother helped with the baby. Except, perhaps not as much lately. Twice when Pearl wanted to go uptown, Minnie couldn't look after Rhonda-Rae because she was going to bingo.

"You never go to bingo," she told Minnie.

"I do now," replied Minnie as she sailed breezily out the door.

If such things irritated Pearl and Fudd, they confused Duddy, whose emotional state ran back and forth between extreme positions. He loved part of the new Minnie, the bed part, where suddenly he was sleeping with an animal. He liked that. Other changes just plain scared him. Minnie didn't seem to need him, or wasn't so concerned about him or his meals. Now he came home and found Minnie reading the paper with her slippered feet on a kitchen chair and not a sign of supper.

"What's for supper, dear?" Duddy asked meekly.

"We're goin' out."

"Again?" Duddy frowned.

"Yes, again."

At one time Duddy would have put his foot down but not now. Not with Minnie ready to do something crazy like kill him. Maybe that's what she was trying to do in bed, give him a heart attack. He could visualize his epitaph:

Here lies Duddy absent of breath,
Died with a smile, he was screwed to death.

"What's going on with Mom?" Pearl complained to Duddy. He replied by fidgeting with his hands in his pockets and rotating his elbows while nodding his head. That was always her father's response when asked a question to which he didn't have an answer.

There were other things too. Minnie had always been abstemious, not only declining offers of alcohol but frowning on social drinking in general. Now, she was showing up at Gabby's and having a beer without bothering to tell Duddy where she was going. Duddy walked into the porch twice to find Minnie sitting at the table having a beer with Edger and Royal. Later, Royal told Gabby that Duddy's eyebrows went right up to his hairline, "As high as Minnie's!"

"What did he do?" asked Gabby.

"Nothing," replied Royal.

Bingo, Gabby's, dishes in the sink, no supper on the stove, having a beer with the boys. Minnie had always been so fussy. For years it was her family's big complaint. "You're too fussy," they used to say when she scolded them for their sloppiness. In the old days, before the new Minnie with the new eyebrows and hair, if someone was going away, Minnie would wash and pack for them and clean their room while they were gone. Now Fudd was leaving and there was no washing or packing and the days were ticking by. Minnie hadn't even gotten the suitcases down from the attic.

"Fudd's leaving pretty soon," Duddy said at the table one night.

"Yes, he is," replied Minnie.

Duddy wrinkled his face and made his chin fidget as only he could.

Fudd relayed these events to Melissa. "I think my mother is sick. I don't think she loves us anymore." Fudd was hoping against hope that Melissa would cradle him to her bosom as a sign of sympathy and support.

"Your mother is searching for herself, trying to find her own identity. She is speaking with her own voice, no longer subjugated to the family as the hewer of wood and drawer of water."

"Huh?"

Relating to his father what Melissa said, Fudd lost much in the interpretation.

"Mom is sub something."

"Huh?"

"She's sub something, she doesn't hew anymore or water either."

"That damn fool girl. What the hell are you talking about?"

"Sub and hew I said, don't you know?"

"Sub and hew, who are they?" Duddy asked, irritated. He hated these new conversations with Fudd.

"It's Mom, she's not sub or hewing anymore. And the water, ah ...."

Fudd stopped as Duddy, chewing hard as he did when alarmed, waved him off. The world had become far too complicated.

There were just the two of them, father and son, sharing a can of beans at the kitchen table. Pearl and the baby were out with Edger. And Minnie? Where the hell was Minnie tonight? It was Thursday. She was somewhere.

Duddy dearly wanted to say something to his wife, but he wasn't certain what to say. Over the years he had given her plenty of reasons to abandon him. She had caught him red-handed. So red-handed there was no point to argue or try an alibi, yet she never mentioned it again. Duddy waited for months, living in fear as he did now, but the years rolled by and Minnie never said a word about the incident on Lambs Hill.

It was a dark and stormy night, rain beating down on the cab of his truck and Crabby Carstairs already had Duddy's fly undone and was pulling his trousers over his knees when Duddy saw something out of the corner of his eye. There in his window was Minnie, her hair in pin curls as if she'd just been roused from her sleep. The image gave Duddy such a start his knee jerked and struck Crabby in the head, momentarily sprawling her across his white underwear.

They were parked as far back on the Lambs Hill Road as you could go, right at the end. Minnie never explained how she got there. Certainly she hadn't walked that distance. She wasn't wet enough. But there she was, out there in the middle of a storm. How she knew where Duddy was, she never explained either. Minnie didn't explain anything. She walked around the truck, opened the passenger door, grabbed Crabby by the hair of her head, hauled her out of the cab and threw her into the ditch. Then Minnie got in and slammed the door. "Home, James" was all she said.

Duddy dearly wanted to talk to his wife, but he wasn't about to accuse her of being a slacker. There was a report in the newspaper about a husband in England who was hacked to death by his distraught wife. Minnie was acting strangely enough and Duddy wasn't taking any chances.

Besides, Minnie wasn't a slacker. She still went to church regularly, worked in her lodge and made most of the meals. She put down preserves and sent a pie down to Mink every week, as she had done for years. It was just that Minnie had mysteriously changed and the big changes were on the inside. It was more than any exterior improvements. Things inside were impossible to gauge and evaluate. Dust didn't bother Minnie. She wasn't telling Duddy and Fudd to wipe their feet. She spent more time away from home and gave less explanation for her absences. She smiled more and whistled while doing the crossword puzzle. This happy, not bothered Minnie bewildered, bothered and downright rattled Duddy. The change in his wife caused him to wake at night with cold chills remembering Minnie's angry face through the wet window on that night, many years ago, on the Lambs Hill Road.

17

L ater the same week, Joe arrived at Minnie's. He would sleep on the couch until Fudd left for trade school. Then he could have Fudd's room and work with Duddy.

Minnie couldn't quite fathom why she decided to bring Joe into her home. She was shocked at what he had done but she was more forgiving now, forgiving and tolerant of others as she had been for years of her husband. Joe could come but she wasn't waiting on him. She felt a growing awareness that giving to others at the total expense of herself was not a good thing.

Looking in the mirror, Minnie had a heightened realization that good-looking women can be both devout and happy. Minnie appraised her life and found the only thing wanting was herself. She was tired of being the family leader. Let it go without a leader. It was time she took control of her own life and as the makeover demonstrated, she was an individual, capable of true emotion without family strings attached. She was also beginning to believe happiness was contagious. If she were truly happy, so were those close to her. She couldn't see it in her children at the moment but they would come around. The very thought made her grateful. She didn't care anymore about leaky roofs. She wasn't worrying about her kids and her husband.

Minnie was picking through her emotions with new powers of observation. She felt fortunate, lucky even. Good health and a good life must be repaid in some way. But the repayment did not mean domestic drudgery. She'd had enough of that. Joe was her repayment in full. It was that simple. Take the boy in; help him make something of himself. Her sisters could not call her lazy and her family could fend for itself because Minnie wasn't staying home hovering over them.

She could see the attachment for each other in Pearl and Edger's eyes. Pearl was ready to take flight. Edger wasn't much, God knows. He had always seemed rather aimless and vacant to Minnie but she now sensed, almost in contradiction, some sort of weird stability growing in the boy. Edger had an inner calmness about him as if he had a big secret nobody else knew. Also, he wasn't conceited like his brother. Whatever happened, Minnie's days as a mother hen were over. She was shaking the feathers off herself, as well as off that old rooster Duddy.

Of course, Joe's reputation preceded him. How could he not be the talk of the entire county? The strong brew of disgust and scandal percolated through the town once again with the news he was coming to live among them. The fresh aroma of condemnation hung in the air and wafted its way down the Whitehall Road to the Snake. Long before he had arrived, Joe had been the buzz of the back porch several nights running. Everybody had an opinion, most of them highly unfavourable.

The most sympathetic observation came from Ivor. "I wouldn't want to be in his shoes."

Royal smiled, "His girl friend doesn't need shoes. Good thing we don't keep cattle."

There was sour condemnation by Mink. "Fucking pervert comes near me, I'll kick him in the balls."

Only Melissa saw Joe's arrival as a hopeful challenge. "Oh help me, Lord. Help me help this poor, sick man who has been dropped into our midst."

There was hesitancy from Gabby and Tess but they had admiration for Minnie too, for taking such a courageous step. Among themselves they talked of their concerns. "What might he do to Pearl or the baby?" Tess asked.

Pearl wasn't the least bit afraid of Joe. He had always been quiet and polite to her, more so than most of her loutish cousins. Pearl's concern was the gossip his living in their house would create until Minnie told her she shouldn't give a damn about the gossip, since she'd been the brunt of so much of it recently what with a fatherless baby and all. "The baby has a father," Pearl replied bluntly.

"Might as well not have."

That made Pearl wince and wish she could get the hell out of the house. Fudd, influenced by Melissa Abbott, said it was a good thing to "spire Joe to a new start."

"Spire?" Pearl asked. "Do you mean inspire?"

"Yeah, that too. But I want my room back if trade school don't work out." Fudd paused, looking hard into his cereal bowl as if he were searching among the milky flakes for the meaning of life's many mysteries. Then he said quietly to his sister, "Pearl, how come Mom isn't getting my stuff ready?"

"You'll have to ask her."

"I did but she told me to do it myself."

"Well, do it yourself then."

"I don't know what suitcase to take, or what stuff to pack, or where to go when I get where I'm going, or how much money I need for the bus or nothing. Can't you help me?"

"I'll help you wash and pack but not right now. I'm going out," Pearl replied.

"Everybody's always going out," Fudd fumed. "Nobody's staying home no more. Goddamn it, you can't get nothing done 'cause nobody's ever here."

"Ahhhh. Better not let Miss Big Boobs hear you swearing. She's got a pipeline right to heaven."

"Don't call her that. You just hate her 'cause she's beautiful and you're instantly jealous."

"If you mean insanely jealous of that holier-than-thou hypocrite, I am certainly not and you can wash your own damn clothes." And so it went between brother and sister.

Duddy wasn't a problem on the question of Joe moving in. To Duddy, Joe's crime was no big deal. Duddy would screw a cow if he got the chance, Minnie suspected. Duddy would screw anything. He had no particular problem with sex – animal, mineral and vegetable. Duddy would screw a clam if he could get someone to hold the shell open. Besides, Joe might turn out to be a better helper than Fudd, although that wouldn't take a great deal of doing.

Duddy was more concerned about Minnie than anything else. He could detect something, but he couldn't readily identify it as the slow realization within his wife that change was possible in everything. He just knew Minnie was different in the way she saw him. Duddy wasn't perceptive enough to realize that the layers of ice that had formed around Minnie's heart were finally melting. Her solace had been diligence, attacking her duties with a smouldering vigour that not only caused her to plunge her hands in hot water, but to scrub the finish off pots and pans. Minnie had been more tightly wrapped than the beds she made. Her fanatical drive for neatness and order had caused her to make the bed so severely she ripped the sheets.

Minnie went back to the beauty parlour every Friday for a touch-up on her new look, and every Friday she knew she was a little more different. She could feel the change, and she was beginning to see that her new approach to her husband had changed him as well. If she could change Duddy, she could change Joe but she wasn't going to die trying.

Tess would work on Minnie while wanting to ask her questions about her new boarder, but she fought her curiosity. "My God, why of all places would he want to come here instead of far away where nobody would know him?" Tess wondered.

The fact was, Joe couldn't move too far away. He was out of jail on condition he would stay where authorities could keep an eye on him, and he had to report in once a month. Besides, he was frightened to go far away, frightened of being alone, frightened of himself and the crazy things he did. Joe wasn't a drinker. He never cared much for the taste. The night of his arrest he was trying to be sociable with his brothers. He wasn't a dreamer either, but that horrible night of his arrest was all a dream – a nightmare with missing pieces, unidentified voices and bits of blurry light. He remembered some things of that night but not the barn really, or even the smell of new hay. He didn't remember doing anything to the cow, yet they said he was caught in the act. But what act? That was never explained to him. In fact, nobody seemed to know exactly who caught him in the act.

Before his trial they had sent him to Dartmouth for a mental examination. A Dr. Fletcher interviewed him at length and finally told Joe, "You're right as rain. As sane as the next man," he added, cheerfully slapping Joe on the back.

Testifying on the stand, the same doctor spent a long time explaining deviant behaviour. As the lecture dragged on, the judge couldn't stifle a yawn and finally told the doctor to get to the point. The point was, in certain individuals, alcohol could lower social standards to a level such that they become animals themselves.

"Is the accused such a person?"

"It would appear so," the doctor replied. "Right as rain" and "Sane as the next man" notwithstanding, Joe was given six months. None of his family was in the courtroom.

After the first week as a prisoner in the Amherst jail, Joe walked unescorted down to the post office and got the mail. Normally, such an outing would be a pleasant diversion from playing cards with the jailer's wife or checkers with Nappy Salter, who had hijacked an Acadian Lines bus with twenty terrified passengers and went on a twelve-mile joyride while drinking rye whiskey and singing Hank Williams tunes. But Joe was extremely paranoid of the outside world. He wondered if he was recognized. Did the good folks of Amherst know that Joe the cowboy, Joe the animal poker, was in their midst?

While he was still at home with his mother before his trial, he often thought of killing himself. He had almost done it once. He had the barrel of the shotgun in his mouth. The taste of blue steel stayed on his tongue all morning. He was such a schmuck. No guts to pull the trigger. Joe the cowboy, the laughingstock of a whole county, would lie in bed in the dark and list the names they'd called him.

"*Hey, cow fucker*" was a favourite of the downshore boys as they drove by laughing.

"*Moo-moo Joe, the farmer's son, kissed the cows and made them run.*"

"*Joe likes his beef on the hoof.*"

It made him cry, and even in the darkness of his bedroom his crying embarrassed him. As a boy he had been punished for crying.

"Real men don't cry," his father raged, shaking him. Joe was ten years old at the time and never cried again until there seemed no alternative.

Joe the desperate cried in the dark. The tears in his mouth tasted more and more like the blue steel of the gun barrel. He didn't understand why no one knew who caught him in the act. He had been very intoxicated, yet through the fog there were pieces of his memory in place. Through the haze of alcohol he remembered fragments. The Mounties had stopped him as he staggered along the road, half a mile from the barn, yet he was "Caught in the Act." Blue steel tasted of failure, just like tears. Joe knew the next time he would squeeze the trigger because death was a better choice.

He was alone. They had let him go home and the days before his trial were the longest in his life. His own mother had turned her back on him. She would not look at him. That was the way she communicated – back to. The shame he had brought her was too much. She could not face him. The family condemnation was contagious. Not a brother or sister visited. There was never a battered half-ton coming in the driveway carrying kin. There was no support, no sympathy, no nothing.

The long hours ticked by and the loneliness seeped inside him, creating an interior as well as an exterior numbness. Joe decided that waiting for justice was worse than the punishment justice demanded.

Life in jail was better than home. Joe didn't expect visitors in jail. Other inmates got company but not Joe. During visitations, Tuesday and Thursday evenings and Sunday afternoons, the place had to look like a jail, the warden said.

"We got to look the part, boys, people expect it." The cells had to be locked and things had to be tidied up, the beer bottles collected and the old phonograph with the Benny Goodman records carried back to the warden's apartment. There were lawn chairs stacked at the front of the jail for family and friends to take up to the cells so they could converse comfortably with their loved ones. It was during those times Joe lay on his bunk, listening to the soft murmur of small talk. Visitors were uneasy with the unusual surroundings and kept the topics on the surface of familiarity: farms and new puppies, kinfolk and crops. They were not the people to hold conversations on substantial subjects at the best of times and few, despite how many visits, ever got the knack of not seeing the bars.

When the visitors left, the warden put a plug of tobacco in his mouth, unlocked the cells and forty-fives and pinochle and Chinese checkers resumed. The warden's wife brought out the phonograph and she and Nappy danced and everyone breathed easier. Visitation was hard on the jailed and the jailers alike.

"I feel so bad for that boy," the warden's wife said. "He never gets company, yet he's got lots of family." The warden was just a little worried about how much time his wife was spending with Joe but he was too proud to say anything. Besides, it wasn't like they were alone except when they played cards in the warden's living quarters at the back of the jail.

Everyone was surprised and the warden was delighted, when in the fourth month of Joe's sentence, Minnie wrote that yes, he could come live with them. The warden said it might mean getting out a bit earlier. Joe had a place to go. He could work with Duddy and learn to be a carpenter.

Joe flopped down on his bunk, digesting the news. There were kinfolk who were willing to give him a chance, people who had some kind of faith in him. It was something he couldn't describe, a pinprick of light in the dark world of Joe the cowboy.

Joe didn't know it, but there was more than a pinprick of light. The entire radiance of Melissa Abbott was burning brightly, ready to beckon him to a higher spiritual plateau.

Melissa was trying on a new turtleneck, a white pullover, a gift from Claudia. Melissa loved the sweater but worried it made her breasts appear even more pronounced. She knew her bust was a stumbling block to new friends. Where her classmates had anthills under their sweaters, Melissa claimed Mount Everest. Her bust had been a problem until Melissa became philosophical. The young married Mountie had liked to kiss and massage her breasts but that was Melissa's mistake. If they made her attractive, then she must use the attraction for higher goals. They had held Fudd's limited attention long enough for him to grow and develop under her tutelage and she had done well with Fudd. But he had been only her preliminary test. Now Melissa awaited a bigger spiritual examination. She had given Fudd direction and hope, had stood him up straight and taught him deportment and etiquette.

But Fudd had graduated, so now Melissa was ready for a new challenge, a step up, another rung on the ladder of heavenly inspiration, and Joe was on his way. The timing was perfect too. Joe was arriving just as Fudd was leaving and that made it convenient all around.

The very day Joe moved in, Duddy brought him over to Gabby's.

"This here's Minnie's nephew, Joe."

Joe shyly held out his hand and Ivor Johnson shook it and said, "Welcome to the neighbourhood, Joe."

Gabby told herself to be brave and she greeted Joe warmly. "Welcome, Joe. Make yourself at home." Royal and Tess introduced themselves and were very cordial.

It was an intoxicated Mink who was caught off guard. He'd staggered in after the initial awkwardness had moved on to restrained appraisal. Gabby had made some lemonade for Joe. The others, as best they could, tried to act naturally in the midst of such a criminal celebrity.

Mink didn't wait to be introduced. He immediately asked loudly enough for all to hear, in a slurring and rather disrespectful tone, who the hell the new guy was. When Joe held out his hand, an alarm went off in the depths of Mink's inebriated brain. Mink's hand actually swung and froze in midair, suspended between his side and shoulder as the bells signalled he was about to thrust it into a bucket of cow shit. "Ah, better not shake hands, mine is covered with grease," Mink mumbled and bent down quickly to grab a beer out of the box on the floor. The movement was too much for him and Mink landed in a lump at Joe's feet. Joe scooped him up as if he were a feather and in that instant the two men locked eyes and studied each other, a man-to-man evaluation. Mink Martin: war hero, owner of a hovel and holder of the biggest hubcap collection in Nova Scotia and Joe: the recently released, totally disgraced, family-condemned deviant.

A strange aura filled the porch at that moment. Joe lifted Mink and gently put him on his feet as if he was handling a rare piece of china. Gabby noticed. Joe wasn't at all what she had expected. He was young, she guessed twenty-five, with brown eyes and sandy hair. He had the same type of powerful build as Ivor Johnson — barrel chest and the developed arms of a weight lifter. Yet there was an overt softness behind the terminal sadness in his eyes. There was a sensitivity too, an empathy in his nature that almost defied definition. He was a man, Gabby knew instinctively, who would stoop and pluck a wounded seabird and hold it in cupped hands. Two things simultaneously collided in her mind. All of her wariness dissipated with Joe's gentle act of lifting Mink Martin off the floor. More importantly at that moment, Gabby knew she liked him no matter what crime he had committed.

Mink, the harshest critic of Duddy and Minnie for letting a deviant into their home, Mink the man who used great profanity concerning animal pokers, meekly thanked Joe and held out his slightly trembling hand and Joe shook it. Mink was flushed and the atmosphere on the porch was so charged it felt like the slightest noise would shatter the room. You could hear people breathing and above their breath was the soft rustle of the incoming tide. Royal finally cleared his throat and tried small talk, while Gabby brushed some imaginary crumbs off the linoleum tablecloth and asked Joe if he wanted more lemonade without noticing he had hardly taken a sip out of his glass.

When Joe and Duddy left a few minutes later, the quietness remained. Each person lost in their own thoughts, conducting their own assessment of the new resident and their personal reaction to him. The wisest among them had some idea of the courage needed to enter a home where a man condemned by society knew no one and everyone knew of him.

Three nights later, Joe came back to Gabby's, but this time he was alone. It was early in the evening, nobody was on the porch and Gabby had her feet up on a kitchen chair reading the paper.

"Mind if I come in?"

"Joe!"

She jumped to her feet, a bit embarrassed he had caught her relaxing. They faced each other in an awkward pause. He swallowed and tried to smile and she hoped she was smiling back. Gabby realized she was a bit taller than him. She could look directly into his brown eyes. She was glad he had come back and uncomfortable that seeing him made her so happy.

"I've still got some lemonade in the fridge."

"Sure, thanks," Joe said, swinging a kitchen chair around and sitting on it with his arms folded across the back, the same way he had often played forty-fives with the warden's wife.

"I want to ask you something," he said. "I've gotten to know my way around a bit. So let me ask you outright and it's okay however you answer, but just tell me the truth please, because I have to know. Do you mind me coming here? With the others, I mean. I thought I made people uncomfortable the other night and that's natural, I suppose. But if you'd rather not have me around, it's better I know, so...."

"No, no. Not at all. You're welcome here," she heard herself say, as if her words were coming from somewhere across the room. She couldn't stop telling him he was welcome. Excitement was bubbling up from somewhere inside her. She was trying to contain it or at least mentally file it away for examination later. She needed material for conversation and all she had were unidentified feelings and unsuitable questions. Plenty of questions. But it was impolite to ask. Gabby wasn't a gossip but her imagination galloped away wondering what was going on inside his head. What he must have been through – the conviction, the jail, the humiliation. Yet despite the disgrace, here he was, willing to be humbled again, willing to have her say, "Don't come back, you sicko."

His soft and serious manner she found almost sensual. There was a maturity about him that didn't fit his age. She detected an underlying vitality that had been dampened down by misfortune. "How old are you?" she blurted out and immediately tried to take it away. "Don't answer that." She laughed, embarrassed, waving her hand back and forth as if to erase the question.

He smiled weakly. "Twenty-four," he replied.

"When's your birthday?" she asked, giving herself time to make up some fib because she didn't know what else to do. She felt a burn on her face. "I mean, I'm just nosy," she said. "That's all. I keep a record of everyone's birthday just so we can celebrate when their big day arrives." It was a blatant lie; she kept no such record. The heat of her cheeks intensified.

"June twenty-fourth. I spent it in jail."

"I'm sorry, Joe." She looked down at the floor and silently cursed herself for being so stupid.

"Oh, it wasn't too bad. The warden's wife made me a cake and everybody sang Happy Birthday. It wasn't such a bad birthday. I mean, it could have been worse, I guess."

She wasn't certain she believed him but he wasn't the type to play free and loose with his words.

He looked away, giving Gabby a chance to raise her eyes and study him. He had a fine face, more cute than handsome, she thought, with a straight nose and firm jaw. She looked at his neatly parted sandy hair. He had a light complexion made pale, she surmised, because of where he'd been. She liked his low, soft voice. Gabby didn't want to but she couldn't help herself. She focused on him, trying to see the monster within. She couldn't find it. She realized he was talking again.

"I just have to know my boundaries."

She wasn't certain if he was repeating himself for her benefit or not. "Yes, I understand," she replied because she had to say something. He was earnest and shy and brave, and suddenly Gabby wanted to hug him. A mothering instinct, she told herself, ignoring that for years she had been convincing herself she didn't have such instincts.

They talked for an hour; they both liked going to the movies and show tunes and the songs of Doris Day and Patti Page. They listened to the same shows on the radio. Joe had worked on a farm and in the woods. Sipping the second glass of lemonade, he finally admitted it had taken every bit of determination he had to follow Duddy into her house that first night.

"I have to do these things. I have to know who will be comfortable with me." He put his head down again and stared at the floor and measured his words carefully.

"You see, they tell me I have to get out with people, that I have to socialize," he continued. "I hope you don't mind."

"No Joe, I don't mind." There was a desperate urge she was fighting to repel. She wanted to reach out and touch him, to reinforce her words with some kind of overt action to give him stronger reassurance. "I open my porch to my neighbours only because I want to. We don't have a social club. People don't want to go uptown. So they come here. You're welcome anytime, Joe." She was trying to look earnest but it didn't feel as though it was enough. If any other convict tried to weasel his way into her home, she would have considered him a con man, but not this guy. He was willing to accept rejection, already expecting it maybe.

When he left they shook hands, almost formally as if they had just signed a business deal. He thanked her. Gabby went to the window and watched him walk up the road. Get out and mix. That's what he was doing, no matter how embarrassing or painful, no matter how humiliating, Joe was doing it. "Good for you, boy," she whispered as she watched him walk away.

* * *

Melissa Abbot, who had been waiting anxiously to meet her new challenge, was taken aback when she finally got her chance. If Joe was not what Gabby expected, he certainly wasn't what Melissa had been anticipating. She was waiting for another Fudd. But Joe was fair-haired, broad-shouldered and his handsome looks caught Melissa a little off balance. For an instant, she doubted her own moral fibre. Fudd was safe, never a temptation, never even a consideration, but this man? Oh, what am I going on about? she asked herself.

"Hello, Joe. Nice to meet you. I hope you like it here."

For his part, Joe was dumbstruck. He had just taken the first baby steps out of the shell it had taken a lifetime to construct and here in front of him was a breathtaking goddess. She was a divine light he had no right to look upon. He had never seen such a beautiful woman. Perfect teeth, perfect hair, and perfect face.

He stiffened his neck intentionally because he dared not look at her breasts, not a pervert like him! Be safe, Joe, he told himself, look down. No, no, not at her crotch, further down. Right to the ground.

He's so shy, Melissa thought.

So the two of them stood on Snake Road in front of Minnie's house, on a warm autumn night, the nubile young woman and handsome young man. She, made slightly unsteady by his handsomeness but confident nonetheless. He, lacking composure and overwhelmed by her beauty, wanting to run but wanting more to stay. For any other couple, the moment might have had the makings of a great romance, except in this case prior conditions caused unusual circumstances. He was a recently released felon, having been incarcerated for bestiality. She was an early blooming teenager who had been the lover of a married Mountie. She had rejected the evils of the flesh for the saving grace of God and desired more than anything, not to physically possess this man, but to save his soul.

Edger was there too but they no longer noticed him. Edger was spending so much time at Pearl's, having dinner with the family, that he and Joe had come to know each other. Joe was more comfortable around Edger than anybody. Edger was quiet like him. There was no need to talk all the time and that was good.

Joe had been exercising his courage. He'd go to Gabby's almost every night, at first knocking on the porch door until she told him just to come in. Each time he returned after a glass or two of lemonade, he felt a sense of growth, a tiny step on the road to redemption.

But standing in front of Melissa Abbott, Joe felt his old self-hatred return as he fought for something to say without having it stumble awkwardly out of his mouth. Melissa spared him the challenge of another sentence.

"I'm going up to the store. You guys want to walk up with me?"

"I can't. Pearl is just bathing Rhonda-Rae and we're going up to see Tess," Edger replied.

"How about you, Joe, feel like a walk?" Melissa asked as casually and lightly as possible. Before the evening was over, Joe found the courage to raise his head, look directly into her face and ask if she was certain she wasn't an angel. It actually made Melissa blush, which alarmed her because the last man to make her blush wore the uniform of the Royal Canadian Mounted Police. Joe's flattery was a long way from Fudd's incoherent mumbles because Joe, reserved as he was, didn't mangle his words. His voice was low but sweetly strong. His question wasn't meant to be serious, but a compliment filled with caring. Melissa felt a wave of heat rush through her. Just for a second she was off balance again, her knees with a little too much spring in them. It alarmed her. Two emotional pellets whirling through her missionary zeal by a man she hardly knew. A man who had done unspeakable, evil things. How could this be?

On their way back from the store, Joe managed, without trying, to fire yet another emotional salvo into Melissa, again penetrating that missionary mantle. He bent over and picked a wildflower, a purple aster, and presented it to her. It was an escapee from Royal's garden. Joe's presentation of the flower, holding it out to her as if it were on a platter, shot through her solidly constructed emotional wall and Melissa could feel liquid coursing in her, much like melting ice. When their eyes came together over the flower, it was only the second time he had really looked into her face. Joe was practising the courage of coming out and it was melting Melissa's defences.

They were standing in front of Melissa's house, talking at the end of the driveway. Claudia watched from the living room window, standing back just far enough not to be seen. As she gazed at them, a small pulse vibrated at the side of her head. Maybe this was a warning signal because there was something about this stranger that bothered her. He was clean-cut and very well-groomed. Not terribly tall, he had the build of a weight lifter. My God, he could be that Mountie!

Claudia took a deep breath. She looked in the front hall mirror but refused to see any sign of panic. She nervously fixed a few strands of hair and went to the door. She concentrated on walking casually.

"Hello," she said, trying very hard to sound relaxed. "I'm Claudia Abbott."

"Mother, this is Joe," Melissa said and her voice had just a touch of coldness that might be imperceptible to others but not to her mother.

"Well, nice to meet you, Joe," Claudia said, knowing exactly who he was. Knowing kept her from saying any of those other social niceties that usually accompany such greetings. There was an uncomfortable moment of awkwardness where Claudia wished she could make a comment to her daughter. A small errand to send her on, a message, any excuse for why she had come out of the house. There was nothing, not a single thing she could bring to bear. Because she couldn't think of anything to say, she muttered an embarrassed goodbye, walked up the driveway and went inside. She shut the front door quietly and leaned against it, breathing heavily.

A thousand snapshots raced through her mind, black and white glimpses of the past twenty-four months. Even though they were edged in pain and deadly accurate, they didn't come to her as occasions as much as feelings. The emotions were stronger than the circumstances.

As mothers do, Claudia carried in her heart the agony of her own daughter and of others as well. The tearful diatribe of the Mountie's young wife withered Claudia's insides. She could never let it happen again and seeing Joe set off those warning bells. Claudia looked up at her newly constructed house, trying to see the sky through the freshly painted ceiling. She whispered as she raised her head and sent a prayer winging through the roof, "Please God, not again. Don't let it happen again."

She was still leaning against the door when Melissa tried to open it. Mother and daughter stared at each other, a deep, lingering look that nonetheless did not really allow either woman to penetrate the other's private thoughts. Melissa didn't speak or complain as Claudia had expected. There was just something Claudia couldn't read in her daughter's eyes, an indifferent emptiness that lacked any expression or meaning.

Melissa went upstairs with her head held high, superiority showing in every step. She desperately needed to hide how shaken she really was. The iron resolve had slipped and she vowed it would never happen again. She knew Claudia's faith in her had faltered, a faith that both had worked on for months. She needed that faith more than life itself.

Claudia leaned against the door and cried.

18

Edger hadn't been totally truthful to Joe and Melissa when he said he and Pearl were going to take the baby over to visit his mother. They were actually leaving Rhonda-Rae with Tess while they ran a secret errand. No one knew except the two of them and the Baptist minister.

They had set their plans in place. It would be difficult, very difficult, but they would somehow make it. Edger had done his homework, conducted his interviews and was ready to move.

Ralph McFadden ran a small, not very prosperous store in Whitehall. Edger had stacked shelves there as a schoolboy. He had piled Ralph's winter wood and shovelled the snow in front of the store and small house attached to it. Ralph always thought Edger was smarter than people gave him credit for, but he was still surprised when Edger came to him with a proposition.

Ralph was at first amazed and, after some thought, he was pleased. "That Edger," he told his wife, "you never know. Still waters run deep."

There wouldn't be many people who would want to take over a tiny, dark, break-even store way down the Whitehall Road. Fewer people yet willing to work their way into ownership. Edger told Ralph he'd work for twenty dollars a week. Ten dollars would stay with Ralph. That money would go toward the price of Edger owning the store someday. They would split the store profits with Edger getting a higher percentage of any profit above what was made last year. Ralph could sit back and do what he dearly wanted to do – retire. They finally agreed the purchase price for the little house and store would be three thousand dollars. Ralph figured it would take Edger six years before the store and house would be his.

"He'll never last that long. Not taking home the pittance he'll make here," Ralph told his wife, rubbing his hands together rapidly as he always did when he got excited.

Edger knew what he was doing. He knew Ralph had been worrying about the store, concerned about getting anything out of it. The little attached house was no bargain either. It was small, its windows leaked and it needed a new furnace.

Edger's proposals initiated a series of discussions between Ralph and his wife Mildred-Bell. "We can retire, live right here for the next six years and have someone run the store. We keep half the profits and that's better than closing the damn thing down without a nickel coming in." He shook his head, agreeing with his own comment and told himself again, "A little bit is better than nothing at all and I'm getting too old to work the hours anymore."

"But why would he do it?" Mildred-Bell asked. "He can't live on ten dollars a week for the next six years."

"He thinks he can increase business," Ralph said. "If he does, he gets better than half the increased profits. If he doesn't, that's his tough luck. Edger is a worker. If he puts his mind to it, I think he can keep this place going." Then he laughed, "Now, increasing profits way down here? Well, that's another matter. But he may run it for a year before he gives up and we can stay in the house."

Bruce Graham – Ivor Johnson's Neighbours

Ralph and MB, as he called her, had often talked of retirement. The store hours were long: seven in the morning until nine at night. At least he and MB had been able to slip into their kitchen for a tea or a quick lunch. Edger would be in the store all day. Ralph felt a little guilty but washed it down with his tea.

Edger wasn't worried. His agreement with Ralph would have to be drawn up in a contract. That's what Ivor Johnson advised him.

"Make it so you can pay him off sooner than six years with no penalty for doing it."

It was a simple agreement, which Ivor helped Edger write and which the lawyer in Amherst said was good. Edger insisted on an out-of-town lawyer because he didn't want anybody to know what he was doing.

Ivor laughed, "You think people in this town don't know already? I guarantee you they do."

Of course Ivor Johnson was right. Mildred-Bell wasn't aware of any confidentiality considerations and she told Mrs. Parsons, who told Mrs. Ripley, who told her bridge club and on and on. By the time Ralph McFadden and MB had considered, debated and signed the contract, thirty percent of the town already knew. Once Edger had the contract signed he didn't care. His only concern was someone else jumping in and making Ralph a better deal.

Edger needn't have worried. There wasn't another soul in the entire county who would consider working the next six years for ten dollars a week. But in fact, neither was Edger. He and Pearl had put together big plans. The store was only the beginning, the launch of their life together.

"Ivor, I want you to know Pearl and me appreciate all you've done for us. You know, the agreement with Ralph, the lawyer and all. We appreciate it."

"Don't mention it," replied Ivor. They were sitting across the table from each other in Ivor Johnson's kitchen.

"We were wondering if –" Edger put his head in his hand searching for the right words to say. "Can you stand for us? You know, ah, be my best man?"

"You're getting married then?"

"Yes."

"Congratulations, Edger. That's no doubt the right thing to do."

"Thank you."

It was a while later in the conversation that Ivor came to the realization Edger's mother and Pearl's parents knew nothing of the coming nuptials. Nor were they going to be told.

"You're not inviting Tess?"

"No, we're eloping. Sort of."

"Why?"

"I don't know." Edger blushed as he answered. "It's Pearl's idea. I think she may be a little embarrassed by all this."

"You should tell Tess. Where are you going to live?"

"With Tess," Edger answered uncomfortably. "At least I hope we are. I haven't asked her yet."

"Let me get this straight. You're not inviting your own mother to your wedding but you're going to ask her to let you and your new wife, plus your new wife's baby, move in with her?"

"Yeah." Edger squirmed as he answered.

"No, I won't stand for you."

"Why not?" Edger pleaded.

"Because you and Pearl aren't being fair to Tess or Minnie and Duddy. You two are thinking of yourselves."

* * *

So as it turned out Tess, Ivor, Minnie, Duddy, Fudd and Rhonda-Rae were all at the Baptist manse on that Friday night. The rain beat on the windows as nineteen-year-old Edger and twenty-year-old Pearl said their vows. Tess and Minnie cried. Rhonda-Rae wailed louder than the rain. The minister lost his place at one point and starting reading a funeral prayer. Duddy's throat was dry and Ivor Johnson smiled as best man.

The reception was at Gabby's and everybody came to congratulate the bride and groom. It was a good evening. They gave the newlyweds gifts and Pearl made a little speech that was so touching, Gabby wiped her eyes and even Mink blinked back some tears. It was a going away party too. Fudd was off to trade school. He was hanging very close to Melissa, who smiled at everyone and sipped her lemonade while she tried to stay as far away from Mink and Duddy as humanly possible. Mink was thoroughly drunk when he arrived and Duddy was giddy as well. Minnie didn't seem to mind. Claudia was helping Gabby with the sandwiches and Tess was talking to Ivor by the window.

"I told him no at first," Tess said and Ivor nodded. "You know, you wait all those years for them to grow up so you can get on with your own life. Then they're ready to go and they turn around and say, 'Hey Mom, can I stay and bring a wife and kid too?'" She shook her head and looked at their neighbours. The party, thanks mostly to Mink and Duddy, was getting louder by the minute.

"I know the truth," Tess said. "Your children are your life. There is no real separation from them, no matter how hard you try. The look on Edger's face when I said no. I don't think any mother could love a son more than I love that boy. I relented of course. I guess he knew I would. He has plans, he and Pearl. Probably hair-brained, but so were mine at their age."

Ivor saw something in Tess's eyes. Not tears really, just the beginning of droplets that had the potential to turn into tears. He put his hand on her shoulder. Claudia, coming from the kitchen with a tray, saw the chemistry between them. She resented Tess at that moment but her attention was very quickly diverted. Mink was moving toward her and just in case that disgusting, smelly, dirty old man wanted to paw her, Claudia beat a hasty retreat back to the kitchen where she poured herself a strong glass of bourbon.

Mink Martin had done a complete about face. He had actually been bathing and shaving two or three times a week, until Claudia told him she didn't want any more rabbits. Then he showed up on her doorstep one night, clearly inebriated and with a case of beer under his arm. She'd foolishly let him in — out of neighbourly hospitality, she supposed. She didn't want to be seen as a prude. God, I've never tried so hard to fit in, she thought.

It hadn't gone well. Mink made a haphazard, awkward pass. Claudia told him to go. He called her a stuck-up bitch. She called him a drunk and the feud between them was back on. Mink threatened to re-erect his hubcap fence. Ivor intervened, Mink relented and Claudia kept the food coming — with one new, major stipulation. Mink wasn't to come near her or her house even if he'd had a bath in the past twelve hours.

"She can just drop the pies and stew off on my doorstep and I don't need to see her stuck-up arse at all," Mink responded.

"You know, Mink, you're using blackmail on that woman," Ivor said.

"How so?" Mink asked.

"Every time you two get in an argument, you've threatened to put up the fence. That's blackmail."

Mink smiled a thoroughly wicked smile, made more sinister by the absence of one front tooth at the top and two at the bottom.

"Word of caution. Don't try it too often, Mink. If she ever really tested it in the courts, I think you'd lose."

What the hell does he know? Mink thought as Ivor walked up the road to his house. Mink was mad at the lecture but he didn't argue with Ivor. When he cooled down, he admitted Ivor knew lots of stuff and his advice was probably right.

19

It didn't take very long to see that Joe was going to be a better carpenter than Fudd. In fact, within a month Joe was doing everything Duddy could do. Duddy could leave Joe, go off to quote other jobs and come back to find that things weren't all screwed up.

Gradually Duddy started bidding on bigger projects. He wasn't building houses, but with Joe working with him, he started bidding on siding and roofing work and building an enclosed sunroom for Mrs. Mason Forbes.

Joe was a good worker and it made Duddy's life easier and far more profitable. When they didn't have big jobs, he could send Joe to do the little stuff like clothesline platforms and back steps, things that Fudd would screw up given half a chance.

In the evenings, Joe would saunter down to Pearl and Edger's store and help out because there was a lot going on. Edger had added a meat counter and brought in more merchandise and vegetables. Joe built bins, fixed the floor and even waited on customers. Joe's notoriety began to bring in new business. The fact that a convicted bovine molester was behind the meat counter wrapping beef, of all things, made the curious drive down from town. Tiddly teenagers came in to size him up and ran out giggling about how cute he was. The gawkers didn't buy much but it gave Edger an idea. Joe's notoriety was publicity and publicity was what they needed.

"We'll do something that will attract attention," he told Pearl.

"Isn't Joe enough attraction?" she asked.

"There isn't such a thing as enough," he replied.

Pearl worried about how much money Edger was spending and more to the point, where he was getting it. Edger was forthcoming about everything except the financial end of things. Pearl was not the sort of person to be put off for very long. Finally, under a constant barrage of questions, Edger broke down and 'fessed up. Anything to stop Pearl's pestering.

"Ivor floated us a loan, just to get us started."

"*Us* a loan! How could he float *us* a loan when I wasn't involved? You've brought in meat and vegetables and bought wood for the bins and, and – "

"You have to believe, Pearl."

She stopped. He could do that to her. He had a way of reassuring her without actually offering any reassurance. When he had conviction, it poured out of him and wrapped around her, making her feel everything was going to be all right. Sometimes when she needed reassurance she had to push him a little, but it was always there.

Pearl believed even when Edger bought a live cow. She believed even if she couldn't stop shaking her head in disbelief.

"He's a Black Angus and I got him at a good price. His name is Stewart."

"Please don't name him!"

"The winter's coming on. Not everybody wants to live on flatfish and deer meat."

They would hold a beef draw. Buy five dollars worth of groceries or merchandise and draw a ticket. Every ticket was a part of the cow: a roast, a pound of hamburger, stew meat, or steak. Everybody would get something. Everybody would be a winner.

"We'll call it The Great Beef Giveaway," Edger said proudly. "And we'll put it in the paper, maybe with a picture of Stewart and a picture of the store too, once we finish painting the front and Joe finishes the sign."

"The sign?" asked Pearl.

"Yeah, the sign. Joe's working on it in your father's basement."

The Great Beef Giveaway at the new E & P Variety Store brought the customers in droves. Everybody was after the free beef.

"You have to buy groceries anyway, so why not get a steak too. Let's get up there quick before the kid goes broke."

Saturday morning, Ralph McFadden and MB peeked through their curtains as cars crammed their driveway and along both sides of the Whitehall Road. A bead of envy rolled over Ralph's heart. MB was darned unhappy too about all the traffic.

"Suppose someone wants to drop by to see us? There's no room to park."

Not that anyone ever dropped by Saturday morning, but it was the principle of the thing. Their driveway, their store, taken over. It wasn't right! Ralph reread the contract he and Edger had signed in front of the lawyer and a cold fear crept over him. He and Mildred-Bell might be moving sooner than expected.

Progress is never smooth whether building a nation, establishing a corporation or getting a financially inept enterprise off the ground. Especially on the outskirts of a town too small to have suburbs. The beef draw was an overwhelming success with some minor hitches. Wilson Meekins and Nettie Kelly from West Bay got in a fistfight over the last ticket. Mrs. Claude MacLeod complained all she ever got was hamburger while others were taking home all the roasts. "It's fixed in favour of your friends," she accused, pointing a bony tobacco-stained finger at Edger.

"I don't have any friends," he replied.

Mrs. MacLeod, who had an acid tongue and was a vociferous writer of Letters to the Editor, wrote a cutting review of the Fixed Beef Draw.

Pearl was ready to drive down the shore and, as she put it, "punch the old biddy in the mouth."

"No, no. It's still publicity," replied Edger.

"You don't mean to tell me you think this is good, this bullshit?" Pearl waved the newspapers over her head.

"Pearl, please don't swear in front of Rhonda-Rae. No, it's not good but it's not as bad as you think."

There was resentment from the merchants in town too. They talked among themselves in low voices. Their criticism was tinged with a degree of admiration. "The kid's got pluck. It must have cost him a lot of money. You won't see that again."

But they did see it again, in mid-winter. This time Mrs. Claude MacLeod won a prime rib roast. Nettie Kelly from West Bay drew steaks one time and stew meat the next. The newspaper reporter from Amherst interviewed Edger and put his picture in the paper along with the story "Local Merchant Beefing Up Business."

Aside from the disgruntlement of other business owners, there were other small setbacks in the retail operation. Somebody tried to break into the store one night but MB's screams scared them off. In the hurry to escape the shrill voice of Mildred-Bell, the thief left a full case of beer sitting on the front steps.

"What kind of thief leaves a case of beer behind?" Pearl asked.

"A drunk one," replied Edger. "One coming from the bootlegger, since the liquor store was closed."

"It should be easy to find out who it was then," Pearl said.

"Not that easy. He had seven customers before midnight. I asked."

"Did you give the names to the Mounties?" Pearl said.

"No," he replied. "Six of them are innocent and I don't want to get them in trouble with the law."

"God, Edger. Sometimes you're too good to be believed." She shook her head as she looked at him.

"What's that mean?" he asked, smiling.

Pearl kissed him. "Nothing."

All winter long, business increased at the E & P. Edger and Pearl were happy. Ralph and MB were not. The showdown came the following spring. Profit for the third quarter increased by four hundred dollars. Finally, Ralph couldn't stand it any longer. He couldn't sleep without seeing all that cash sliding through his fingers. He and Mildred-Bell had time to convince themselves they'd been duped by that sharpie Edger. They ignored the fact the sharpie was working fifteen hours a day, had made many improvements inside and outside, and had used promotions and advertising. Edger had done more, much more, than Ralph and MB had ever expected. They were overwhelmed by his accomplishments and at the same time convinced that anything Edger could do, they could do too.

Once he had worked up a good head of steam by pacing back and forth across his small kitchen, Ralph finally took the contract to a lawyer. It could be broken, perhaps, if he had grounds.

Ralph went home to consult with Mildred-Bell over grounds. Did they have any, or could they find any? They suddenly, desperately, wanted their store back. It was a gold mine. Ralph was seventy-two, but the winter off had made him restless. He was tired of *Pepper Young's Family* and *Ma Perkins* on the radio and tired of the sports pages. Tired also of listening to Mildred-Bell whine all day long. The money Edger was suddenly taking in and the booming business he had developed made Ralph bitter.

"I've been tricked."

Ralph couldn't stand it anymore. "The hell with grounds. I want my damn store back," he shouted at Mildred-Bell, who shouted back.

"Don't shout at me!"

Ralph confronted Edger in the driveway at 6:45 in the morning on the first day of May. With a dribble of tobacco juice running down his chin, Ralph said, "I want you off my property now. This is my store and I'm taking it back."

Edger was so stunned he couldn't answer. When he tried to put his key in the lock, Ralph pushed him away.

"Get out."

Edger silently turned and slowly walked away. He went up the Whitehall Road, turned on to the Snake and walked past Minnie and Duddy's, past Royal's place and sat on Tess's front steps. He was at a loss, bewildered beyond belief. He looked across the street and saw the light in Ivor Johnson's kitchen.

At exactly twenty after ten a truck pulled in the driveway of the E & P Variety. Two men got out: Ivor Johnson from the driver's side, Edger from the passenger seat. They walked in and Edger slapped a cheque on the counter. Ivor did the talking.

"That's the remainder of what Edger owes you, Ralph. He's paying you off and he wants you out of his house by the end of the month. You understand? The store and the house are his and if you aren't gone by the end of the month, he's going to charge you rent."

Ralph's mouth opened and closed several times as he tried to speak but Ivor held up his hand. "I just talked to my lawyer. We're bringing action against you if you don't vacate this store at once. I mean right now! There will be no more profit sharing. The store belongs to Edger."

Because he had to do something, Ralph picked up the cheque with his shaking hands. The bank had certified it with Edger's name on it. Where did the kid get the money?

Mildred-Bell went into hysterics when a stone-faced Ralph walked through the adjoining door into their soon-to-be-vacated home. She flew into the store where Edger stood looking rigid and white. Then she met the cold fire in Ivor Johnson's eyes.

"Leave this store," Ivor said.

His voice was hardly more than a whisper but there was force behind it, a threatening power that made MB back away. She pointed her finger at them.

"You'll never get away with this."

"Get out," Ivor roared and MB flew back through the door.

It was the last time Ralph and MB ever used that adjoining door. Before they finished calling their lawyer, they heard hammering as Edger drove a quarter pound of five-inch nails into the gateway to their lost enterprise.

"I'm going up to Jack Cameron's," Ivor said, "to buy you a new set of locks. One for the cash drawer too. The situation calls for higher security." There was a touch of a smile as he patted Edger on the shoulder.

When he was alone, Edger walked around touching things. He lightly brushed his hand over the molasses and pickles, mustard and cans of green beans and beef stew. The store was his and Pearl's and it had all happened so suddenly, Pearl didn't even know. What would she say? He could hardly explain it to himself. Ivor had just taken him to the bank, written him a cheque and told him not to worry. Edger was glad there weren't any customers at the moment because he started to choke up. He fought tears until he could no longer hold back. What kind of storekeeper cries?

He moved away so he wouldn't stain the bags of sugar.

There were threats of a lawsuit of course, but they didn't amount to much. Ivor instructed his lawyer to proceed with due diligence and in a very aggressive manner. The day before the end of the month, Ralph and MB, bitter but assuaged with the money they hadn't expected quite so soon, moved into a little apartment uptown. As MB put it, "Away from those dreadful people in Whitehall."

Edger and Pearl moved into the little house attached to the store and Edger pried the quarter pound of nails out of the adjoining door.

Every fall there was a beef draw and every summer a lobster draw. The store prospered. So did Edger and his family.

20

While Edger and Pearl were making the store a success, many things were happening in the world outside during 1954. The Cold War raged and people worried about Communism, although very few had any idea what it actually was. Some well-known movie stars stated they'd never been Communists and didn't like Communists. Along the Snake, Communists weren't seen as a big threat. Life rolled along with the usual ups and downs and a certain predictability. Fudd dropped out of trade school and came home to find his parents had become different people. Joe had his room and Pearl was gone. The furniture was rearranged and Minnie had new pictures on the wall. Their cat Oliver had died and been replaced by a yellow tabby that snarled at him. Now it was Fudd who slept on the couch and "Oh, no," he couldn't have his job back with Duddy. Fudd wasn't too concerned about the couch or the job but what really wounded him was Melissa. He couldn't put it in words but he could see something he didn't like. A more articulate observer might have described it as the wearing away of the young woman's moral fibre.

The fibre was threadbare in places and through its thinning exterior, Melissa Abbott could feel lust. Yes, it was lust all right. The kind that had surged through her veins with the twenty-three-year-old married Mountie in North Sydney. Tall and handsome, he had taken her innocence and much more. Along with the loss of her virginity, Melissa had lost faith in herself. The young Mountie had been very cruel and he refused to leave his family for her as he had first promised. He had hurt Melissa deeply and in her hurt she sought revenge. What she did then had caused her to lose faith in her own faith. Her actions, she soon realized, were more vile than anything. The fact that she did it had shaken her emotionally and created a series of tremors across the entire community.

That anger had left a pretty and very pregnant wife weeping bitterly at her front door. Her revenge resulted in Claudia's intervention and prompted a blistering reprimand for her ex-lover from the superintendent of the RCMP that threatened his career. It had left his marriage in shreds, caused her mother to find another job in another town and strained their mother-daughter relationship almost to the breaking point.

Melissa knew it was her fault they lived next door to a drunken maniac who would probably murder them in their beds. If she hadn't thrown herself onto a higher plane, as the man of God advised before he put his hand on her leg, if she hadn't had a few remnants of her tattered faith to patch together she would have been lost. But things had become so complicated. Fudd had failed in the wider world and Joe, a gentleman in every respect who she felt was blameless, had rekindled the fires of lust. The flames were turning into an inferno so powerful, Melissa would retreat to her bed and give in to her body's desire, then curl in a ball and weep at her weakness.

She permitted herself to have fantasies about Joe. What he had done to the animal she visualized him doing to her. She had a crazy dream that shook her to the very core. She was involved in a *ménage-à-trois* with Joe and the cow.

"How's that, you sick bitch?" she heard the devil scream.

As winter turned to spring, Melissa remained miserable. Fudd and Ledger were miserable too. Fudd showed it, Ledger didn't. When Ledger came home in his paratrooper's uniform for a short leave, Fudd felt his brass buttons and thought what he might have done.

They had a homecoming party for Ledger in Gabby's porch. Tess was very proud. Her sons were turning out all right.

"Here's to my boys, the merchant and the paratrooper," she said in an impromptu toast. Everybody lifted their bottles.

There was something else in the air that spring of the Cold War and rainy nights. It had to do with Gabby, the perpetual host, whose back porch was the neighbourhood watering hole. She had spent the long winter nights fighting feelings she didn't want. She was, after all, a rejected woman whose man had walked out years before. Rejection leaves a mark. More than a mark – a scar. Her husband had taken his clothes, his power tools and with them, her passion. In the intervening years there had been a few dates but never anything even remotely serious. Gabby wanted to keep it that way. She wasn't going to ruin her life again. Yet she knew there was a force growing in her. She finally acknowledged it and that made her run to her bedroom for a good cry. She cried standing up because somehow that made it less like giving in. She cried standing up even when her legs became weak and her knees almost buckled. She wouldn't give in. When she finished, she straightened her hair, put on new lipstick and went out to the porch. That's what kind of winter it had been.

Gabby had opened her house to her neighbours because it was better than being alone. The nightly gathering had been her remedy. Just knowing people were there was enough; she didn't need to be constantly available. The situation was much more relaxed that way. Royal or Ivor often dropped by, sometimes together, sometimes alone, had a beer and left. During the winter, Ivor stoked the fire in her little stove to take the chill off the porch. Deep down, Gabby needed them to fight off the wound that had carved up her insides the night she found her house empty of all male belongings. The tools, boots and chainsaws were gone and she knew he wasn't coming back. The porch had been a solace and it had worked well enough until the last few months. It was natural, she supposed, that one day a man would catch her eye. But this feeling was too strong and the man wasn't right. She hated herself for what she was feeling. She considered it a weakness. But self-hate is an admission. At Ledger's party she stood next to Melissa Abbott. Two women, twenty-five years apart chronologically and inches apart physically, fighting the same internal struggle. It's a wonder each couldn't feel the other's competition and suppressed passion.

In Gabby's case it had started the night Joe came over by himself. Her admiration for his courage slowly transformed her feelings from admiration to a smoldering fire that quickly burst into flame. The more she got to know him the more she could feel love blooming. She was forty-one, seventeen years older than he, but it wasn't just their ages that was the problem. Everything was impossible. Joe was not suitable on any level. Her reputation would be ruined. Of all the men during all the years, why him? Why, why? She fought her feelings, fought his kindness, his consideration, his soft manner and his easygoing nature. The more she fought, the more she grew to love him. She held his hand once when they were alone, on the pretext of reading his palm. The roughness of his skin and the firmness of his fingers excited her. She could feel the starting point of the strength going to his arms.

Gabby appealed to her own strength nightly. She had made a life for herself without a mate and it was a good life. She had a little respect and a reputation as a good woman.

Don't wreck it all, she kept saying in the silence of the darkness with the covers pulled over her head. Don't wreck it all.

A thousand feet away, Melissa Abbott had wrapped herself up in a ball of her own bedcovers, giving herself a similar message. Both women would wake well before dawn: Gabby with a headache, Melissa with a wetness between her legs.

* * *

It wasn't all recrimination on the Snake as summer reluctantly arrived. On the contrary, like a Baltimore Belle or a Maiden's Blush, sometimes love is allowed to bloom uninterrupted. The afternoon of July fifth was a case in point. Royal had anxiously waited for his new climbers to arrive. They were old stock from England and he worried about them. But they seemed fine and he worked the ground getting it ready for their new home. He had picked a special place. His early ramblers and the white roses he had purchased in Boston already gave his yard the fragrance of tropical sweet winds and exotic spices. Royal was in his glory, digging in the dirt, listening to Kitty Wells on the radio. He was so happy and preoccupied he didn't notice the car that had passed his house several times.

She had driven by before after finding the house by accident. Stopping in town for lunch on her way back to Sackville, New Brunswick, she got awfully mixed-up leaving, going south instead of north. It only took a minute to realize it was the wrong road and she pulled into the Snake to turn around. That's when she noticed the roses. She stopped and marvelled at the whites and deep reds, the dwarf pinks set between six-foot yellow climbers. When she got home she did a charcoal sketch of the yard from memory and the next summer, just for fun she brought her camera. From the photographs she had done two oil paintings. She had no idea who lived in the little house. She thought of knocking on the door but didn't. This year, however, someone was in the yard. A tall, middle-aged man, thin and balding. He resembled the African voodoo doll that hung in her living room, a small head for such a long body. Before she lost her nerve she pulled over to the side of the road.

Royal didn't know he was her inspiration, that his botanical handiwork had given birth to another fanatical rose fancier. She was fifteen feet away when he first noticed her. Selling magazines, probably. She was too well-dressed for a Jehovah's Witness or a tourist. She smiled at him. Clutching her purse she had the appearance of a woman on a mission, coming to meet her mentor.

Royal stood up with the spade in his hands; his knees were hurting more each year. If this lady were selling kneepads, she'd have a customer.

She had reached him before it occurred to her what she should say. She didn't function well without a plan. Every term, it took her weeks before she could go into a classroom without a rehearsed opening, some icebreaker she had memorized. Once she got past the first few minutes it was alright, but she needed an opening and she didn't have one.

He was even taller up close.

Oh dear, she thought as she stopped directly in front of him. Too close in fact, almost stepping on his toes. He was the man who had made this magnificent yard, there was no doubt of it. She knew her colours and this man had earth written all over him. His forehead was browned by the sun; he was all shades of red clay and rich loam. He obviously cherished beauty as much as she did. His sleeves were rolled up and the top three buttons on his shirt were undone. She could see the reddish hair on his chest and it momentarily distracted her.

"Hello" was the best she could do, addressing his chest hair because she was a foot shorter than him.

"Hi," Royal smiled.

She looked up into his face. There was a rough and wrinkled texture to him, part happiness and part pain. She silently condemned herself for being so stupid. She should be talking, not trying to analyze him. He was waiting.

"I, ah, I just stopped because I admired your roses so much. Ah, I just stopped to ask you something."

"Yes," said Royal.

She realized he was thoroughly enjoying not helping her out. She had an awful flashback then. She could hear her mother. "Quick girl, quick. Don't stand there stumbling. Speak up if you want people to hear you."

"What do you feed them?" she asked firmly.

"Food," he replied.

His abruptness made her blush, the way some of her students did when they told her an off-colour joke. When she blushed she went scarlet with little crimson runners travelling off the hot centre of her cheeks, creating blotches like rose petals that lasted an hour. She had fought this curse until she understood, at age thirty, that it was useless. Blushing was a handicap, a cross she would carry and as she got older, less and less of life embarrassed her. But she could feel the burn beginning.

"What kind?"

She didn't mean it to, but her voice had an edginess in it and Royal knew she was more uncomfortable than he'd meant to make her. He didn't want to scare her away. He loved talking about his roses.

"Come on, I'll show you."

He turned toward his garden shed and she followed, relieved his back was to her. It took him fifteen minutes, a mini-lecture almost, to introduce and instruct her on his rose food and his systems of feeding. He had different foods for different roses. There were the constants of course; even the application of simple bone meal took a bit of care. He showed her how he mixed the meal with water. He condemned some commercial brands that drained the vivid colour out of the deep reds. Be careful about that, he warned. They went around the house and she admired each bush and Royal smiled. He told her stories. How he had dug an old rootstock out of the ground on an abandoned farm and got chased by a bear. He showed her his new climbers from England and how he was lovingly putting them in the ground. She helped a bit and by then she was relaxed and laughing and the crimson etchings had faded.

"So you're really interested in roses?" he asked.

"Thanks to you."

"Me? Really?"

"I first saw your roses a few years ago and they were an inspiration. I read up on them and the next year I bought a few. One died, the others are doing all right – sort of."

He offered her a glass of iced tea and as he handed it to her he said, "By the way, my name is Royal."

"Hi, Royal. My name is –" She paused. "Don't laugh. My name is Rose."

He didn't laugh. It was a beautiful name. He had always thought that if he had been lucky enough to have had a daughter he would have called her Rose.

Rose Quackenbush was a professor of Fine Arts at Mount Allison University in Sackville, New Brunswick. She was thirty-seven and had never married. There were numerous reasons for this. No one she cared for had ever asked her. She had loved a man once and loved him completely. He had deeply disappointed her. It turned her off men and at one point she wondered if she might be a lesbian. When she discovered she wasn't, nothing really changed. The men she was attracted to were married and she certainly didn't intend to become the faculty tart. It was all right. She had her teaching, her painting, and her little house on the edge of the Tantramar Marsh. She had her cats. "If I'm going to be an old maid, I might just as well act like one."

She had her gardens, which in recent years included roses.

Rose and Royal dangled their legs over his back steps, intent on unearthing all the mysteries of the tea rose from roots to stocks, to depth of planting.

"Forget the books," he told her. "You can't plant them too deep or give them too much water." Yet she learned he was judicious in watering some varieties.

Bruce Graham — Ivor Johnson's Neighbours

"The roses will tell you, just pay attention."

She stayed so long her stomach started growling and she was embarrassed again. Royal laughed and fixed them lunch. She liked the way he made lobster sandwiches with sliced tomatoes and cucumbers on the side. They ate outdoors under his big maple tree. She laughed at his jokes and he folded a rose petal into a heart and gave it to her. She said she should go but instead he took her down to Gabby's. It was all very strange, she thought, a porch like a little pub with people sitting around drinking. A box of beer on the floor and a glass with money stuffed in it on the table.

How trusting, thought Rose. She met a young man in an army uniform, a bull-like man with cool grey eyes and a barrel chest plus an intoxicated old-timer named after some animal.

The sun was sinking below the Cobequid Mountains when Rose finally got in her car and drove away. She was coming back next Saturday to pick up some cuttings and he promised to come to Sackville sometime soon to inspect her plants.

Neither of them quite knew how to say goodbye. It was somehow difficult to emotionally untangle themselves from the day. Royal didn't want her to leave and she really didn't want to go. They started to shake hands and stopped and laughed. He kissed her on the cheek and she kissed him back on the mouth. Just as their kiss came to an end she felt happy and outrageously wild and quickly kissed the soft curly hair of his chest. He waved as she drove away. In her rearview mirror, his white roses resembled little puffs of smoke that bracketed his silhouette in the growing darkness.

In the dead of night, as the barn owls hooted in the hills across the Whitehall Road, while Melissa and Gabby tormented their bedcovers and struggled with personal demons, Royal awoke and shot straight up. He saw Rose Quackenbush's face and for an instant wondered if she was real or just a warm, happy dream.

* * *

The next weekend, Fudd saw Rose and Royal sharing a laugh as he left his house to go uptown. Fudd was very uncomfortable. Coming home had been even more distressing than he'd anticipated. It wasn't just that he hated trade school and had zero interest in plumbing, and it wasn't just that he was coming home a failure. He had always been a failure. He was used to the role. But in some imperceptible way everything was different.

When his mother stopped looking like his mother, she'd stopped being his mother. Instead of hollering at him for his failings, she hugged him and hardly seemed to care. Fudd couldn't put his finger on it. His mother was so, what was the word someone had used – "breezy"? Now more devil-may-care in her approach to everyday life, all the things that used to be important to his mother – his messiness, his leaving the top off the jar of peanut butter, those type of things – didn't matter anymore. It all made Fudd furious. Then there was his father. Duddy didn't disappear anymore for hours on end; he wasn't drinking on the job or chasing women.

"The skin dog is dead" was the way his father put it to him.

"Why?" demanded Fudd.

It was bad enough to have one parent transformed but two was way too much. Duddy just smiled and patted him on the shoulder. Duddy had removed the usual chin stubble as he had removed the dirt and dust on his old truck. His parents went to dinner and didn't ask him.

"It's a date," his mother said. "You don't take your kids on a date."

"Old married people don't go on dates," he retorted.

"Life is what you make it," she responded and she was out the door before he could reply.

There it was again, that breeziness, that not caring anymore. The old mother was gone; the old dad had disappeared too. Melissa was preoccupied with Joe. Pearl and Edger were busy with the store. Ledger had joined the army.

Of all the different things at home he was the most comfortable with Joe. At least he could talk to Joe, who had finally moved into Pearl's room so Fudd had his old room back. But even that was different; it looked smaller, as though the walls were sneaking closer to his bed.

Goddamn it, Fudd said to himself. He was left out of life.

He didn't hold a grudge against Joe. Melissa explained things and he would do nothing to block the work of his sweetheart. Fudd would do nothing to diminish himself in her eyes anymore than he already had. He would not become a plumber.

"Life can be a dirty sink. Sometimes, Fudd, you just have to grab that cloth and that soap and clean it. Everything you need is within you," she had told him.

Maybe it was in him but Fudd was having a tough time finding it.

Fudd hung around with Ledger a bit but Ledger was weary of Fudd slowing him down.

"I do better tracking chicks on my own," he said as he slapped Fudd on the shoulder.

"Yes, I suppose you do," Fudd said and went home.

Ledger did take Fudd to Springhill one night and they met a very old woman who took them both to her bed. Fudd got the clap and his testicles turned into baseballs.

Ledger, on the other hand, was fine.

"I had VD shots in the army. They give them to you whether you want them or not."

Fudd got shots too, after the fact. His affliction gave him a different gait. It was not the walk he had taught himself when Melissa changed his posture during those many hours with a book on his head. It wasn't posture but painful swelling, intensified by the slightest testicular rocking between his legs. Fudd walked in a bow-legged squat, as if he were carrying a plate of food on his lap. Lady luck certainly wasn't smiling on Fudd. A trade school dropout with the clap, who couldn't tell the woman he loved why he was walking in a sitting position. His parents were strangers, he had failed Melissa, he had failed himself, his cock had seepage and his balls were blue and swollen.

Poor Fudd.

He needed to reach his parents. He really wanted to reach his mother but she seemed too far away. With her arched eyebrows and her pixie cut, she was beyond him. Of the two of them, Fudd decided his father was less changed and he waited for the right opportunity. He went down the shore with Duddy one day to price a small job in Wards Brook. It was a chance for them to be alone. Fudd wasn't certain what he was going to say, but he was going to say something and he was trying to give it some thought. Everybody was moving on with their lives. Only he was stuck. It was troubling to him why his parents didn't give a damn. Had Joe completely taken his place in the family? Was Fudd out and Joe in?

Duddy was whistling what he always whistled, "The Camptown Races." The words were going through Fudd's mind, distracting him from his mission.

"The Camptown race is five miles long, do-da, do-da, the Camptown race is five miles long, la-do-da-day."

Duddy had been whistling the same tune for a quarter of a century and he had it in perfect pitch. As he repeated the tune from the top, Fudd broke in, a little too strongly.

"So what do you think I should do?"

Duddy stopped whistling. "About what?"

"What should I do now? Now that trade school is out. What next? I know, get a job, but doing what? That's what I want to know."

Duddy was silent. Fudd thought his father was giving serious consideration to his inquiry, but it was nothing of the sort. Duddy starting whistling again.

"Will you stop that fucking whistling and talk to me, for Christ's sake?"

"There's nothing to say. I can't tell you what to do. You got to find that out for yourself."

Fudd stared at him. "That's it? That's all you got to say?"

"What else is there to say?" Duddy replied.

Fudd pressed his teeth so tightly together his jaw ached. "Stop the fucking truck," he roared. His door was already open and he was out before the truck completely stopped. Fudd landed on his ass but got up quickly enough to run and slam the door shut and watch Duddy drive off.

"Son of a bitch," he yelled after Duddy.

Fudd was so furious, so upset, so frustrated he hardly noticed the pain in his groin. It didn't matter, for at that moment he had a bigger pain and it kept building.

He hadn't walked more than half a mile when the dam burst and he began to cry. He just couldn't help himself. There wasn't a soul around and he had more than three miles to hoof it back to town. He thought of trade school and the fact he couldn't handle the basic math. How he tried but kept falling behind and how his instructors kept saying he needed to apply himself. How he hated his boarding house with his drunken landlady and her two sons who had even less education than he did. The oldest, the loudmouth, couldn't read or write. He thought of how he had missed Melissa and how he hated Halifax with its sailors, whores and pickpockets. He thought of walking in the Public Gardens and pretending Melissa was with him. Fudd was crying because he suddenly realized the truth, the whole truth and nothing but the truth. Melissa would never be his. He would never have anyone. His parents had forsaken him.

He was on his own.

The old Minnie would never have admitted it, but the new Minnie was honest and forthright. She was deliberately keeping her son at arm's length. It alarmed her when Fudd returned. It wasn't that she didn't love him. He had been a handful all his life. Minnie had done her best, battling his battles, fighting his fights, taking on his teachers and even his Boy Scout leader who wanted to expel Fudd for behaviour unbecoming to Lord Baden-Powell. She had fought them all and had brought Fudd as far as she could

— a passing grade of 54.7 average in grade nine. She had gotten behind Melissa and encouraged trade school. But he'd come home. She knew he wanted his old mom back. He wanted the return of the slave, the cook, the cleaning lady, the washing woman. He wanted the creature comforts he had known as a child so he could stay a child. So he could move back and stay home and she would be his slave forever. Sorry son, that lady has hit the road. She's gone, gone, gone and she isn't coming back. Minnie had a new life now. A better life and she wasn't going to let anybody pull her back to the woman she was, in the marriage she had.

So Minnie hugged Fudd to let him know she loved him but she didn't wash his clothes or clean his room. She didn't let on she worried about him. She didn't want Fudd to settle into comfort because she wasn't going to let him languish at home, working at seasonal jobs and living the rest of year on pogey. No, definitely not. She was not going to allow her son to slide into a lesser life because he wasn't the sharpest knife in the drawer, or because he was too damn lazy to do better.

So when Fudd slammed the door on Duddy's truck it was expected; Duddy had already been given his marching orders. He was not to cave in to Fudd, not to offer him his old job or even advise.

"First of all, Joe has the job and is working out fine and secondly, Fudd needs to be on his own. Out from under our wing."

Minnie heard Fudd rummaging around up in the attic and then in his room. She knew he was packing. Bureau drawers were slamming, the closet door was slamming, Fudd was making all the noise possible. Minnie pressed her lips together, put on her best bonnet and went out the door. If she stayed, mothering love might rise to the surface and smother her good sense. She might weaken and rush upstairs and smother Fudd with the love he was looking for.

Minnie really had no place to go so she thought she might find Gabby at home. Gabby looked dreadful.

"Are you sick?" asked Minnie.

Gabby shook her head. There were dark circles under her eyes and her frizzy hair was sticking out in all directions.

Gabby had been roaming around the house half the night. She made coffee and watched the first rays of the sun creep over the horizon. She even wrapped herself in a winter jacket and walked down to the shore. Gabby and Fudd had one thing in common; they both needed to face reality. It can be as hard as granite when you're up against it. Reality can have a bite like a snapping turtle. Reality can take a chunk out of you.

They were an odd-looking pair that morning: Minnie in her new Persian lamb coat and her black hat with the pheasant feathers and Gabby in a ripped and faded floral housecoat. Minnie's makeup was perfect. Gabby wasn't wearing any.

Gabby considered blurting out her problems, telling Minnie everything but she rejected the idea. If she was going to confess it wasn't going to be to Minnie who might, one of these days, revert to her old judgmental self. Gabby didn't completely trust this new Minnie, or maybe didn't completely understand her. The transition from shrew to glamour girl had been too quick for Gabby, who didn't understand the ticking of Minnie's inner clock. How could she be so damn happy? Gabby asked herself. What she really meant was how could Minnie be so damn free. How could anybody living with that deadhead Duddy walk around with a smile on their face, sipping tea in a new hat that had enough pheasant feathers to take flight. Gabby acknowledged that Duddy had changed too. He hadn't tried to feel her ass in three months but she trusted his change even less. No, if she were going to unburden herself it would be to Tess or maybe even Claudia, but certainly not Minnie.

She was at the point of telling someone. Gabby was wretched. She had almost blurted it out to Joe a dozen times. There was opportunity but Gabby had bitten her tongue. Sometimes when Joe walked past her, there was a desire to brush against him. She didn't give a damn anymore what he'd done. Gabby needed some connection with him. Her desire was so strong it scared her. It was concentrated inside her some place she couldn't quite locate. Listening to Minnie, looking at Minnie, Gabby knew it was time to do something. When Minnie left she couldn't remember a word either one of them had spoken, except for her little embarrassment when she passed Minnie the shortbread cookies and saw the surprise when she said, "Have a Joebread, Minnie?"

* * *

Fudd hadn't written many nasty notes in his life. When he finally found a pencil, the lead broke as he was trying to spell unworthy. That ultimately came out, "to my unworldly parents." Fudd tore up the paper bag he was writing on and jammed the pieces in his pocket. He left the house, angrier than when he arrived, and managed to slam the door so hard that Mink Martin, recovering from a bad hangover, heard it at the other end of the street.

Fudd had little money and no direction. He only knew he was heading out of town and just stuck out his thumb to hitch a ride. Over the next few months he had many jobs. He worked washing dishes at a diner in Truro, and then he got a job as a bush cutter near Lunenburg, making six dollars a day. Next he worked at a service station in Lockeport, and from there he got hired on a lobster boat. It would be some time before Fudd cooled off and came home. When he did, he would be a vastly different man.

* * *

Meanwhile, Ledger's leave was coming to an end and he also was dissatisfied with his life, but not nearly as much as Fudd. Ledger had only one problem: Melissa Abbott. She still wouldn't give him the time of day. He convinced himself he hardly cared. Being home had rebuilt a great deal of his old confidence. More than one married woman was willing to succumb to his charms. He was again smug most of the time. However, he looked out his kitchen window and saw Melissa with that way of hers – that swinging gait, those swaying hips and the best breasts is the world. When he got his eyes full of Melissa, and she was definitely an eyeful, that anti-smugness worm crawled through Ledger and devoured his superiority in no time flat.

"She's a fairy," he told himself. "She walks around with Joe and Fudd, her dysfunctional bookends, bodyguards for the spiritual wonder woman because they're safe. She couldn't handle a real man and she knows it."

Melissa wouldn't even go for a Coke, for God's sake. And him in his uniform.

Claudia was also concerned about her daughter's dysfunctional bookends. Melissa had no girlfriends, no friends her own age. If she wasn't reading or doing schoolwork, she was with Joe or Fudd. To Claudia, Fudd wasn't so bad because she could never picture Melissa in a relationship with Fudd. The boy just looked too dumb for words. But Joe was another story. If it hadn't been for the horrible thing he had done, that unnatural, perverted thing, Claudia would have been even more concerned. She wondered what part Joe's past played in Melissa's mind. She hoped it meant everything, but she noticed the way Melissa looked at Joe. Claudia wondered about her previous misgivings about a man convicted of a beastly crime coming into her home. He was older than Melissa. They were often alone. And yet he was so very much a gentleman. If he had raging hormones he hid them well, unlike that horny Ledger whom Claudia couldn't stand, prancing around in his uniform and parading back and forth in front of her house in the middle of the night. She had a good mind to phone the police. She wouldn't trust Ledger. But Joe was so damn trustworthy. But what if he snapped again? What if he came down on her daughter like he had done to the cow?

How crazy, she said to herself because she needed reassurance. Joe went to AA although he didn't drink, reported to the authorities although he didn't misbehave, had counselling and was trying to better himself. He was polite, respectful, charitable and cheerful. He was such a, well, a nice guy.

Claudia thought of having a birthday party for Melissa but there were no friends to invite. Gabby said they should have a party anyway and invite the neighbours. Everybody came including Pearl, Rhonda-Rae and Rose Quackenbush, who was now a steady weekend guest at Royal's.

It started as a typical evening. The traditional birthday stuff: a cake with eighteen candles, a few presents, the singing of "Happy birthday, dear Melissa, happy birthday to you."

But beneath the surface there was tension and below the tension, there was turmoil, brewing and bubbling like a witch's potion. Smouldering underneath the turmoil was a thickening layer of wounded pride, irrational considerations, guilt, secret thoughts, and just plain horniness.

Melissa made a little speech and cut the cake. When she said she was glad to be living on the Snake, she realized she would have to pray fervently later.

The birthday party gave Ledger the first real opportunity to see his daughter up close. Rhonda-Rae was dressed like a little Scottish doll in a pleated tartan skirt, white blouse with little frills on the front and a tartan tam. Her beauty sent an arrow straight through Ledger's heart. She smiled at him. She had his eyes. She was the best part of Pearl and him, and Pearl looked pretty good too. She had slimmed down and there was an appealing glow about her.

The glow was more than her happiness. Pearl was pregnant. She was just a few weeks along but she had dreaded telling Edger, who was working so hard, and there was so little money. But he broke into a wide smile at the news and it made her weep with joy. God bless this wonderful man. Only Edger could turn her to mush in a matter of seconds.

Happiness can shine through you, just as turmoil can block the brain. What Ledger saw in Pearl was completeness, and that can make anybody look good. But Ledger told himself not to get distracted. He wanted Melissa and if given the opportunity, before the night was over he'd make a final assault on the Fortress Abbott.

Other people had different objectives but similar goals. Maybe it was the tilt of the constellation that was bringing forth this desire to act. Gabby had made up her mind it was time to tell Joe. She was not sure what he would do. He might laugh or just snicker. No, not Joe. He would not hurt her. He wouldn't snicker.

Melissa had come to the same conclusion. It was time to tell Joe. She knew what she wanted for her birthday.

Both women had vital concerns. Gabby had been reading herself the riot act for months about her reputation, the fear of rejection, the difference in their age. Melissa was concerned only about the drastic difference in her message. She had always told Joe that the real world, the important world, was the spiritual one and now she going against all that. She was going to get down to animal instincts and kiss him. She was going to tell him it was okay to touch her, to caress her, to put his hands all over her and take her completely.

How life changes. Poor Joe, from perversion to popularity. It can be a rough ride. Joe the cowboy was in for quite a night.

21

Melissa's party was in full swing – the porch was crowded and noisy. Gabby, beside herself after three glasses of bourbon, had given up on rationale. She was a little wobbly on her feet and her speech might be a touch slurred, but by God, tonight was going to be the night. She was going to lay it out for that man, tell him exactly what she thought of him. Her feelings were important and he had a right to know. Then she would feel better, even if he laughed. But Joe wouldn't laugh, she kept telling herself. He wouldn't.

It was Melissa's party and she was the centre of attention with Joe a fixture at her side. She couldn't be pried away by Ledger. To make things worse, except for Edger, Pearl and Rhonda-Rae, nobody seemed to be leaving. People got up after the birthday cake but another box of beer mysteriously appeared and everybody stood around, laughing. Royal and that funny woman from Sackville were even dancing and, by God, so were Duddy and Minnie. That had never been seen on the porch.

Patti Page was singing "The Tennessee Waltz." Ivor Johnson and Tess were dancing and so were Joe and Melissa. Ledger grabbed Gabby and the back porch became a crowded dance floor. Everybody was dancing except for that war hero Mink Martin, who had passed out with his head in a piece of birthday cake.

There were other tunes and more waltzes and Ivor whirled Claudia around in a spin. People cheered. During one slow waltz, Ledger could feel Gabby's heart beating hard. That was because Gabby was watching Melissa holding Joe so very, very tightly.

Joe could hear Melissa's heart too. It was pounding like the heart of a racehorse on the home stretch.

Is it normal for a young woman, a girl really, to have a heart working so hard? Joe wondered.

"Cut in," Gabby whispered.

Ledger nodded, only too happy to oblige. Then the music stopped just as he got his hands on Melissa. The announcer read a commercial for Carter's Little Liver Pills and everybody stood around awkwardly, waiting. Then there was a swing tune no one could dance to except Ivor and Tess. Finally, another slow waltz and Ledger went for Melissa, just as Melissa and Gabby went for Joe. More awkwardness until Joe said he should dance with the hostess. Gabby was relieved she hadn't physically pushed Melissa away. The bourbon was making her head spin. If Joe refused to dance she would have broken down right there and punched the guest of honour in the mouth.

They had been dancing a few seconds when Gabby blurted out her request. "Joe, can you stay behind tonight after the others leave? I need to talk to you." The question made her lips quiver. All evening she waited to say it. There was no turning back now.

"Sure," said Joe.

And that was all. His reply was so casual, without alarm or concern or curiosity that it made Gabby relax. The bourbon warmed her. She put her head on Joe's shoulder. It was the best moment of the night.

Claudia had a dance with Ledger, who, for a brief dirty moment, wondered what it would be like to have the mother of the daughter he desired.

Finally, Rose and Royal left. Ivor got Mink to his feet and took him home and the party broke up. Ledger was trying to stick close to Melissa. It was cramped quarters because every time he turned around he bumped into Joe.

"Oh, excuse me, Ledger," Joe would say.

"Joe, walk me home," Melissa said in a flat voice in front of Ledger. She made it very plain which man she preferred and Ledger's face burned with the insult.

Badly needing something to do, Ledger followed Ivor out the door and took Mink's other arm.

"I'll give you a hand," he said.

Joe touched Gabby's arm. "I'll take Melissa home and drop in on my way back if you still want me to."

"I do," said Gabby.

"What did you say to her?" Melissa whispered.

"Oh, she wants to have a word with me."

"We're going to be a while, Joe."

"We are?"

"Yes, we are."

She put her arm through his. "Joe, let's go down to the beach. There's a blanket under the driftwood that we can sit on," she whispered.

"There is?" Joe said curiously.

"I put it there this afternoon," she replied

"We're going for a walk, Mother," she called to Claudia, who was walking slightly ahead of her, before Joe had time to answer.

"Got your sweater? It's getting cool," Claudia replied as she unlocked her front door. She looked back into the darkness in the direction of her daughter and Joe. She wanted to say something more, something motherly, even something reassuring but she couldn't find anything that sounded appropriate.

Bruce Graham – Ivor Johnson's Neighbours

"I'll be warm," Melissa called and hugged Joe's arm.

Claudia listened as a ruckus broke out in the other direction. Mink had suddenly come to life and was fiercely resisting all efforts by Ledger and Ivor to get him past his own front door, claiming the enemy was hiding in his hovel. Claudia wished Ivor would come over for a while. There were many things swirling in her at that moment. It was the first time in years she had danced and it felt good to be held by a man, to have strong arms around her. She didn't want to go in her new house. She wanted to go help Ivor. She wanted to call out to her daughter. Different forces tugged at her and she felt helpless.

She had watched the way her daughter clung to Joe while they danced at the party. They moved very slowly, swaying to the music. Joe smiled and talked to other people, seemingly oblivious to the fact Melissa's face was buried in his shoulder. That scene made Gabby envious and Claudia ill at ease.

She and Melissa had talked about Joe a number of times whenever Claudia had broached the subject. She could probe only so far before she reached that zone within her daughter that she wasn't allowed to penetrate. Melissa's feelings for Joe were in that zone somewhere and her feelings for Fudd never were. That made Claudia extremely nervous.

She wanted to call out to Melissa and Joe, to ask them to come back to the house, but – "But what? She is my daughter, damn it," she muttered out loud.

"Melissa," she cried out. "I don't think you should go down there. It's cold. Come back to the house." She tried to make it sound light, not a command but a warm, loving suggestion. Her words were lost in the wind as if Mother Nature herself rejected the silly suggestion from this overwrought woman. The ruckus next door was getting noisier. Mink was putting up a stiff resistance against Ivor and Ledger at the threshhold of his hovel.

Claudia stared into the darkness, trying to see Joe and Melissa. She wasn't certain the black forms on the beach were them or only tangled driftwood. She closed her eyes, sighed and convinced herself it would be all right. She had no reason to worry. Not that kind of concern, anyway, the kind that steals a child's innocence, that takes away her chastity. Melissa had already been relieved of all that. Innocence and chastity had long gone and been replaced by an uprightness that at times can scare a mother more than any married Mountie. Melissa always made the highest marks in her class. She didn't need help with her homework anymore. She didn't need her at all. Her mother, the Mountie, girlfriends, close connections had all been replaced by something Claudia couldn't identify and couldn't reach. It both reassured and terrified her.

Melissa pulled a blanket from under the bleached roots of a big piece of driftwood. In the moonlight, the roots were a mosaic of twisted images. It was a favourite place of theirs where Melissa had instructed Joe on the higher meaning of life. They had discussed what images the roots held for them: angels in flight, trumpets, the fish – the sign of the early Christians – and even the burning bush. She had used the roots as an illustration that many things can be seen by those who will only look. Only those who listen can really hear.

Joe had been a good student. Unlike Fudd, whose attention span ran no more than a minute and whose dirty little hands tried to paw her, Joe had never done such a thing. There had never been a twitch or a quiver to indicate such a desire. Joe had been more forthright than Fudd. He had told Melissa everything about his early life, the brutality of his father, the bullying of his brothers, his nightmares and finally how his mother had treated him and how she had refused to look at him. They lived in the same house and she kept her back constantly turned. Joe spoke of his arrest and the hurt he had caused. He told her about the embarrassment, the ridicule, the taste of blue steel and his lack of courage. He told Melissa about his life in jail. How it wasn't anything like he expected. How he played cards every day with the jailer or his wife and how, once they knew him, they let him walk uptown to get the mail.

The more he talked, the more her moral resolution crumbled. Its decline was the almost imperceptible evolution from sympathy, to sorrow, to admiration, to endearment, to love and to lust. With every stage the physical drum beat in her, pounding out a message that in the last stage reverberated through her body. She had held his hand during their talks the last few days and she caressed the back of his neck. He had not responded or even seemed to notice. If she had to be in the driver's seat, so be it. Melissa had the place picked out, for she wasn't anything if not organized. The seduction of Joe was worked out to a finite detail.

There was only one small hitch. She didn't know the dialogue. The words, always her strong point, were unwritten. She hadn't or couldn't put them together to reverse her original message. How could she contradict or deconstruct the world she had promoted, a world above mere physical feelings and personal pleasures? She was a hypocrite but didn't want to sound like one. She didn't want to belittle herself in his eyes. But her drive was such she was willing to take a chance and spoil everything, undo everything she had accomplished with Joe and herself. She knew it could all come unravelled in a minute. She was willing to chance it. That's how much she ached for him in her heart, in her soul and between her shapely legs.

There was a place along the beach between two large rocks that would give them privacy and shelter. She led Joe there, tightly holding his hand. Joe was silent but concerned. He was uncomfortable with the way Melissa was holding his hand. It was unnecessary and so unusual considering what she was saying. Besides, he promised Gabby he'd show up and Joe was a man of his word.

Melissa put the blanket down between the two rocks. "Sit down with me," she said and he obeyed. The minute they were side by side, Melissa took his face in both her hands.

"Joe, there is something I want to tell you."

"Yes?" he replied and his coolness put her off a bit.

"I know that we've spent a lot of time talking about higher reasons and elevated purposes in life, and you know I believe those things with all my heart."

"Yes," Joe said.

"But I have feelings and so do you. Feelings that need to answered. I have great passion, Joe, strong feelings. I love you, Joe, and I want you to know that."

She kissed him hard, pressing her lips on his, her tongue forcing his mouth open. She tasted his breath. She pressed her breasts against him then she lunged, climbing on top of him. The dam within her had finally ruptured.

Joe was having none of it. He squirmed off the blanket, twisting and turning, until his face went into the gravel. When he finally had enough leverage, he crawled and pushed and pulled himself away from her grasp. He got to his feet, feeling disoriented and dizzy.

Melissa was wrong. As a teacher, she had sold herself short. Joe would not come apart. The demons may have gripped his spiritual guidance instructor, but they would not grip him.

"Melissa, what are you doing?" he sputtered, the specks of gravel flying from his mouth.

"Joe, don't be upset. We have a right to have feelings. You have a right to express those feelings. That doesn't take away from what we've discussed these many months."

"Yes, it does. Yes, it does," he replied in a voice full of shock and displeasure that she had never heard before.

"Joe," she started to say.

"Listen to me, Melissa. If we're going to be just another couple doing it on the beach, then what sets us apart from all the other people? Where is our spiritual life? Where is the higher plane?

Bruce Graham – Ivor Johnson's Neighbours

Why is all that stuff important if we're just going to screw the same as everybody else? We're not like everybody else. We're going to be different. Isn't that why I've gone through all that I've gone through? Isn't that what it's all about? You call it my personal journey and now you want it to end on the beach. No, Melissa, it can't end here. You can't end it."

He was running, disappearing into the dark. She could hear his footsteps on the gravel. The burning of her skin told her she had moved to yet another state, that one between numbness and panic.

* * *

Gabby was turning out the lights. Joe wasn't coming. In a way she was almost relieved. The effect of the bourbon was wearing away and taking what confidence she had with it. She put her face on the cool wall and took some deep breaths.

God, life could be nerve-wracking. The tension in her was beginning to wane because she would not have to tell him the truth. At least she was safe for now. She would not have to face a man seventeen years younger and tell him she loved him. Not that night, anyway, and maybe she would die in her sleep and never have to face it. Then she heard the back door open. Joe was on the porch.

"You wanted to talk to me, Gabby?"

She swallowed hard. She was so certain he wasn't coming she had started to relax.

"Turn off the porch light, Joe. Let's sit in the living room."

There was unhappiness, a gloom draped over him she had never seen before. He was always impeccably neat yet his clothes were now dishevelled; his hair was tousled, the usually controlled cowlick standing erect. Gabby wondered if she should have another glass of bourbon. They sat together on her chesterfield, Joe a respectful two feet away, sitting upright, ramrod straight. Gabby moved closer. She took his hand and she bowed her head. There has to be a way. There has to be, she thought and she felt tears and held her eyes shut tightly because she truly didn't want to cry.

Joe was rigid as Gabby feverishly gripped his hand. What a night he was having. First Melissa squeezing the life of him while dancing, then struggling on top of him on the beach, shamelessly throwing herself at him like a tart. Now Gabby, trying not to cry but crying nonetheless. Was he going to die, Joe wondered? Was this the last night of his life and they all knew, and in their own way they wanted to say goodbye?

"Gabby, what's wrong? Why are you crying?"

"I'm not crying."

"Yes, you are."

"No, I'm not."

"Yes, you – "

"Joe, shut up, just shut up."

Joe shut up and Gabby wiped her cheek with the back of his hand. Then she kissed his hand that she held firmly. Joe looked at his hand. It was getting quite a workout.

And then, because she didn't know what else to do, Gabby grabbed Joe with both arms and kissed him. She forced his mouth open and tasted his breath and she had a better grip than Melissa because this time, Joe couldn't get away.

Timing in life is everything. Ask a trapeze artist in mid-air waiting for the swing, or ask a tear-stained, blurry-eyed Melissa who, on her eighteenth birthday, had stumbled back along the beach past her house and past the dark windows of Mink Martin's shanty. She had followed Joe but had to stop and cry and bite her lip. Then she had to stop because of beach stones in her shoe.

Her timing was such that she stumbled into Gabby's small yard just in time to see the top of Joe's head through the living room window. Melissa found a wheelbarrow to stand on just in time to see the man she loved in the arms of another woman – an older woman. A woman old enough to be his mother and they were kissing and at that moment Melissa Abbott renounced all of her spiritual vows, the pledges of the past twenty-four months, the love for her fellow man and fellow woman. All was renounced at once as she, like a raging bear, picked up a stick of hardwood from Gabby's woodpile and threw it with such force that it shattered the plate glass living room window. The window of the woman who, earlier that evening, had hosted her birthday party.

The noise was heard all over the Snake. Across the street, Ledger was smoking and fuming on Tess's steps. He thought it was an explosion. Tess heard it in the house. Claudia heard it in her bedroom. Two girls walking home on the Whitehall Road heard it, and Dover Linkletter and his son Lester heard it while they were digging shad worms by flashlight way down on the shore. The shattering sound was heard by so many because it was distinctive, quite unlike other noises in the night: the barking dog, the backfiring car or the slamming screen door. The shattering glass carried the compelling crack of a rifle, followed by ten thousand tinkling bells as tiny shards hit the hardwood floor. After the last tinkle, there was still the shrill wailing of the banshee, screaming into the night.

"Bitch, bitch, bitch!"

Inside, Gabby and Joe were paralyzed in the embrace. Gabby had not relinquished her hold and Joe had stopped struggling. They were trying to make sense of the noise and digest the shock. The glass had fanned out in front of them. From outside, the wailing banshee continued her hellish cry of "Bitch, bitch, bitch."

Gabby was shaking. She released Joe and got to her feet, the bourbon rapidly dissipating from her system. Warily, they both approached the broken window, slowly and without saying a word. The shrieking continued and the tension in the room mingled with the light breeze and smell of sea air rushing at them through the gaping hole. They walked on glass, breaking it into smaller pieces. Slivers penetrated Gabby's rubber-soled slippers and the crunch of the shards sent shivers down her spine. She couldn't distinguish details in the darkness. At forty-one, Gabby was at the age where corneas start to harden.

Joe could see. He could see too much. He was breathless. There was tightness in his chest. His spiritual advisor was walking in circles, waving another piece of hardwood above her head like a warrior going into battle. His spiritual advisor was a blaspheming vandal. What in the name of God was going on tonight?

It was as bad and confusing as the night he was arrested. So many things were similar. Again, he faced too much confusion, half-understood things, so much swirling outside and inside him. He could still feel the handcuffs of Gabby's grip, while Melissa's animal sounds and breaking glass were like the slamming cell door. Too much, too much! It all was happening again.

Claudia was running toward the noise. With the same certainty a wild animal has for its young, she knew the distress call came from her daughter. She could taste fear mingled with sea mist as she stumbled in the darkness. She only ran faster, instinctively trying to answer the agony she heard in the voice of her daughter.

Ledger also recognized the voice, but he believed it must be Joe that the love of his life was ranting about with such curses and accusations.

"How could you, goddamn you? How could you?"

Ivor Johnson had his shoes on and was across the street by then. He lifted the hysterical girl off the ground and carried her home, meeting Claudia as she rushed from her house. Melissa put out her hands to Claudia. Now she needed her mother. She was delirious, beside herself with grief.

"I'm sorry, Mommy. I'm sorry."

At that moment Claudia Abbott felt she was the worst parent in the world, the most incapable person alive to raise a child, especially a child so exceptional academically and so very, very different.

Bruce Graham — Ivor Johnson's Neighbours

Within days of the window breaking a composition evolved from some frustrated poet and ditty writer who lived along the Whitehall Road.

> *For when she is good, she is very, very good and really excels in class,*
> *When she is bad, she is very, very bad, and can cost you a lot in glass.*

But that was later, when people had time to reflect. Within minutes of the breaking glass there was no time for reflection.

"What happened?" Claudia asked breathlessly as she ran up to Ivor who held the weeping girl in his arms.

"I'm not sure," answered Ivor. "There's a broken window."

He nodded towards Gabby's, but Claudia had already scooped Melissa out of his arms and was heading home.

Ledger was on the scene and Gabby was outside by the time Ivor got back. Tess was there too.

"What's happened?" everybody asked.

How much was Gabby willing to reveal? Did she know herself what had happened? Was Joe willing to talk and where was he, anyway?

Gabby felt the crush of responsibility. Could she get away with saying nothing? She knew why Melissa had done it. Could she lie? Could she say she was just sitting in her living room at eleven-thirty at night, when a God-fearing Grade A student, for whom she had just hosted a birthday party, decided to throw a stick of hardwood through her plate glass window? Would anyone believe it? She didn't think so.

"I don't know" was the best Gabby could do. "I just don't know." She said it so often she almost believed it herself.

Ivor went to get cardboard, tape and canvass to cover the window. Ledger stood around in his paratrooper's uniform and even though it was strictly against military regulations, he put his hands in his pockets because he suddenly felt cold. Who the hell cared about regulations at a time like this? There might be a wedge where he could climb in between Melissa and Joe. Maybe, but he wasn't sure.

Across the street, Claudia hugged her weeping daughter in her arms.

* * *

There is a certain thing that happens to people after an accident or an incident. Following a murder, a car mishap or a drowning, even after the body has been taken away, people still stand around, bonded by the tragedy. Such was the case at Gabby's. The assembled crowd was not just her neighbours, but also Whitehallers walking home from a dance and a couple of townies driving by. No one knew much about what had happened but no one wanted to leave. People milled around talking amongst themselves.

Ivor, Tess and Ledger sealed up the opening where the window had been. Gabby was cold and Tess took her inside. Then Ivor and Tess went down to Claudia's to see how things were, but the house was in darkness and they decided not to knock on the door.

Later that night Ledger went down to Claudia's too. He didn't knock either, but stood at the end of the driveway, smoking a cigarette in the dark. He was taking the train tomorrow. He'd be gone a year. He'd missed his chance and he told himself again that he didn't care. Now he had new ammunition for his emotional defence. That girl was crazy, nutty as a fruitcake. She had done him a big favour. What a waste, so damn gorgeous and crazy as a bag of hammers, Ledger said to himself as he crushed out his cigarette with the full force of his boot. He twisted and stomped the dead butt into the ground. "Crazy," he whispered and went home.

Inside the darkened house, Melissa was trying to convince her mother, through long sobs, that indeed she was crazy.

"I'm mad, mad."

She rolled herself into a ball, weeping and begging her mother to have her committed quickly. When it had all come out about her daughter and the married Mountie, Claudia had seen the same routine. It was Melissa's defence and it was not going to work this time. The more Melissa sobbed the more her mother's heart hardened. Everything spun through Claudia's mind, a kaleidoscope of the past twenty-four months. Her embarrassment over the hubcap fence, Mink's obscenities, the cost of the new house and the loneliness she felt away from the few friends she had in North Sydney. When she thought of the sex scandal and the damage done to her good name, Claudia felt only anger.

"Snap out of it," Claudia roared and Melissa literally jumped as Claudia released her and came to her feet.

"Why the hell did you throw a stick through Gabby's window? I want an answer and I want it now." Claudia could feel her fury rising. She was not running away again. No more packing up and moving. She had let Melissa dupe her these last two years. That spiritual repentance nonsense was just an act to keep Claudia at bay, a way for her daughter to avoid responsibility for having had an affair with a married man. It was a convenient avenue for Claudia as well. She could escape the unpleasantness of constant strife with her daughter. I didn't follow through and now there's this, thought Claudia. But what was this? Was there some sort of a feud between Melissa and Gabby? How could there be? Gabby had just hosted the party and Melissa had hugged her when they left. Then, like a streak of lightning, the jarring jolt struck Claudia.

Joe.

She pointed a shaky finger at Melissa. "Joe, it's Joe, isn't it? Is it Joe? Get up here and tell me, damn you. Get up here and tell me. It's Joe, isn't it?"

She grabbed and shook Melissa. Melissa didn't resist and simply cried more until finally, through gigantic sobs, she blurted out what Claudia wanted.

"Yes, it's Joe, it's Joe, it's Joe."

Claudia stepped back to prevent herself from striking her daughter. She wanted to lash out at someone because she had failed both herself and her daughter. She had found it easier not to believe those unpleasant things that pounded against her conscience like the beating of a drum and she deliberately had refused to heed the warning signs.

Claudia turned off the lights and both women wept in the dark.

* * *

Finally the novelty of the broken window was wearing off and the instant bonding was breaking down as quickly as it had formed. The little group disintegrated, going through the final stages of what holds bystanders together. In the silence, there was only the tarp, flapping slightly because the wind had come up and the gawkers had run out of questions and conversation. The main characters had already left the scene – Tess had taken Gabby inside. Ledger was gone and so was Ivor. Nobody missed Joe because nobody knew he had been there.

Joe, the centre of so much that night, the object of such strong affections, the guy squeezed hard by two women, was gone. Joe – the reason for the broken window, the bewildered neighbours, the daughter's heartbreak, the mother's misery, had just wandered off into the night, unnoticed.

Joe's lips were sealed about the night's events, but his insides were coming apart.

22

There was plenty of talk resulting from the broken window and it had the scent of scandal that permeated up and down Whitehall. Why would a good girl, a righteous girl, throw a stick of wood through a neighbour's window? People looked to Gabby for answers and all Gabby felt was a sharp pain. Something was curling up inside her, a vital organ gone astray. She could feel it turning and twisting, the heat on her face. She was both embarrassed and beyond embarrassment.

Joe had drifted away during the commotion never knowing her true thoughts, leaving her wounded and feeling vulnerable. She hadn't seen him since and she had to tell somebody, because she was bursting inside. She finally confessed everything to Tess and the remnant of that rogue organ seemed to grow as if it were about to tear through her flesh.

Gabby and Tess had been longtime neighbours, if not exactly close friends. Sometimes an arm's length relationship is best for pouring out heartfelt emotions. A detached observer, free of encumbrances, is a better contractor for building defences against public humiliation.

Everyone would know sooner or later. It wasn't her broken glass that Gabby minded but her broken reputation.

"That crazy girl. She had no right to break my window."

Tess fixed them bourbon and Gabby started slowly, methodically she thought, but before she realized it, she was racing at breakneck speed, gasping and blurting out things in rapid fire sentences. She confessed her feelings of shame that she would be called a cradle robber. She told Tess of her sleepless nights, even hinted at erotic fantasies and finally revealed her attempt to construct a defence for herself when she realized she was going to push ahead, prepared to take her chances with Joe and then with the world outside. And when she took a break from the rapid-fire revelation she would restate, "She had no right to break my window." Those were her cushion words to fill in the silences, between her machine-gun sentences. When Gabby finally stopped, the only sound was the ice cracking in the bourbon. Tess was a good listener from years of practice, part of the hairdresser's trade. Finally at the end of her story, Gabby was breathless but could no longer feel the pain.

* * *

Joe could feel it. His pain was the breaking of tiny membranes that had been healing over his original wound, the membranes Melissa had moulded and Gabby had reinforced. Minnie and Duddy and Edger had contributed too. All those people who had come to his aid. They had held out hope that despite everything he could still have a life. Joe could not conceive of Melissa or Gabby as objects of affection and certainly not with any kind of physical arousal. He owed them more for building in him the belief that he could be healed.

It was Melissa who had given him the steadfastness to venture farther into the world. She encouraged him to try new things, to read new books, to understand poetry and to learn to dance. It was

Gabby who gave him the belief he was capable of normality. For Joe, these women were above sex and beyond physical desire. They were on a pedestal and they had let him down, dropping their pedestals on him like pillars of unwanted stone. Joe was shattered like the glass in Gabby's window, the shards loose and jumbled inside him, threatening to cut him open. He tried to hold himself together, to avoid losing vital life liquid. What had happened, he asked himself, what had suddenly gone so wrong?

That night of the broken glass Joe walked for hours. He turned off the Snake onto the Whitehall Road and passed the darkened windows of Edger and Pearl's store. He passed the house with the crazy sisters who yelled at passing cars and he walked by the bootlegger's shanty where the porch light was always on. Sleeping dogs awoke and barked from steps with peeling paint. Joe ignored everything. He looked straight ahead. He walked the length of Whitehall. He went down to the beach at the foot of Blockhouse Hill. There was no other sound but the soft drift of water over pebbles and the crunch of his footsteps on the gravel. The bubbly swirls of the first waves, pushed by the new tide, lapped at his shoes. Joe didn't care. Joe the cowboy, Joe the object of so much affection was going to do something. He didn't know what but it was going to be big. Joe needed to make a statement.

Ninety minutes later the tide was taking over the beach, pushing him closer to the bank. The moon came and went, playing peek-a-boo by slipping behind silvery clouds and exposing itself a minute later to cast a milky hue on the water and the beach stones at the high watermark.

Joe didn't notice the moon or tide. He wanted to shout something, to make a declaration all the earth would hear: the wicked, the unfaithful, the pious, and the holy. One strong, clear message that pitiful humans, and he was one of them, more pitiful than most, could carry in their hearts and take refuge in its meaning.

Near exhaustion from the strain of the night and the miles he had covered, Joe tripped over a piece of driftwood and fell, face first into the rough gravel. He got up and for the second time that night he was spitting pebbles out of his mouth. That's when he finally noticed the sky. The clouds were backlit by the moon, turning the heavens into a silvery blackboard. Joe knew what he must do.

It was mid-morning by the time Joe started back along the beach. He had walked to West Bay, fourteen miles along the curving, jagged coastline. He walked through tidal streams running off the steep banks of the Minas shore. He watched the birth of the day start as a sliver of crimson in the eastern sky. Tired and betrayed as he felt, with wet feet and hair damp from the morning mist, there was a spring in Joe's step. He had settled his inquiry. The challenges were purely physical. The hard part was over.

* * *

Seventy-five miles away, Mel Smart couldn't sleep. It was another night listening to the regular breathing of his wife. Louise never moved in her sleep and Mel wondered how someone so riled and in a state of constant irritation during the day could find such peace at night. Mel wore his wristwatch to bed. With the illuminated hands he could keep track of how many hours he stayed awake and give Louise an exact accounting of his insomnia.

When I finally die from lack of sleep, she'll be sorry, he thought. But he doubted Louise would really give a damn. Winning the biggest battle of their sixteen-year marriage had not settled her down as Mel had hoped. He had finally relented and they had moved down east to be near her family. It was give in or give up his kids.

To quote Louise, "By God, I'm going with or without you."

Worn out by their bickering, Louise had finally put her foot down and they starting packing.

Not that Mel had a lot going for him where he was. Business was only so-so. There was a lot of competition in crop dusting, but at least in southern Ontario there were a lot of crops. In New Brunswick they grew potatoes, for God's sake. Mel decided the only way to augment his slim income was to buy an old smoker and start Smart's Skywriting.

It was a novelty the first month. Mel made a little money. But as Louise pointed out, in truth he wasn't very good at skywriting, and the second-hand smoker he picked up for a song wasn't such a bargain after all. The money still wasn't enough and Louise complained about how much he spent on fuel to practice manoeuvring his old Cessna through the various letters. Looping *L*s were easy, *A*s were not. Louise said his writing looked funny.

Mel's first job had been "Happy Birthday, Gloria." It had come out all right. But his next, "Donna will you marry me?" didn't impress Donna with either the proposer or the proposal. The rejected guy wouldn't pay because he said the skywriting looked like "Dianne will you marry me?" To make matters worse, there was a Dianne somewhere in the guy's background. She happened to be Donna's best friend.

Mel was out the money and Louise was starting up again about selling the Cessna and getting what she called a real job, like other people.

Mel was angry the day Joe phoned. Louise was discovering that living close to her family was not as rosy as she expected. For one thing her sisters, so loving and kind on the telephone a thousand miles away, were in Mel's eyes a bickering, greedy and grasping lot. There had been a family fight with Louise, of course, taking her frustrations out on Mel.

"As if I wanted to move this close to your family," he retorted.

"Get a real job, for God's sake, so we can live," she snarled.

"I had a real job back home. Remember?"

"You were making peanuts," Louise shouted and slammed the door. She could take refugee at her mother's, the family fortress of last resort. God knows what Louise told her mother about Mel. He could not begin to comprehend the depth of his wife's animosity.

Mel was just heading for the bar when Joe called. It was only eleven o'clock in the morning but Mel needed a drink, and his good for nothing brothers-in-law had cleaned out his liquor supply and of course they never replenished a drop.

At first Mel refused Joe's job. It was too complicated, too many looping letters but Joe would pay in advance, unlike others.

"All in cash in advance," Mel barked.

"Yes sir."

"And what is it you want again? Let me write this down."

"Be diligent ...."

"No, no wait. I haven't got a pencil. Just a minute. Okay, okay, let me have it."

"Be diligent in prayer."

"That's it, 'Be diligent in prayer,' that's it?" Mel asked. Religious nut, he thought to himself. But what the hell, their money is as good as anybody's.

It took everything Joe had saved, as well as an advance from Duddy, but it was enough. After a long sleep and phoning Mel, Joe went to see Gabby and Melissa. Melissa wouldn't answer her door but Gabby leaped into his arms, relieved he wasn't angry. Joe wasn't angry, just let down, he told her.

"There's no hard feelings, I hope," he said.

"Hard feelings, hard feelings? What you don't know about feelings would fill a book."

"Are you angry with me?" he asked.

"Angry, no I'm not angry with you. I'm mad at myself for being such a simpleton."

He hugged her. "You're the nicest person I know," he told her and she could feel his breath on her face.

"Oh, yeah! Would you tell me that if we were the same age?"

"What's that got to do with it?" he asked.

"Everything," she replied almost silently. "Everything."

"I've got a lot to do today. I have to go to Moncton."

"See you later," she said, without looking at him.

He started away and came back. "You know –" he said and pressed his hand on her shoulder. He became silent and she wasn't

Bruce Graham — Ivor Johnson's Neighbours

sure he was gone until she heard his footsteps walking away, because she could still feel the firmness of his touch.

"The nicest person I know," she said softly to herself. It was something. Not enough, but something.

Joe picked the place and time for maximum impact. If conditions were right it was to happen just as folks were arriving in town for their Saturday night shopping.

Saturday night was the highlight of the week. More than economic, it was social too, a time for meeting friends and swapping stories or points of view on everything from crops to politics. Saturday night shopping was the central fibre of small town life. It was the connection, the human contact that kept people close. As Ivor Johnson said, "Saturday night is the glue that holds the community together."

Seven o'clock was the optimum time. It would still be daylight and there would be plenty of people around for maximum impact when Mel's Cessna buzzed the treetops on the Cobequid Mountains and swept down, in a long vertical glide, over the town's church steeples, stores and rooftops. Turning in a horizontal loop, Mel clicked on the smoker to start the letter B.

People stopped in mid-conversation. It was unusual to see a plane right over the town flying so erratically. The players and gawkers poured out of Sam McLeary's smoky pool hall to have a look. Some of the patrons in the tavern at the Cumberland Inn, keeping a wary eye on their beer, went to the windows. "What the devil is that thing doin'?"

Mel didn't know it, but the flight was to be his last job as a skywriter. There was a combination of things that contributed to make it his last flight. He was feeling lousy with the flu. He had chills one minute and was burning up the next. Then there was that damn smoker that kept cutting out so his loops wouldn't stay together.

As people strained their necks to watch, Joe's heart sank. The first B didn't curl and turned into a D. The next letter, which was supposed to be an *e* curled too much and became an *o*.

215

Mel got it right the next time and made a beautiful D. By then, however, the sweat was pouring into his eyes and Mel thought he was going to vomit. Then he made errors in quick succession. The *i* turned into an *r*, the *l* fell in on itself, looking like another *r*. The word *in* went completely haywire. The *i* corkscrewed into a jiggle that resembled a *y*.

Mel managed to make a beautiful P just before he hurled the contents of his stomach onto his hands, arms and flight instruments and mangled the *r*. Then the smoker quit completely and Mel, covered in his own vomit, left the mess he had created, knowing Louise was right after all. He did the only thing he could do. He pointed the Cessna towards Moncton, climbed above the Cobequid Mountains and high-tailed it for home.

At least Louise hadn't seen it.

The startled citizens saw it. Years later they still talked about it. Some said it was the quietest moment ever witnessed on Main Street. Men, woman and children, mouths agape, gazed skyward in awe. They said dogs stopped barking, frightened by the silence.

Reactions varied.

"Who would write such a thing?"

"Somebody's idea of a joke."

"A sacrilege, filth."

"The funniest thing I ever saw!"

"Disgusting."

"Do you see it?"

"What the hell?"

"Somebody's got a sense of humour."

"It's the end, I tell ya, the end of the world. You wait and see. The end."

Floating above the town as far as Riverside, Beaverdam, Long Hill and Whitehall, where Joe had already closed his eyes to yet another defeat, were his hoped for heavenly words. In large, fluffy letters across a clear blue sky was the message, "Do Dribble Your Pee."

The impact stayed long after the letters slowly expanded and pulled apart in separate tufts like pieces of cotton candy.

Who was responsible? There was finger pointing everywhere but the locals could find no logical answer. No one could offer anything close to a plausible explanation. Without a rational reason, a community can tilt towards the irrational. Wild rumours began and they got wilder with each re-telling. One old man, who had trouble with incontinence, was certain the message was directed at him. A family plot he said, by his no-good boys to have him put away wherever they put people with pissing problems, so they could grab his lobster boat.

At the end of the Saturday night dance at Manning's Hall, several versions of the ill-fated flight had been fuelled by excessive alcohol, and the Cold War didn't escape those with wilder imaginations. The mysterious writing in the sky was a code by the Russians. The more sober and rational believed the town was neither a likely spot for Communist codes, nor would the Russians be quite so obvious. But never underestimate the surging power of a rumour no matter how ridiculous. By Monday, aliens had replaced the Russians and some children in grade three were kept home from school, just in case. In high school, boys played hooky because another rumour had the plane crashing by the Farrell River.

"Government agents are looking for bodies."

* * *

Melissa did not see the skywriting. She had been confined to her room by her mother and confined to her bed by her doctor.

"The child is under strain, which is unusual for her age but not without precedent."

That was the story. Strain. Nervous agitation caused by pressure from her mother. Claudia was blamed for pushing the kid, demanding academic excellence. She readily accepted the lie over the truth.

It was a time of discomfort in the town. Wild rumours were running rampant. While duck-tailed high school boys in black leather jackets searched for dead Commies or aliens or any bodies they could come up with, Claudia was making her apologies to Gabby and writing out a cheque for the window. The two women embraced stiffly. Claudia was smart enough to put things together.

Passing Gabby the cheque she said casually, "So what's with you and Joe?"

She could see the fear in Gabby's face that another person knew.

"Do you love him?" Claudia continued. "Not that it's any of my business."

"Yes," Gabby broke in, "I do. He's younger, I know, and that's a problem, but yes I love him and I guess Melissa does too."

"Yes," replied Claudia. "It appears so."

There was an awkward pause as both women sipped their tea and Claudia adjusted her dress. She was perched on the edge of her chair, biting her lip, her shoulders rigid. "If you ask me, I think Melissa is too young as far as Joe is concerned."

"And I'm too old?" Gabby said, putting down her teacup. "I'm forty-one and Joe is soon turning twenty-five."

Claudia nodded and saw something else in Gabby's eyes. A hardness of will had come into her expression.

"For a long time," Gabby continued, "the difference in ages was the factor that kept me away from him. I didn't care about other things. I fought my feelings night and day. I resisted because of what other people would say. I didn't want to be the brunt of jokes. It bothered me so very much, but not anymore. Joe has had enough public humiliation to last a lifetime and if I can carry part of it for him, all the better. I no longer care what people think, what they whisper. I woke up one day and wondered why other people's opinions were so damn important when it was me who was suffering, it was me who needed to tell him how I felt. I started to do that when Melissa fired the stick."

"She says you were kissing him," replied Claudia.

"I was, and what's it to you or to Melissa? She doesn't have ownership papers saying Joe is hers."

"No, she doesn't." Claudia got up and walked around the back of her chair. "But she's closer to his age than you are."

"Are you here to fight on your daughter's behalf?"

"Certainly not! Do you think I want her in a relationship with a –"

"A what?"

"Never mind."

"You know your problem, Claudia? You're proud," Gabby said.

"And you're not proud enough," Claudia shot back but Gabby didn't flinch.

"I'm proud enough to go after what I want, which is a hell of a lot more than you would do."

"I think I'd better go."

"Yes, I think you had better."

Claudia felt she could never be close to Gabby again and she regretted that. Gabby had been good to her, the only real friend on this twisty little street with its peculiar, if not downright strange, people.

Living on the Snake, battling with Mink Martin and recognizing she had let things slide with Melissa, plus Gabby's words still ringing in her ears all had an effect. Claudia would not run away as she had done in North Sydney. No matter what rumours swirled around her and her daughter, they would hold firm. Melissa would be off to university in the fall. She already had a scholarship. Any field she chose was open to her. Delinquency is messy but it can be dealt with; it can be boiled down to rational, sociological terms. While disagreeable, delinquency is at least understandable enough to be palatable, even if for parents it leaves a taste that is bitterly sour. Melissa might be as unsettled and unpredictable in university – unless the academic level was so stimulating she could lose herself in her studies. That was Claudia's hope. She was pushing Melissa towards medicine, the more academics the better.

Claudia needed to talk. She needed an ear to listen, a shoulder to lean on. Under medication from Doctor Ryan, Melissa slept soundly. Claudia couldn't sleep at all. She sat in the dark with her back door open looking at the stars. Gabby was right. She didn't have the courage to go after what she wanted.

23

It came as a shock to Minnie and Duddy when Joe announced he was leaving. "We thought you were happy with us," Minnie said while Duddy walked back and forth, fretting and stewing and twisting his rubber face into the look that said he had just swallowed a bad prune.

"I can never repay your kindness," Joe said while he hugged Minnie. He gave no other explanation. He was going home. One more time he was going home to have his mother turn her back on him. He wanted to tell her she was right to reject him, because he really was unworthy. That was all. He was going to make his mother understand how right she had been. Then he was going to do something and this time he would not fail.

Ivor Johnson had just finished the crossword puzzle in the newspaper when the sof t knock came on his door. It was late and he wasn't expecting anyone. The look of dejection, almost hopelessness, on Claudia's face didn't require comment. "Come in," he said and stepped aside.

Even through her misery she marvelled at the cleanliness and tidiness of his kitchen. Not a thing appeared to be out of place. Could he be even fussier than her?

Claudia's candidness reached new heights that night. She didn't hold much back, and it was very unlike her. He made them tea as she told him all about herself, her daughter and her physical attraction for him. "Is there a chance that you and I might try to be something more than friends?" she inquired.

"I'm afraid not," he replied. It was as direct and as kind as a rejection can be. They talked for hours. She did, anyway. As he was making tea she had given him a preview of her life, but in the following hours she gave him chapter and verse. Her husband's sudden death and his family's help putting her through Teachers' College. She was the only widow there and when they learned she was pregnant they gave her the diploma a month early to be rid of her. Student teachers were not allowed to have sex until they had their teachers' license.

Claudia didn't mean to tell Ivor about North Sydney and the married Mountie; it just came out with all the other stuff. She talked and then cried, and at one point held Ivor's hand and asked again if there was any possibility of a future for them, or even just a test to see if they could be a couple.

He shook his head and patted her hand and said, "No, there isn't any possibility."

"Do you find me unattractive, is that it?" she asked.

"Not at all. There are other reasons."

His answer hurt, but there was so much hurt already inside her at that moment she couldn't quite distinguish or separate it from the rest. It was an open wound and she fought it by returning to her biggest concern.

"Children can be so difficult, such a handful, it's a wonder we ever have them." She started sobbing, uncertain what was making her cry at that particular moment. Walking home she wondered if she should have pressed her case for the two of them, but he had been so quietly resolute in his rejection, she didn't see how she could counter it. Claudia Abbott had never asked a man such a forward question. His response had been bad but her unburdening had been good, at least good enough. The veil of depression had lifted temporarily. She could at least sleep.

When Claudia was unburdening herself to Ivor Johnson, Gabby was knocking on Minnie's door. Minnie was plucking a few rogue hairs that had ridden away from her new eyebrows. She hadn't finished but Duddy was snoring, so Minnie got the door herself.

"I want to talk to Joe," was all Gabby said.

There was no "Hi Minnie, how are you?" from the usually outgoing, personable Gabby. "I want to talk to Joe" was all she said, her expression deadpan and solemn. Minnie responded as bluntly. She didn't know why, she just did.

"He's not here. He's gone home. Packed up and left us."

The two women stood looking at each other. "You want to come in?" Minnie finally asked. Gabby shook her head and backed away.

"That woman is acting queerer and queerer," Minnie told Duddy in the morning.

As she watched Gabby walk away hurriedly, almost running down the Snake, all Minnie could do was shake her head and confirm to her new cat that at least she had her life together. "But the rest of them. My Lord!"

As Claudia was having her fourth cup of tea at Ivor Johnson's table, Gabby was driving wildly through the night, passing the placid fields and small farms of Diligent River. She knew what Joe might do. Her hands gripped the wheel tightly, blinking back sleep. She closed her eyes and could still feel Joe's hand on her shoulder. She was tempted to regain that feeling, or go further and pretend he was massaging her neck, relaxing her, when a young deer shattered her fantasy by jumping in front of her headlights. Gabby swerved quickly, squealing her tires as the white spots on the frightened animal loomed like snowflakes inches from her face. She brushed the fawn but didn't hurt it. Nonetheless she shivered from the experience, as the night loomed large in front of her. Tufts of fog hung over the road where the land was low, making a path for the sea mist. The yellow eyes of some indistinguishable animal peered at her from a woody thicket. She rolled down her window to stay awake. The mist was wet and salty. An owl hooted from somewhere in the woods and Gabby bit her lip, pressed down on the accelerator and gripped the steering wheel more tightly.

She didn't know where the house was. Down a dirt road somewhere off Fox River. She knocked on doors, asking directions. Dogs howled at her, rousing chickens in a hen house until it became such a racket the man cursed at the fowl to shut up. It didn't stop her. She knocked at other doors. Startled country folk rose from their sleep. Gabby didn't care; she was not going to be deterred by chickens, dogs or tired farmers. Through half open doors she asked directions of women in curlers and bleary-eyed men with stubbled chins, who had hurriedly whipped on wool trousers and wide suspenders over their white long johns. She picked up pieces of information. She had missed the road a mile back, they told her, and pointed gnarled fingers into the darkness. After watching her drive off in the night, they looked at their spouses, shook their heads and went back to bed.

Joe's mother listened as usual with her back turned. She said nothing but Joe knew she was listening. They'd had no contact in the two years he'd been living with Minnie and Duddy. She was right, he told her. She was right to reject him because he was unworthy, evil, unnatural and perverted. His mother listened and said nothing. She stoked the fire and went up to bed.

Joe stood alone in the cramped kitchen wondering where the shotgun was.

Yet, once again, timing is everything. Gabby's timing was such that her knock on the door interrupted Joe's search.

"Joe, we've got to talk."

"Gabby!"

Joe stepped back as she had already barged into the room and grabbed his arm. She hugged him and wouldn't let him go until finally he didn't resist because he was somehow past resistance. He whispered to her, "There isn't anything left to say, Gabby."

"Oh, yes there is," she said softly. "There's a lot to say."

"Such as?" he asked.

"Like my feelings for you. My actions in my living room, my—" Gabby suddenly started to shake. It was just a small vibration that gave her voice a staccato quality. "My entire stinking life, that's what we need to talk about."

She started to weep and Joe held her tightly. They stood in their embrace for a long time. Long enough for the three dogs to get bored and settle down; long enough for Gabby to stop sobbing and start breathing regularly. In fact she was breathing deeply and there was a little sigh each time she exhaled. She had fallen asleep in his arms and at that moment Joe realized he could finally identify his feelings. He was suddenly free of anxiety and knew how that had happened. Because she had come to him, had saved him at his moment of utter despair. A woman who loved him had arrived in the nick of time. That was his omen, the sign he needed. He had been looking for his shotgun and he had found Gabby. As he searched for the gun he had vowed he would not stop, but Gabby vowed she would not stop either. He scooped her up in his arms and carried her to the battered chesterfield by the stove. The dogs lifted their heads but didn't stir.

Joe's mother had endured a hard life. Even as a child she worked long hours. She married a man to escape a brutal father and found her husband worse. She kept their small farm together while he drank and raged and frittered away his life on hairbrained schemes. When he died, Joe, his brothers and sisters were small and wild. She raised them in dirt-poor circumstances. The daughters got pregnant young and moved away to be married. Some of the boys, the wilder ones, just ran away without ever saying goodbye. She sold the farm and moved into the ramshackle house that would have collapsed had it not been for Joe.

Joe had been her last hope, her only support. He was the youngest one, the quiet one and her life's work rested on him.

He had been her only hope and when he had turned out to be abnormal she lost all hope. He had been sent away for violating an animal. A cow of all things! What did she expect? Nothing, that's what. Nothing.

Joe's mother was an early riser. She never varied in her routine. The day they came with news her husband had staggered onto the road and been run over by a lumber truck and was dead as a nit, she continued hanging out her wash.

"Why hurry, he's not going anywhere."

She rose at five-thirty every morning, never a minute later. The dogs were waiting as always at the foot of the stairs. They had a routine too. She let them out and went into the kitchen. Except that morning there was her son with a strange woman. The two of them asleep on her chesterfield with their arms wrapped around each other.

The old woman moved closer. She studied Gabby, making sure it wasn't a man with a wig. No, this woman was real. For the first time in years there was a flicker of warmth in the old lady. She bent over even closer, an inch from Gabby's face. She saw the crease under Gabby's chin and the small crowsfeet at the corner of the eyes. She was no kid but Joe's mother wasn't bothered by slight signs of age. Especially if there was a chance, just a small chance, her son was normal after all. She had stopped hoping for anything the day Joe went to jail. But studying him with his arms wrapped around this woman, she sensed this was a good thing. There was a certain relief, the only emotion aside from loss and shame she had felt in a long time.

It was Gabby who woke first because the bravest of the three dogs was back from his morning pee and sniff and was nuzzling her with his big, black nose. She opened her eyes to look directly into the large amber eyes of the eight-year-old German shepherd. The dog was delighted and started to lick her face. She tried to shoo him away.

"Nice doggie. Go away, go away."

"Gus, leave her alone" came the command from a brittle little voice, so dry and wraith-like, it sounded as if it hadn't been used in years.

Gabby's second gaze met the beady eyes of Joe's mother, sitting an arm's length away. The granite grey, weather-beaten face so startled her she let out a small involuntary yelp.

"Excuse me," she said.

"Would you like some tea?" Joe's mother asked, never taking her eyes off Gabby, who was untangling herself from the still sleeping Joe. Gabby got to her feet and smoothed down her rumpled skirt, rearranged her sweater and tried to press down her tangled hair. She would love some tea and could she use the bathroom please. The old woman pointed.

"It's out there around back. Just walk down the path and don't fall in the brook."

Along the narrow twisting path ran a small stream that bubbled over mossy rocks. Sparrows and goldfinch were bathing in one of the little pools. A morning mist hung in the trees. Further up the glen, Gabby could hear the work of a downy woodpecker getting its breakfast by hammering a tree trunk. Under the canopy of the hardwoods, the air remained cool.

The outhouse was a two-holer and Gabby wondered how sociable a family would have to be to share such a facility. She felt strangely happy without knowing why. Her head ached but she didn't care. She wasn't sure what was going to happen but she thought it was going to be good. She didn't want to investigate any further, not at that moment; she just wanted to be. Walking back along the path she realized how well she'd slept.

Joe's mother had poured steaming tea and Gabby, after an awkward silence, introduced herself.

"Are you his woman?"

The question was so quick and direct it startled Gabby.

So did her reply.

"I want to be."

"Ah," the old lady said and when she smiled, Gabby could see most of her front teeth were missing. "That's good. That's very, very good."

"Thank you," Gabby said and felt a little foolish.

When Joe awoke, the three dogs, Gabby and his mother were all watching him intently. He tried to focus through the haziness of sleep. She was there all right, with his mother, the two of them, staring at him. His mother was actually looking straight at him. It gave Joe the strangest, happiest sensation.

"There's tea, Joe," his mother said and got up to make them breakfast.

Joe wondered, just for a second, if he had died during the night.

24

There are certain signs of success when running an out-of-the-way business in an out-of-the-way section of a small town. If your store becomes the neighbourhood meeting place, it's a good sign. The E & P Variety had become the kind of establishment where old timers hung around having a chew of tobacco, swapping stories and occasionally passing a bottle in a brown paper bag. Pearl complained about tobacco juice and made Edger supply a spittoon. One day a couple of kitchen chairs mysteriously arrived at the front of the store and somebody brought down an old car seat in the back of their half-ton truck. It could seat three comfortably.

Some of the old timers were veterans of the "Great War" as they called it. Many had been in the trenches in France. A couple had been couriers and had the bad luck to be at Ypres when the Germans first used mustard gas. They were the grizzled guys with handkerchiefs in their hands, constantly wiping away the water that collected in the corners of their eyes.

It became an ongoing contest between Pearl and the veterans. When necessary she would read them the riot act. If they missed the spittoon or got tobacco juice on the steps, Pearl would let them know. She certainly wouldn't allow any swearing in front of Rhonda-Rae. Of course, that only led to them teasing her to the point where Pearl couldn't come out of the store without being greeted by a chorus of wolf whistles.

As she got older, Rhonda-Rae would dance on the top step and curtsy, something Edger had taught her. The old guys would applaud and give her a nickel for ice cream.

"She got a stomach ache because she's had about a dozen ice creams cones," Pearl complained.

Edger smiled but didn't stop unpacking cans of sardines. Edger never stopped working. He had expanded the business, knocking out walls and turning the little garage into what he called the hardware department. Besides meat and fish, he added millinery products, needles and thread. E & P sold string and twine, paint and brushes, fishing line and rods, bobbers and spools.

Even when the old boys passed around a bottle and called Edger out to join them, he didn't. He was busy.

Pearl remembered the day her second child was born. She would talk about it years later. It was the day they were supposed to go to a wedding. Pearl was packing to go to the hospital, worrying about her water breaking when a commotion below drew her to the window.

At least thirty people were standing in the store's driveway, jeering and cheering as Muggy Fitzgerald and Jumpin' Jimmy Hicks circled each other like a couple of banty roosters, both with their dukes in the air. Muggy was well over eighty and Jumpin' Jimmy hadn't jumped in half a century. Onlookers had gathered. Little boys, gawkers in training, were spellbound by the excitement. Older teenagers on their bicycles tooted the little squeeze horns on their crossbars if one of the disputants landed a punch. There wasn't much tooting because there wasn't much punching, just a lot of circling and noise. The two crazy sisters contributed to the circus-like atmosphere by singing the Perry Como hit "Don't Let the Stars Get in Your Eyes." This had nothing to do with anything but was distracting some of the onlookers. The crazy sisters were told to shut up by Mrs. Bertie MacGrath and her niece, who was known only as Jugs – for obvious reasons.

Pearl waddled downstairs, yelling at Edger, "Go out there and stop those guys." Halfway down the stairs her water broke and she grabbed the banister as moisture ran down her legs. Edger, usually so cool and deliberate, went berserk. He ran back and forth, yelling outside for assistance and those watching the pugilistic veterans kept looking into the store where there seemed to be more excitement.

Pearl thought she was going to give birth right on the steps. All she could remember was mass confusion, a dozen people running around each other shouting orders. Jumpin' Jimmy was jumping again and shouting at her to breathe.

Muggy was shouting at Jimmy, "Of course she's going to breathe, you idiot. What's the alternative?"

Wet and embarrassed, Pearl ended up going to the hospital in Muggy's old Dodge with Edger holding her tightly. Jumpin' Jimmy looked after the store.

"I'll get back as soon as I can," Edger told Jimmy, who demanded that everyone who wasn't buying something get out of the store.

On the way to the hospital, Muggy told Edger not to worry about the store. It was in good hands with Jimmy running it.

"Weren't you just fighting with him?" Edger asked and Muggy looked hurt by the question.

"Yeah, I suppose I was but that don't mean nothing. We been fighting for sixty years and we're still friends," Muggy said.

"Really," Edger replied. "Looked to me like you two were going at it hammer and tong."

"Tah, that's nothing. You should have seen us when MacKenzie King was Prime Minister, we fought all the time in them days. You stay with your wife and don't worry none about the business. I'll spell Jimmy off after a bit so he can go home and have his supper, 'cause he gets crabby if he doesn't eat. We'll look after things. You stay with Pearl."

"Thank you, Muggy," Pearl replied. "I thought you two forgot about me and this baby I'm having any minute," and with that Pearl let out a little cry because she was having a contraction.

Edger held her tightly. "Are you alright?" he asked as Muggy turned the corner on Main Street at the drugstore at such breakneck speed, the old tires screamed and he narrowly missed the rear end of Mrs. David Smith.

Between gasps, Pearl ordered Muggy to lay off the horn.

"You'll wake the dead," she told him and Edger couldn't help smiling because at that moment they were passing the Anglican cemetery.

Before anybody could say anything else they were at the hospital and Muggy applied the brakes so hard both Pearl and Edger went flying into the windshield.

"That ought to do it," Pearl said, rubbing her forehead.

"This is exciting," said Muggy, racing around the truck to help. "Better than handing out rum at a federal election."

Edger continued talking while holding Pearl tightly. Every thirty seconds he asked again, "Are you alright?"

"Edger, stop asking me that."

Three hours later, as Rose Quackenbush and Royal were married among the roses, Pearl delivered an eight-pound boy.

When Duddy brought the news, the wedding guests toasted the birth. Only forty guests were invited but half the town turned out anyway to see the wedding on Royal's front yard. Flash bulbs popped, people applauded and punch was served even to the uninvited.

"I've never seen Royal so happy," whispered Minnie.

Duddy nodded and gripped her hand. "And we've got a grandson. I'm getting him a hammer for Christmas," Duddy whispered. "Might just as well start him early."

"He's not going to be a carpenter."

Minnie's statement wiped the smile right off Duddy's face.

Pearl and Edger named their son Ivor Justin. When he heard the name, Ivor Johnson turned his head away from Tess.

With two children, Pearl and Edger needed a bigger house, but Pearl wasn't prepared for her husband's response when she broached the subject. She hated to bother him. She worried about his constant working. But when she mentioned a bigger house someday, saying, "It's nothing we have to worry about right now," it was clear Edger had already been planning.

"We need more than a bigger house," he replied. "We need a bigger store with a section for clothing."

"Clothing?" Pearl asked.

"Yes, work wear. You know, there is an empty building up by the Whitehall Bridge."

He kept talking and even in the dim light of her bedroom, she saw that ray of hazel that penetrated his eyes when he got excited. She had noticed it the night he told her he'd look after her. It was present at their wedding and at the birth of young Ivor. She saw it now as he talked of a new store. There would be no point in arguing.

There was a point, however, Pearl would argue about and argue fiercely.

Early the next year Ledger came home. He had broken his ankle during a jump. Tess got the call. They said he'd never be a paratrooper again. His military career was over.

"It's bad for Ledger. He's depressed but I told him this might be an opportunity," Edger said to her one night in bed.

"What do you mean?" Pearl asked.

"Maybe Ledger will come into business with us."

Pearl's stomach twisted. She didn't harbour any ill will toward Ledger. Not on the surface anyway. She didn't really know what she felt. Deep down she wondered if she could be harbouring anything else like flickering embers from her past. She wasn't certain because she didn't think about him. She loved Edger, worshiped him in fact, and admired his ambition. But to have the father of your firstborn, a man you once had feelings for, in such close quarters day in and day out? Pearl didn't know exactly why, but she didn't like it.

Edger had never asked her about Rhonda-Rae's father. They never actually talked about it. Edger had legally adopted her. So why was Pearl beside herself?

"I don't think we should invite Ledger into our business. That's not fair to us."

"But he's family, Pearl. He's my brother."

She turned away, afraid to say more because she didn't trust her temper.

* * *

Ledger was on crutches, hobbling no farther than the front yard at first. He didn't want to work in a store, didn't want his brother's charity. He certainly didn't want his mother's sympathy or to be where he was. He didn't want to walk with a limp. Didn't want, didn't want, didn't want.

Tess watched him from her kitchen window as he tried to take a step without the crutches. She could see his lips moving and she knew he was hurting and cursing. She was more worried about his bitterness than his limp. The ankle would heal but inside her son? Well, that was something else.

Ledger's return was causing turmoil in Pearl as well. For the first time in their marriage, Pearl felt far away from Edger's plans. He had always been secretive until he was ready to reveal things. That was just the way he was. But he often took her advice, particularly regarding the advertising and how the merchandise should be displayed. She was good at displays and ideas and was proud of her contribution. Pearl was more than Edger's wife, she was also his business partner. But another partner was looming. The Big Shot Ledger who wasn't such a big shot anymore. She didn't have faith in him as a businessman either. She didn't think he'd be as dedicated as her husband. How could he be? The store wasn't his idea. He didn't even want it. Her husband had wanted it and worked at it. This was Edger's dream and she shared it. Now Edger was expanding their dream to include his brother and Pearl didn't like it one little bit.

She was more uncomfortable because she wasn't certain what transpired in private between the brothers. She hoped Ledger had rejected the idea of a partnership but he started hanging around, giving Edger a hand stocking shelves. A week later he was waiting on customers. That was it! Pearl had enough Minnie in her that things didn't sit on the back burner too long. She confronted Edger.

"We're just trying it out to see how it feels. Ledger isn't sure himself."

"But you asked him, you invited him into our business without asking me."

Edger hadn't seen Pearl really angry since the day he'd put the spider down her back, the day her forehead pulsated.

"Pearl, we're just trying this out, that's all. No promises have been made."

"Edger, do you know he's Rhonda-Rae's father?"

She shot it at him without warning and regretted it instantly when he flinched, almost staggered. He breathed hard, trying to recover.

"I suspected. Yeah, I guess I knew. I hoped it wasn't so."

Edger slumped against the wall and Pearl, sorry as she was, couldn't stop what she had started.

"He left me pregnant to fend for myself. That's the kind of man you want to bring into our business."

"Ledger is Ledger." Edger exhaled deeply as if expelling a lifetime of exasperation. He had turned white and his paleness scared her, as if long-buried suffering was making its way out of his body and taking his life with it. He stared at the floor and his voice came out flat and lifeless.

"Once when we were small," he said, "Ledger and Nuts Allen tied me up in the woods by the old reservoir. It was Saturday afternoon. I know because they left me there while they went to the movies. I struggled to free myself because I wanted to go to the movies too. I cried and swore and screamed all afternoon. I told myself that day I'd hate him for the rest of my life and we would no longer be brothers. I struggled with the knots until my fingers bled and I swore to God that I would always hate him. But you know, Ledger came back before suppertime. I could hear him coming, walking through the woods whistling, without a care in the world. He came up to me and smiled and I watched him cut the knots with his hunting knife. I was so glad to see him I wasn't even mad. We walked home together. I knew that day I'd never hate him, whatever he did. He's the only brother I've got."

"I'm your wife," Pearl said softly, not wanting to be angry.

Edger nodded, "Yes, you are. The first among all others."

He was quoting their wedding vows. She wanted to kiss him then. Partly because she was so sorry he had been picked on and partly because she had contributed to the unhappiness of his past.

"If you don't want him in the business I'll tell him. But Pearl, whatever he did to you, you weren't tied to a tree. It turned out all right for both of us."

He walked out of the room and the tears she'd been repressing for days because of anger, frustration and hurt welled up in her eyes. It had turned out better than all right. It had turned out splendidly. She cried because she knew, more vividly than ever before, that she had married a very, very good man.

25

Ledger could taste bitterness when he woke each morning. He tried to leap out of bed as though it had all been a bad dream. But when he hit the floor, reality rushed at him faster than the ground rushing up to meet an unprepared paratrooper. He'd gone from being a military jumper to a limping civilian. He had traded the brass buttons of his army uniform for the white apron of a storekeeper. He was just a gimpy clerk in a little part of a little town. So the bitterness filled his mouth each morning and he could never quite get rid of the taste throughout the day.

Then there was the ignoble experience of accepting help from his brother, the weaker one, the one who could never swim as far or run as fast or wrestle as well. The one he protected when he wanted to show off or picked on when he needed to vent his hostility. The brother he had tied up in the woods now offered him a future of sorts, who talked about a partnership between them in a bigger enterprise, who offered him a goddamn life, if you could call it that.

Bruce Graham – Ivor Johnson's Neighbours

There were other things too. How was he supposed to act around Pearl? He could tell she loathed him. Edger was raising his child, had taken the unwanted baby and mother off his hands. His brother had adopted the child Ledger didn't want. How did his brother get to be so damned good, so superior, so noble? The indignity was too much. How did you walk around people and ignore their pitying looks? Ledger, who had been so fleet-footed, so athletic, now felt so damned empty.

The emerging partnership brought the brothers into daily contact. Ledger bounded out of bed every morning and when that reality hit him he dreaded the day ahead. He was all bitterness and Edger was all business. Happy and Grumpy, driving all over hell's half acre looking at buildings because Edger was bent on moving into bigger quarters whether Ledger came in or not. They talked to the bank manager except Edger did all the talking. Ledger just listened to how well his brother handled himself. They carried out what Edger called "spying missions" on retail stores in Amherst and Moncton, fishing for new ideas.

Ledger's bitterness didn't slow Edger down nor did it get him down emotionally. Edger packed enough happiness for both of them. He hired Winnie Wasson to work three evenings a week so he could spend more time with the children. He helped Pearl with the babies and even showed up at Gabby's occasionally for a beer.

Edger was all enthusiasm and he had confidence now, a belief in himself that he could do it, that he could handle a bigger business and make it a success. He dragged his brother across the county looking at counters and clothing lines. Sometimes in the car they were silent, Edger concentrating on their next step and Ledger, tight-lipped, packed in his own gloom. Other times for unknown reasons, when the conversation veered away from business they could find a light note, even occasionally laughing about shared good times in the past. Ledger could even find a smile for a few minutes until he remembered that in the past he was the top dog of any pack.

It was in one of those rare times when they were sharing a memory about their mother that, like a bolt of lightning, the realization hit them both simultaneously about their unknown father. They had been seventeen the last time they approached Tess together, believing a combined force might bring additional pressure to bear. It was a long shot. Her only response had been that they would know when they were twenty-one.

"We're twenty-two," Ledger shouted, pounding his forehead. "Twenty-two! A whole year past the deadline. God, what have we been thinking? How could we forget? God, what's the matter with us? How could we possibly forget?"

"Maybe it's not so important for us now," Edger said. "Not like when we were young and all the kids had dads. It's been so long without a father. I mean, I don't miss what I never had."

"It's important," countered Ledger. "Don't you want to know? We've waited all our lives. I want to know and I want to confront the guy. I want to know right now!"

"Now?" asked Edger.

"Yes, you're damn right, right now. Let's find out tonight. We've been waiting a lifetime, haven't we?"

"I don't know," replied Edger. "I don't think we should gang up on Tess. Besides, we've got so much else going on right now."

"Listen, she's always set the time, told us when. She set the ground rules. I don't get your problem," Ledger said, twisting in the passenger seat and rubbing his ankle. "It's time, Brother. It's time."

They didn't speak the rest of the way home, both brothers lost in their own thoughts of discovering their father. Ledger rehearsed what he would say to him and Edger worried that his brother was sighting in a new target, another bull's eye for his bitterness. It didn't cross their minds that their father might be dead or living in a foreign land. Their thoughts, their rehearsals, were personal and imminent. That's the way they looked at it.

They drove through town without talking. The moon was on the water in Whitehall. Two little boys were sitting on the rail of the bridge as they themselves had done years ago. They drove into Tess's driveway.

"Wait a minute, wait a minute," Edger burst out, trying to smile and put a lighter touch on his brother's determination and seriousness. "Don't fly off the handle, Ledger, just think about this. Are you sure, absolutely sure, you want to know right now at this time? Can't it wait? Suppose, just suppose, it's somebody – well, somebody we don't like."

"I already don't like," said Ledger, "so what's your point?"

Edger tried another approach. "Suppose it's somebody, you know, like – like – oh, Mink."

"Mink!" exclaimed Ledger, punching his brother on the shoulder. "That's our mother you're talking about, buddy. I like the old guy but you don't really think –? Give our mother a little credit, will ya? Come on!" He was out of the car.

Tess wasn't home and Edger was relieved. "She can't be far, she didn't take the car," Ledger said, hobbling towards the street. They headed across to Gabby's. "There she is, coming out of Ivor's." Ledger pointed and started towards her.

Edger ran ahead because he wanted to get to her first and warn his mother somehow of what was coming. Ledger hobbled after him. They met their mother under the streetlight at the end of Ivor Johnson's driveway.

"We want to know," Ledger said breathlessly. "We demand to know who our father is."

Even in the streetlight they could see the shadow of shock that passed over their mother's face. She drew in a sharp breath as if she'd been hit in the stomach. It took the excitement out of the question and the air seemed to go brittle around them.

"You want to know who your father is?" Tess repeated slowly, pausing after every word as if she was waiting for something.

"Yes," Ledger said, slightly subdued by her reaction. "Yes, we do. Who is he?"

"I'm your father," said a soft voice in the darkened driveway.

It was Ivor Johnson.

During those first seconds of stunned silence, Edger felt that every secret of his life had finally been revealed to him. There were no more mysteries left. A great flood of relief swept over him and caused him to shudder. He thought he was going to faint and he took a step forward in order to steady himself. He was flooded with emotions – happiness and sadness. How could he tell the difference? In the streetlight he could see the hard look in his brother's eyes as Ivor Johnson came up behind Tess and put his arm around her.

Both brothers were reliving a lifetime of wanting and waiting for the father they never had. Yet, curiously enough, they did have him. Who had done more for them? More than most dads. Who had fixed their bikes and sharpened their skates and put Band-Aids on their scraped knees? Ivor had taught them how to fly kites and catch flounder. He had financed the store. He had always been there, like a constant star shining right across the street. It was no surprise, really, yet incredibly surprising and embellished by their life-long ignorance of their own parentage.

"You're Dad?" was all Edger could manage to blurt out. The words hung in the air and sounded silly.

"What kind of weird fucking people are you two?" snarled Ledger, finding his own voice and feeling the fury build in him. He turned away hurriedly, muttering to himself, profanities pouring out of him, then he hobbled back with so many feelings welling up in him he couldn't untangle them. He was full of fire and wasn't finished.

"I'm going to say it again, what – ?"

Tess quickly stepped up to him and put her hand on his arm. Ledger deflated and there was silence. Edger was still uncertain if he were going to faint or not. The night was cool but he was sweating profusely.

They could hear each other breathing. Two young men, twins, their mother and dad, the neighbour. A family of sorts standing under a streetlight, studying each other as if they were meeting for the first time. Off in the distance the foghorn sounded.

"Why?" Ledger pleaded. His fury had been replaced by gut-wrenching misery. He swallowed, trying to recapture his hostility. His knees were weak. A quivering thickness engulfed him. A rising cloud choked him.

"Why?" he sobbed, embarrassed for crying and deeply regretting he had ever broached the subject of his father.

"Let's go inside," said Ivor.

"Come on," said Tess.

Ivor took Tess's arm and Tess put her arm around Ledger, leading him toward the house and Edger didn't mind because he understood who needed their mother the most.

For the first time in his life Edger felt older than his brother. It was curious but he was looking at his family through new eyes. He had never seen his parents arm in arm. Not like a couple, a man and his wife.

"Was I blind?" Edger whispered. "All these years right under my nose and I never suspected."

The truth was, at times both brothers had suspected and shared their suspicions. They talked about it more when it mattered. When Edger was seven, eight and nine he hoped with all his heart that Ivor Johnson was his father. At ten he wasn't certain about anything and for some reason it didn't matter so much. At fifteen it didn't make much difference at all and at seventeen, as he tried to bring perspective to his identity, it mattered a very great deal.

He slowly followed his parents and Ledger, who was overcome with emotion, into Ivor's kitchen where Ledger, so visibly shaken he was trembling, asked again.

"Why?"

"There were complications," his mother said.

"Third parties," Ivor Johnson said and turned on the stove.

"Third parties?" Ledger repeated. "You mean there was another woman?"

"Yes," Ivor responded. "My wife."

"I heard you were married but I didn't know for sure," Edger said, wanting to break the strain.

"Nobody here knows for sure."

"We made a pact years ago," Tess said. "Your father, ah, Ivor and I made a pact that we would wait for each other. Except his situation took so long to sort out. It took a long, long time and by then you boys were five years old." Tess looked at her sons. "Well, by then I was hurt from all the waiting, hurt it had taken so long. I felt I had kept my part of the bargain and I didn't want to go ahead anymore. So I deserted the deal we had made. Ivor wouldn't take no for an answer. He moved in across the street. By the time you were ten, I had learned to love him again. It took a long time, but he kept his end of the bargain. It had just become too complicated."

"But you cheated us out of a father," Ledger interrupted.

"No, Ivor was your father, just from afar. I know it wasn't perfect but neither are your parents."

Tess tried to wipe away her tears and Edger was crying too, along with his brother because he had never seen his mother cry. Even the night she shot the man, she didn't cry. They had given her a hard time, but she had never cried. She was not a woman to weep. Edger leaned down and kissed her. He hugged Ivor too. They turned to Ledger hoping for the same from him. There was a long look between mother and son before Ledger shook his head.

"No," he said. "You'll be getting no sympathy from me." He glared at them and went out, slamming the door behind him.

"I'll go get him," said Edger, still wiping away his own tears. "He'll be okay." He started to leave then turned.

"By the way," he said, "are you two ever going to get together, live together like husband and wife?"

Without hesitation, both Ivor and Tess answered simultaneously, "No."

"Why not?" asked Edger.

"We work better like this," Tess responded.

"Who wants tea?" asked his father.

"No thanks, ah, Dad. I'm going to find my brother." Edger turned at the door. "Do you mind me calling you Dad?" he asked.

"No son, of course not," said Ivor Johnson.

Ledger hadn't gone far. He was only a little way down the road, limping from side to side searching for something to kick with his good foot.

"Jesus, that's too much for me," he said, shaking his head. Edger could see he was still trembling.

"You can't say she wasn't a good mother," Edger said. "It just wasn't complete somehow. She kept telling us life doesn't always deal you a perfect hand."

"No," Ledger snorted, his voice filled with contempt. "It sure as hell doesn't.

They didn't speak for a long, long time, walking slowly down to the shore. They sat together on a piece of driftwood and watched the water.

"Well, we wanted to know," Edger finally sighed, hardly realizing he had broken the silence.

"Maybe I needed him the most," Ledger said softly.

Edger couldn't hide his surprise. "You? You had it all."

"Maybe I didn't have as much as you thought," Ledger said.

They were silent again as the fog came towards them – a low creeping cloud covering the shore and turning the more remarkable driftwood, the long dead tree roots, into smoky silhouettes that resembled sea creatures with five hundred deformed and slithering arms.

The brothers kept looking into the darkness, remembering a lot of things about their mother, their father and themselves.

The next day, they found themselves unable to concentrate. Even the hardworking Edger couldn't keep his mind on business. Ledger sat on a carton of spices he hadn't unpacked.

"Let's go to Gabby's and have a beer," he suggested. Surprisingly, Edger agreed.

"Want to drop into Dad's?" Edger asked.

"No," came the reply.

When they arrived, Joe nodded at them. He was standing in the back porch with bags and suitcases around him.

"Joe, what are you doing? Moving in?" Edger asked jokingly.

"Yes," Joe replied.

"You're going to board here then?" asked Ledger.

"I'm going to live here," Joe said.

It was the way he said it that made it clear to them. He was not boarding as if Gabby was his landlady.

Gabby came up behind him, looking radiant, and put her hand on his shoulder.

Ledger looked at his brother and leaned against the porch door. "Goddamn it, I can't stand any more!" he said and Edger began to laugh.

"It's been quite a twenty-four hours, hasn't it?"

"Gabby, how about a shot of that bourbon of yours?" Ledger asked.

"Yes, I think a toast is in order," she replied.

They stood in a circle, three with a glass of bourbon and Joe with lemonade.

Edger took it upon himself to be toastmaster. He looked at Joe who no longer carried the weight of the world, and at a beaming Gabby who had obviously regained her girlish enthusiasm. He wanted to include his bitter brother because he wanted his words to include all of them, but Ledger wasn't waiting for any toast. He was guzzling his bourbon. Edger raised his glass and said, "Gabby, Joe, there aren't two people on earth more suited for each other. You didn't just find each other by accident. May you always be happy and may I always be counted as your friend." Then, still holding his glass his eyes met Ledger's and he continued, "There are times that you know will change your life forever. This is one of them for all of us."

They toasted and for the second time since he and Edger had met with the bank manager in town, Ledger finally understood something that had escaped him his entire life. How smart his brother really was.

26

The scandal about Joe and Gabby simmered through the unusually hot autumn of 1957. It wasn't just the difference in ages, although that was a shocker. Gabby had been single so long. She was a fixture as a single woman. But more than anything it was Joe's conviction, his unusual crime, that really got tongues wagging and wag they did.

"That a respectable woman would take up with someone like that!" It got so bad at the beauty parlour that a fed-up Tess did something she had never done before. She told cackling customers to "Shut up!" and when Barb came to the stunned customers' defence, Tess stripped off her smock, took her coat off the rack and walked out the door.

Despite the gossip and some dirty jokes, more than a few women were secretly envious. Not just because Joe was a good-looking guy with good manners, but because Gabby had the courage to take the man she wanted, regardless of public opinion. Some old biddies were spiteful and catty. But many women looked at their own husbands and whispered to themselves, "Good for you, Gabby, you've got more guts than me."

Then the Russians launched Sputnik and people had other things to talk about. After all, a juicy story can only hold its juice for a certain length of time before the liquid evaporates. The fear and loathing of the Russians dried up the juice rather quickly. Never before had people been able to stand on their front steps and watch a Commie contraption travel across the sky above their heads. They couldn't touch it, but by God they could see it and that was enough. Night after night folks gathered and watched and whispered. Imaginations ran wild. "If the Russians were right up there they could soon be right down here." Sputnik dried up local scandals faster than old crackers left in the sun.

New scandals arose of course, and as often as not they centred on the Snake. In November, Melissa Abbott dropped out of university and came home. She was pregnant.

"She refuses to give up the baby," wailed Claudia, breaking down in Gabby's arms. The two women had been estranged since the window breaking, but it had been to Gabby that a teary-eyed Claudia had come during yet another crisis.

"I've threatened her, told her I'd kick her out and change the locks on the doors. No matter what I say, she refuses."

Mink Martin reported there was awful shouting coming from the Abbott house. "Sounds like a couple a roosters on castor oil. Gets my dog all worked up," he complained. "It's got so a fellow can't have a quiet drink anymore."

Mink's report was accurate. Melissa and Claudia had some awful arguments with Claudia seeing her daughter's potential go down the drain. Melissa, overwhelmed and rebellious, threw books, pillows and even a lamp that made so much noise Mink Martin's swig out of the bottle trickled down his chin.

Melissa stayed behind closed doors and screamed. Finally, out of desperation because Claudia feared for her daughter's health and mental stability, they made a pact of sorts. Melissa would stay home and have her baby. It was an uneasy time and both women retreated to their own rooms and wept.

Melissa was never seen. She didn't walk up the road or stroll around her yard or go down to the shore at night. Ledger limped by very late. He'd sit in the ditch across from her house and hate himself for doing it. "Why am I here?" he asked himself and bit the inside of his lip as a form of punishment. He even sat there in the cold when dew covered the ground and sea mist chilled the air. Some nights a light was on in what he believed was Melissa's room. He waited longer in those times, shivering, hugging himself to stay warm. His ankle throbbed. He never saw even her silhouette in the window.

Ledger tried to lose himself in things for which he had little interest. His brother didn't seem bothered by things the way he was. Edger wasn't put off by the revelation of their father's identity. He was too busy. He and Pearl had finally purchased an old building and were converting it to a store. Ledger was helping them but hadn't made any commitment to be a partner, and it was awkward being around Pearl. It was all too much. Things were eating away at him. He had some money from his army discharge. It was time to buy into the business or back out.

"I don't know" was his reply when Edger asked him. Pearl gave an almost audible sigh. "What the hell is your problem?" Ledger snapped at her.

"You go to hell, Ledger! You're my problem. If you don't want in the business, get out."

Edger tried to be the peacemaker but all he did was delay the inevitable. A few days later Ledger and Pearl got into it again. "I don't want you here," she screamed. "I don't want you in the store period, as a partner or even a customer."

"You think I want to be here?" he shouted and picked up a can of soup and hurled it at her. It shot by her head and she looked at him so startled she was speechless. Ledger just felt weak. He actually thought he was going to faint and rushed out of the store so he didn't embarrass himself in front of her.

At Christmas, Ledger asked Faith Armstrong to marry him. Fast Faith, as they called her around town, cast around for a day or two and couldn't see a better prospect. She accepted. It was not that he loved Faith, but she was all right, he guessed. Ledger just wanted something or someone to hang on to.

He brought Faith to Gabby's porch a couple of times but she didn't fit in. In fact, the whole atmosphere on the porch was different. It was Gabby and Joe's now, more like a home than a watering hole. Even Mink's visits became less frequent. Ivor and Tess dropped by sometimes but Royal and Rose kept to themselves, reading their gardening books and going to bed early. Minnie and Duddy seldom came over.

One night, when a few of them were there sitting around on one of those occasions when it was more like the old days, Duddy came in with someone following him through the door. It took a minute before they recognized him.

"Fudd?" Gabby said and ran and hugged him. He looked different with longer hair, cut and styled like a movie star. He was wearing an expensive suede jacket.

"You look like a million dollars," Gabby said and Fudd beamed and took a beer out of the box.

"What are you doing exactly? Minnie says you're in some sort of business."

"My own business," replied Fudd. "I sell lobsters. I was working on a lobster boat in Lockeport. The guy asked me to drive some lobster up to Halifax for him and that's how it started. Now I supply most of the restaurants. I just bought a new truck and I make three trips a week."

A month later, Fudd came home again, this time bringing his wife and daughter. People thought his wife, Joan, bore a small resemblance to Melissa.

Not as beautiful but not bad either, Ledger said to himself and immediately did a comparison with Fast Faith, who had drawn up a list of qualities she expected in a husband. Sobriety was at the top of the list.

Fudd had other news too. He had won the Liberal nomination in Lockeport and was running in the next election.

"Jesus," Royal said to Ivor, "Jesus."

Minnie and Duddy threw a party for their son and daughter-in-law. Pearl made Fudd a cake shaped like a lobster. After the party, Fudd took his wife down to meet Melissa, but he too was unable to penetrate the permanently locked doors of his very pregnant, former spiritual guidance counsellor.

A month before Ledger's wedding, Fast Faith, encouraged by her mother, broke off their engagement. She told her friends she couldn't live with Ledger's awful temper and drinking. The real reason was her mother's constant barrage.

"You can do better than him, dear. Somebody from Snake Road? Really! You can do better."

Ledger thought it was his limp. "I don't walk like a man," he told his mother.

"You walk just fine," she said.

They were all concerned over the fires burning inside Ledger and the amount of liquor he used to quell them.

"Self-pity is an awful thing," Ivor finally told him.

"Fuck off, Father," Ledger replied.

"It's all right, son," Ivor said.

"It's not fucking all right at all," Ledger screamed, flinging the telephone book across Ivor's kitchen. "All right for you maybe," he cried, his intoxication slurring his words. "All right for you," he continued in a tirade, "sitting here in your cosy little white house watching the world go by. All right for you. But it sure as fuck is not all right for me!"

"It will be if you let it," Ivor replied.

Ledger, astonished that his father failed to get angry, stormed out and slammed the door.

Ledger began showing up at the store with bloodshot eyes.

"Where have you been? You smell of booze," Edger said.

"I don't have to answer to you. I'm not your servant."

Bruce Graham – Ivor Johnson's Neighbours

Edger said nothing and for Ledger, that also made matters worse.

He would go uptown at lunch and sit in the tavern at the Cumberland Inn or arrive at Gabby's in the early evening, already loaded and with a pint in his back pocket. Tess would find him asleep on the side steps some mornings.

When Ledger was drinking, people steered a wide path around him. He was argumentative. He was thrown in jail one Saturday night for breaking up the tavern, which gave Fast Faith's mother great satisfaction.

Pearl begged Edger to withdraw the offer of a partnership with his brother but Edger wouldn't. "No, Pearl, I won't."

It was the only issue on which he would not bend and Pearl only pressed so hard. She didn't slam doors and cry, although she thought of it. But she had enormous respect as well as a lot of love for her husband. That stopped her and she swallowed her discomfort, partly because she knew Edger and Tess were so worried about Ledger, who seemed to be going over the brink.

It got worse. Ledger didn't show up at the store. He'd disappeared for a day or two and couldn't remember where he had been. Ivor Johnson and Edger had patrolled the Whitehall Road at night, picking him out of the ditch. They'd taken him to Ivor's so Tess wouldn't see and washed the vomit off him and cleaned his clothes. The last time it happened, Ledger was so sick he'd fallen asleep in the big La-Z-Boy chair in Ivor's kitchen. He remained in bed for three days. Weak and still groggy, he woke up in Ivor's guestroom. His father brought him chicken soup and fresh rolls Tess had made.

"Why are you doing this?" he asked Ivor one morning, propping himself up in bed, still weak but no longer so sick with that aching in his head and gut. "Why?" Ledger asked again.

"You were in the ditch. I'd never leave you in the ditch," Ivor said.

"No matter how big an asshole I am?"

"No matter how big an asshole you are."

"I don't deserve it," Ledger said.

"There goes that self-pity again."

"You never give in, do you?" Ledger said.

"Never," Ivor replied.

"I'm sorry what I said the other day."

"I know, you were feeling bad."

"I can't seem to see any light at the end of the tunnel."

"Stop trying to see it and start trying to feel it," Ivor said.

"Huh?"

"Look around you, Ledger. You've got plenty to be thankful for. You just can't see it."

"Tell me, what have I got to be thankful for? Just give me one thing."

"Well, Fast Faith dumped you. That's a good start."

Even Ledger had to smile. "Got anything more?"

"Okay. You had an accident that broke your ankle. You weren't killed," Ivor replied.

Ledger didn't respond for a while, then he said hardly above a whisper, "Why do I wish I had been killed?"

"Because the fall broke more than your ankle. It broke your spirit. Your ankle is as good as it's going to get, but your spirit still needs repair," Ivor replied. "If your spirit gets repaired, your ankle won't matter."

"Won't matter if my spirit gets repaired?" Ledger muttered thoughtfully. "I didn't know you were religious."

"I'm not, not in the church sense," Ivor replied.

"But you believe in a spirit."

"Yes," Ivor said.

Ledger closed his eyes and wondered where his spirit was.

With his eyes still closed he asked. "Ivor, where exactly is my spirit, what part of me?"

"All over you," Ivor replied.

"All over me," Ledger repeated.

"Yes," said Ivor.

Ledger fell into a deep sleep and his father watched his son breathe. Even though Ivor Johnson wasn't religious in the church sense, he prayed for his boy's well-being.

The next day, Ledger joined AA. The same week he apologized to his brother, his father and mother, to Gabby and Joe because he hadn't been very nice to them. But mostly he apologized to Pearl. He apologized to her for everything. "Particularly Rhonda-Rae," he said.

Pearl lost her hostility and became embarrassed by his comments. She finally tried to get him to stop. "Rhonda-Rae has a father now, Ledger. It's all right really, everything is all right."

"It's not all right for me, Pearl, not until you tell me I'm welcome in the business."

"That's up to Edger," Pearl replied.

"No, it's up to you too. I've been a shit. I almost died before I saw that."

"It's fine with me, Ledger," Pearl replied.

A few hours later, at the close of the business day, Ledger told his brother he had finally made up his mind. He wanted to buy into the business. Over Ledger's shoulder, Pearl nodded her approval to her husband and Edger reached out his hand.

"Partners, then."

"Yes," said Ledger, "partners."

Ledger worked hard. He had to. He had no social life and quitting drinking wasn't easy. He had no idea of the difficulties ahead of him. There were times at night that he didn't know what to do with himself.

"Is there any way I can help?" his brother asked.

"No, I just need to do a lot of thinking," Ledger said.

"You know, this sounds silly, but there's a place I used to go when I needed to think. It's where we smoked those stolen cigarettes when we were kids."

"Where?" Ledger asked.

"Under the Whitehall Bridge."

Several nights later when he was breaking down, Ledger started walking to the tavern, convinced he couldn't live without a drink. He stopped at the bridge and just stood there in the dark. He touched the rail and the wood was wet from the deep mist. He looked up and down the road and listened for any footsteps in the fog. Embarrassing for a grown man to be crawling under a damn bridge. When he was finally there it was as if he had stepped into another world, filled with the sounds of his childhood. Joyful noises connected with happy times. Normal tones were reshaped and reverberated under the bridge, giving them a mystical quality. Running tides, squawking seagulls, the wind pulling in the water, all mingled through the timbers and were muffled by the tar. Sharp sounds bounced through the pylons and the low rumble of cars overhead had the sound of slumber. It all left him with the sense he was revisiting a place he had lost a long time ago.

It hurt him to get there but he kept going back because it was there, up against the centre pylon, that many things seeped out of him. All the contradictions of his life rolled away with the outgoing tide. At low water he'd often sit and wait for the leading ripples of the incoming trickle, which led the way for the deluge of water behind it. Some nights Ledger fell asleep under the bridge. He awoke damp and shivering with the tide lapping at his feet, but he was sober and went home with the sense he had beaten another day.

One night he walked up to his father and hugged him.

"Thank you," he said.

"I see your spirit is under repair," Ivor replied.

"I haven't got to that yet. I'm thanking you for teaching me how to drive, all the other stuff, I guess."

"You're welcome. Want some tea?"

After several weeks with his spirit well under repair, Ledger needed the bridge less and less and kept it for those times when he found himself at loose ends or when the unidentified emptiness threatened him. Without putting too fine an edge on it, Ledger was a young man who had lost his youth too quickly. He had been jolted from one existence to another without any transition period. The kid was gone too quickly. He could almost touch the place where the young, brash brat used to dwell, that place in his chest where a very cool guy used to live. That guy who had the world by the tail.

He worked hard and put in long hours so he'd have less free time and less temptation. When he wasn't working he'd hobble around the neighbourhood trying to pass the time. He'd sit with Joe and Gabby but the love radiating from them often made him lonelier. He'd wander off to his father's for a game of checkers, even drop in to Royal's or Duddy's just to see what was up. But some nights he needed that special environment and he'd be back at the bridge. His procedure there was always the same; it had a military discipline to it. A long reconnaissance to guarantee he was alone, a quick manoeuvre under the structure and up to the centre pylon to rub his ankle and think. He'd take his shoe off and get the exact spot where the break had occurred. When he rubbed it hard, it made his toes tingle. He closed his eyes because it gave him such a strange sensation.

Sometimes, the pulsing pain would correspond with the lapping of the incoming tide. Ledger liked that experience, as if the tide was taking his pain away when nothing else could.

He was having such a night, rubbing his ankle vigorously with both hands, trying to create the rhythm of the incoming tide. The water was halfway up the slope, filling the space between the banks when Ledger heard something.

Footsteps? Someone was coming down the other side of the bank. Loose pebbles were scattering on the gravel embankment. He could see a dark form across the water. The light steps: a woman he thought. She was weeping. Ledger squinted to see better but all he could make out was someone having a problem with their footing and sobbing uncontrollably. The figure was stooping, carrying what looked like a bundle. The dark form slipped and scrambled up the embankment as high as possible and plopped against the pylons, sitting down quickly, directly across the water from him.

Ledger could hear the sobbing and something else mingled with it. Another sound. Was it a baby? A baby crying? Why was somebody under this bridge with a baby? Sudden alarm shot adrenaline through his veins. He did not want to be discovered, trying to explain why a grown man was under a bridge in the dark of night with one shoe off. The sobbing became desperate. It sounded vaguely familiar but Ledger couldn't concentrate on identification. Every nerve in his body, every hair, every filament became taut. Was this distraught form going to throw the baby into the tide and jump in too? Both of them in the water?

Silently, without knowing why, he slipped his shoe on. Would he run or swim? He wanted to say something, shout something, some message of reassurance. But what would he say? The crunch of the gravel and what he could see of the form told him she was getting up again. The water was deep enough, cold enough, bleak enough to consume a woman and child in no time. Would he run or would he try to do the right thing? And what was the right thing? If she wanted to go, to end it all, who was he? No, goddamn it, no! He was a former paratrooper, but with his ankle could he save both woman and child in that dark tide on this frigid night? Was he a hero, he wondered?

At that moment Ledger understood who he really was. The throbbing of his ankle stopped because his feet had gone numb. The water was very, very cold.